RATTLER!
THE DAKOTA SERIES #3

THE DAKOTA SERIES: #3

RATTLER!

by CAP
IVERSEN

Boston ⚭ Alyson Publications, Inc.

Typeset and printed in the United States of America.

This is a paperback original from Alyson Publications, Inc.,
40 Plympton St., Boston, Massachusetts 02118.

This book is printed on acid-free, recycled paper.

First edition, first printing: July 1995

5 4 3 2 1

ISBN 1-55583-228-8

For Sahedran

When brother stands with brother,
a war is already half won.

—INDIAN PROVERB

PROLOGUE

Heat waves danced off Richard Mecum's mosquito-infested pond. It was a man-made pond, twenty feet wide, and the envy of every inhabitant of Broken Wagon Wheel. Maintaining a pond in an area thick with dust and dry chaparral was an endless burden. On most afternoons, when the sun swept across the sky like a river of fire, Richard Mecum had to run off overheated children, thirsty horses, and stray cattle. Sometimes he had to chase away a loafing cowboy who stopped to soak his swollen feet in the tepid water. Richard didn't mind sharing the water – there was certainly enough for a cowboy to soak his feet in – but children, cows, and cowboys didn't have much respect for a man's flowers.

The pond was a temptation, and Richard knew it was irresponsible to provoke his neighbors with cool water and sheltering foliage, but horticulture was his hobby. He couldn't indulge his love for exotic plants without plenty of water. In this part of Texas, even with the Rio Grande a day's ride south, surface water, like shade, was scanty.

He had ordered some strange feathery ferns from California and palm trees from Florida. Addison and Sons Mail Order Company shipped the plants via railroad, then stagecoach to Broken Wagon Wheel. *Rush Order! Live Plants! Deliver at Once!* the parcel fervently declared, and the stagecoach driver, a crusty but professional fellow by the name of Riker Sims, would dash the coach across the hot Texas flatlands and deliver the plants to Richard's door. The seedlings would arrive wilted, bruised, and barely alive, but Richard would lovingly plant them around his pond where they could drink deeply of the murky water and spring back to life.

Broken Wagon Wheel was dry and brown in the sunlight. When the sun disappeared against the western flatlands, the town possessed no color at all; it was just flat gray. In the midst of this colorless town, Richard Mecum's pond sparkled like a Swiss tarn; like a Rocky Mountain lake at daybreak, cool and colorful. Miraculously, some of the plants flourished, and the palm trees stood ten feet tall. Ferns and lilies struggled to grow in their shade. But most of Richard's hobbies perished under a merciless sun.

The challenge, of course, was to keep the plants alive. For the better part of his day, Richard Mecum was a dull, insignificant bank accountant, and he needed a challenge. His hobby cost him most of his banker's salary, but it was well worth the envy of his neighbors, who sweated in their small boxes of shadows and licked the salt from their lips when they glanced down the street and saw Richard Mecum's flowery oasis.

Today Richard was expecting orchids to arrive on the afternoon stage. He was also expecting a boy. Not from the stage. From the As the Crow Flies Saloon.

The Crow, as it was commonly referred to by its customers, was more than just a passing cowboy's watering hole. It had a kitchen in the back. Coffee and hot breads were served at breakfast, and, if the cook was in the right mood, he'd stir up frijoles and fried chili peppers for supper. There were three rooms upstairs at the Crow. The proprietor, a lean, big-voiced woman, and her baby brother lived in two of the rooms. To make ends meet, the smaller room was rented out on a weekly basis. Come suppertime, the cook would stoke the fire, stuff the large adobe oven with sweet-smelling breads, and the rooms upstairs became insufferably hot.

Clay James rented the room above the kitchen. The compact little chamber was sweatier and dustier than it had been yesterday, and yesterday was hellish enough. One of the local ranchers had driven a herd of longhorns right down Main Street past the Crow, and the dust settled an inch thick on the bureau and faded quilt and Clay's fine canvas coat. Clay long ago gave up trying to sweep out the dust. Once he succeeded in cleaning the room, the cowboys brought in another herd and the task would have to be done all over again. Clay grudgingly learned to live with the dust, as he learned to live with all the other annoyances that came with being stranded in a town like Broken Wagon Wheel.

Downstairs, the cook was stirring up a mess of sowbelly. Now sowbelly was something Clay would never get used to. Both the smell and the idea nauseated him. Clay was a native of Washington, D.C., a city that boasted elegant restaurants, theaters, and French wines. What Texans were capable of eating and drinking endlessly amazed him. They seemed to take pride in their own discomforts, as if eating an animal's innards and drinking liquor that ought to be used for the sole purpose of lighting lamps made them tougher and meaner. One could argue that it did.

Texans flatly disgusted Clay, and only the frustrating matter of being without forty-five dollars and some-odd cents kept Clay James from being on a ship across the gulf and up the coast back to Washington. Forty-five dollars and a clever constable.

Clay fanned himself with a newspaper and checked his pocket watch for the time. The pocket watch, like his city of origin, was a source of sizable pride, and as each day in Broken Wagon Wheel dragged sweatily by, pride was a sensation Clay felt very little of. The watch reminded him that he was a worldly man, cultured and educated. It was genuine gold, not gold-plated like the five-dollar pocket watches the cowboys flashed when they wanted to show folks they could tell time. In place of the number twelve was a small diamond, but what Clay found most charming about the watch was when he opened the gilded casing the watch sang a pleasant Chopin tune.

The watch was a gift from Timothy Addams, a congressman's aide in Washington, D.C. Timothy had also given him a gold locket. Clay wore the locket as religiously as a priest wears a crucifix of some saint that's supposed to save his soul. Timothy had an endearment inscribed on the back of the locket: *To my dearest friend ... all my love, Timothy.* Clay was waiting rather impatiently for Timothy to save his soul from Broken Wagon Wheel.

Timothy was generous, all right, and Clay appreciated the trinkets, but what Clay really needed from Timothy was forty-five dollars ... or a one-way ticket home. The unspoken agreement among the congressional aides in Washington, and, indeed, among some of the congressmen themselves, was they did not want Clay James to come home. Not yet. He carried too many secrets with him, knew too many names, had too many addresses, too many personal letters in his possession. Clay James had created a scandal, a scandal few polite people cared to speak of. And until the scandal faded away, like most scandals in the nation's capital usually did, Clay was not welcome among his wealthy gentlemen friends. He was too dangerous.

It was Timothy who first suggested that Clay leave Washington, D.C. "Getting out of Dodge City," Timothy laughed in an attempt to make light of a very serious situation. When he noticed Clay's solemn expression, he quickly added, "It will just be for a while, darling." But the "while" turned into weeks, the weeks into months lost in a hot, dirty border town where the perpetual aroma of sowbelly and perspiration and steer manure blended sadistically with heat and dust. Broken Wagon Wheel, Texas, was where Clay James went broke, and Clay was now convinced there was a conspiracy among his gentlemen friends to keep it that way. He was right.

Sighing deeply, Clay snapped shut the watch, sharply ending the tune. He hated Broken Wagon Wheel, hated Texas, and he dearly missed Timothy Addams. He would have gladly sold the watch for the money he needed to get back home. But the saddle tramps who visited the Crow didn't know a diamond from a chunk of coal and wouldn't offer him more than ten dollars for a watch well worth a ticket home.

Thankfully, it was time to leave, before the cook put the biscuits in the oven. Clay didn't know Richard Mecum. He had met him at the bank when he attempted to get a loan on the watch. Richard was tall, with white hair, and a face as gray and wrinkled as an old petticoat. But he dressed sharply and lived in a yellow, two-story board house. That made him the best man Broken Wagon Wheel had to offer. By the size of his garden, and the luxury of owning a pool of water of his own, Richard Mecum seemed like a man who could afford to be generous. If he was given the opportunity.

Clay James was without argument the handsomest boy in Broken Wagon Wheel; perhaps in the state of Texas. His light blond hair and clear blue eyes clearly distinguished him in a town where brown eyes and black hair were the main dish on the menu. Some of the other *gringos* had fair hair and light skin, but most of them were old or already married. There was none as fair as Clay James, not even the ruddy-faced marshal who, until Clay arrived on the afternoon stagecoach two months ago, was considered Broken Wagon Wheel's most eligible bachelor.

Clay stepped out of the Crow. The sun stung his eyes like acid, and he considered stopping by Hattie's Needle Shop and having her sew him a felt derby. But everyone, and he did mean everyone, in town knew he was penniless and was relying solely upon the kindhearted proprietor of the Crow just to have a roof over his head. He was sure the seamstress, Hattie Liverpool, would not be as generous.

He glanced over at Pappy's livery stable and watched a young boy play tag with the little girl – or was it a boy? – stablehand. Then he glanced a few feet down at the stage depot, which was sloppily connected to the livery stables, almost as an afterthought. The townsfolk began to gather in front of the depot in anticipation of the arrival of the afternoon stage. Few people came in on the stage, and those who did were of little interest, but the stagecoach rolling into town once a week was Broken Wagon Wheel's biggest event.

As he stood on the boardwalk waiting for his body to adapt to the assault from the sun, a group of dirty-faced wranglers galloped wildly up to the Crow, stirring up a cloud of eye-watering dust. They swung off their horses, rudely shoved past him as if he were nothing more than a pole standing in their way, and then, with their spurs jingling and their smells trailing behind them like faithful dogs, they stomped into the Crow, where they instantly took up a shout for whiskey.

Texans were always galloping, always stirring up dust, always stomping their high-heeled boots and twirling their big, Mexican spurs and shouting demands. Clay blinked the sting from his eyes. How did a boy like him, a boy with so much potential, end up in a place like this? He had made only one mistake in his young life. It was a big mistake, he had to admit, but still it was only one.

The Washington, D.C., policeman had been a meticulous man with shy, downcast eyes, and a pocket full of gold pieces. With the promise of sharing that gold, the policeman timidly persuaded Clay to go into a darkened alley where other boys like Clay congregated. Then, when Clay unbuttoned his pants, the policeman frantically blew his whistle, and Clay was suddenly surrounded by other constables. Clay could still hear the scream of the whistle, feel the humiliation of being carted off in a jail wagon, hear the slamming of the jail doors. If it weren't for Timothy Addams, who arrived cloaked and secretive in the middle of the night to post his bail, Clay would probably still be rotting in jail. Instead, he was rotting in south Texas.

Well, to hell with Timothy Addams. To hell with the skittish congressmen and senators and their unsuspecting wives. Clay James would make it out of Broken Wagon Wheel on his own. He didn't need them. He didn't need anybody. He had Richard Mecum.

As he walked towards the muddy-brown pond, Clay's only hope was that Richard Mecum didn't stink. Or serve sowbelly for lunch.

With nervous anticipation, Richard stood at the front window and watched heat waves do a jig under the palm trees. Half of him was waiting for Riker Sims to deliver the orchids, the other half was waiting for the blond boy to finish sauntering up the dirt path. Richard grunted irritably when Clay leaned over and plucked a lily off its stem and stuck it in his buttonhole.

When Richard pushed open the screen door, Clay found the old man nervous, irritable, and in a hurry. Clay smiled through vanilla white teeth. That's the way he usually found them: nervous, irritable, and in a hurry. But Richard Mecum had serious worries. Next to the mayor, he was Broken Wagon Wheel's most prominent citizen. What if some of the townsfolk glanced his way while wishing they could rest next to his pond and saw Clay James, bold as a rooster, strut to his door and pick his precious flowers?

Richard rushed Clay inside, then indignantly scanned the streets for gawkers before slamming the door. After quickly closing all the curtains on the bottom floor, he stopped to admire Clay. The boy had cost him more than the orchids, but he was just as lovely and had arrived more fresh.

Scarcely ten minutes later, Clay lay propped up in bed, carefully counting his money while Richard hurried around the room, cleaning up. Now he needed Clay James to leave before Riker Sims came to the door with the orchids. If Richard didn't answer when the stagecoach driver called out, he would leave the package with Hattie Liverpool at the sewing shop. Hattie was a bona fide, blue-ribboned busybody, and she would tap – hell, she would bang – on Richard's door until the late hours of night and demand to know where he had been all day. He hadn't been at the bank – she looked. And, "don't you know your orchids are plumb shriveled up by now? Might as well make jelly out of them."

The children swore that with Hattie Liverpool's penetrating vision she could see clean through walls. If she saw Clay lying in his bed, she would gasp, faint on his doorstep, and the entire town would rush over with smelling salts.

What a dreadful, dreadful thought. The thought alone made Richard wring his hands and pace the floor. Ten minutes of pleasure wasn't worth the anxiety chewing at his belly like chiggers. The anxiety of not knowing whether orchids could survive the harsh Texas sun was one thing. This anxiety was of a whole different class. It could mean public humiliation, the loss of his job, even imprisonment. What was he thinking when he had nervously arranged for Clay James to meet with him that afternoon?

He needed to get the boy out of his bed and out of his house before Hattie showed up with the dead orchids. He hadn't heard the rumble of the stagecoach passing by, or the bark of Riker's voice informing him he had a parcel, but it was hard to hear the rumble of anything with a boy like Clay James on top of you.

"It's not enough," said Clay.

"Pardon me?" Richard wasn't listening. He was moving from window to window, keeping an eye out for Hattie waddling up the boardwalk.

"I said, old man, it isn't enough." It was the tone of Clay's voice that made Richard turn from the window. It wasn't friendly like it had been when he first arrived.

"I don't understand," Richard stammered. "I'm sure it's the correct amount."

"No ... you owe me five dollars more."

"Five dollars! Why, that's robbery."

Clay grinned smooth at him. In his pants lying on the floor, the gold watch suddenly jingled a brief tune, warning of the hour. "It's getting late, sir."

"Oh, all right." Richard rushed to the dresser where he kept his plant money. Keeping his back to Clay, he peeled off more dollar bills. "Here. Take it."

Still lounging in bed, Clay accepted the money. "Thank you."

"You have to go now," said Richard. "I'm expecting..."

"Go?" said Clay. "I'm in no hurry to go. It's cool in here. Cooler than it is above that damn kitchen. How much money do you have in that drawer over there?" Clay sat up with just a tangled sheet wrapped around his bottom and pointed at the dresser. If there were thirty-five dollars more, Clay could be out of the fires of hell by tomorrow afternoon.

"I've paid you quite enough," said Richard, firmly. Anger was beginning to mingle unpleasantly with nervousness. "I've paid you twice the amount we agreed upon."

"That's debatable. Perhaps we should take it up with the marshal." Clay's smile was still lazy.

"The marshal? Good God, how can you suggest such a thing?" Angrily, Richard pulled the rest of the money from the drawer and threw it at Clay. "There's ten dollars more. It's all I have."

Finally, Clay rose lazily and beautifully sculpted from the blankets and began to search in the dim light for his boots.

As Richard watched the boy move unconcerned around the room, the chiggers again began to grumble unmercifully in the pit of his stomach. If Clay James had broken their agreement over the amount of money he was to be paid, what was to stop him from breaking his promise of remaining silent? How could Richard trust him? Broken Wagon Wheel was a small town. Clay need only whisper the secret to one soul. Whispers, like feathers, could be carried on the wind.

"You won't say anything to anyone, will you? Like you promised?" The words came out sounding more timid than he wanted.

"That depends." So far Clay had pulled on only his pants. Washington, D.C., was still twenty-five dollars away.

"Depends on what?"

"If you have five dollars for me next week. And five dollars the week after that..."

"That's blackmail!"

"Call it what you want," said Clay calmly. Damn Western men. An Eastern gent would have gladly given Clay the money without being coerced. Western men quibbled and whined over every halfpenny in their pockets. Only a fine horse seemed to get them excited. Clay had watched a cowboy part with a year's wages for a sorrel with a blaze on its forehead, then turn around and gripe over the price of sugar. "Five dollars next week, five dollars the week after that, and the week after that..."

What was Richard Mecum to do? Five dollars every week was his entire plant money, and he just placed an order for mountain bluebells, payable upon delivery. How was he to pay for them? And how was he to live with this devilish boy looking over his shoulder week after week? How was he to sleep with the fear that Clay might tell someone – the authorities, the newspapers, Hattie Liverpool, for chrissake?

Clay bent over to pull on a boot. An iron lantern sat on the table next to the bed. Richard moved quickly. Snatching up the heavy lantern, the banker closed his eyes and swung it blindly. He heard the dull crunch as the lantern smashed against the boy's head. When Richard opened his eyes, Clay was lying prone on the bed, dazed, disoriented, a large gash above his temple. A slight groan escaped his throat, and then he struggled to get up from the bed. Richard jumped on him, placing his fingers around Clay's smooth throat. Clay clasped the old man's wrists, tearing into them with his fingernails, but Richard continued to squeeze. The thin chain on the gold locket snapped and fell into the folds of the sheet. Eventually, Clay's beautiful body stopped kicking and became limp on the mattress.

◆

The desert sidewinder peacefully sunned itself on a smooth, flat rock. It was asleep, basically minding nature's business. It had already eaten that day – some rodent that it quietly sneaked up on and seized without much of a fight. Now the rattler was ready for the cool of the night to drop across the desert.

The sound of wagon wheels crunching through loose shale awakened the sleeping snake and its tongue darted in and out, sensing its surroundings for danger. The snake watched warily as the wagon stopped ten feet away, across a gully. Protectively, it slithered under a boulder, into a hollow, shaded area. An old man with a bright shock of white hair jumped out of the wagon and swiftly moved to the back. Hidden under a canvas was a large bundle wrapped in a blanket. With some difficulty the old man lifted the bundle, dropped it out of the wagon, and, using his boot, pushed it down the short slope of the gully. The blanket fell away when the bundle landed at the bottom.

It was a body. A human body. It came to a stop inches from the sidewinder. Defensively, the rattler coiled and struck at it. But it was already dead, harmless.

At the top of the gully, the old man searched the bluffs and the cliffs of Dead Horse Canyon for witnesses to his crime. Satisfied that no one had seen him, he wiped his hands on a neckerchief and climbed into the wagon. When the man was safely at a distance, the snake crawled back to its bed on the flat rock, cooling itself under a slowly sinking sun.

◆

Judd Brooks hunched over the low, flickering flame of his camp-fire. He didn't need the heat from the campfire – Dead Horse Canyon would hold its heat well into the night. He was trying to fry an egg without lard in an old tin pan. It wasn't working, and Judd was getting impatient. With idle curiosity, he watched the wagon approach the gully hundreds of feet below him. Vaguely, he wondered why the old yahoo was riding this far into the desert this late in the afternoon. When the old man pulled the body from the wagon and dumped it down the gully, Judd Brooks abruptly dropped the egg in the fire and scurried behind a ridge to get a better look. He stayed hidden there until the old man climbed back into the wagon and drove away. Then he slipped onto his horse and galloped out of the canyon and across the flatland.

He saw an old rattler sunning itself on a flat rock and started to take a shot at it, but he wasn't sure how far the wagon had traveled. He didn't want the sound of gunfire to bring the old man back to the gully.

Judd dismounted and slid down the incline. The body was lying facedown in the sand. Judd turned it over. It was a kid. Maybe nineteen, twenty, hard to tell. Immediately, Judd began to rifle through the boy's shirt. He didn't find any money. He lifted his hat, cursed at the sun taking its time sinking behind the canyon, then looked at the rattler again. Really, he should kill it. Rattlers weren't worth a damn.

Judd leaned over again and went through the kid's pants pockets. He pulled out a gold pocket watch. When he flipped open the cover, the watch played a sweet melody.

"Ain't that dern purty," said Judd, before sticking the watch in his pocket.

I

My dear Benjamin,
...your wholehearted enthusiasm for LEAVES OF GRASS and your letters delight me ... the copies of your poetry arrived yesterday afternoon ... i read them in the garden with the moon as my light ... remember, Benjamin, simplicity in all things ... i await our visit over tea when at last we meet! sincerely,

Walt Whitman
Camden, New Jersey
1875

Bennie Colsen sighed and put the letter back in his breast pocket. He had read it, say, about one thousand times now. He smiled wider than a jack-o'-lantern, one pleased boy. Normally, when Bennie smiled like that, I got an uncontrollable urge to wrestle him to the ground and take a taste of it. But we were rumbling along at ten miles an hour on the Southern Overland Express and we were not alone. The stagecoach held the blistering heat of the flatlands like a good canteen holds water, and it was encumbered with heavy-breathing passengers who were graciously trying to be tolerant of the heat and of each other. Course, most of them could afford to be tolerant; they were scheduled to disembark in El Paso or San Antonio. Bennie and I weren't that lucky. Our destination was the East Coast – Camden, New Jersey – to have tea with a poet. And I would rather have been skinned alive by Comanches.

Knowing what that smile was capable of doing to me, Bennie did it again before looking out the window at the passing scenery. We had left the cool, adobe relay station at the border of New Mexico and crossed into Texas. We were traveling fast, making good time, thanks to the skill of Riker Sims, the stagecoach driver. Thirty years prior, Sims had guided wagon trains into the new country. He led settlers into Oregon and Mormons into Utah. He fought the Ute and the bloody Cheyenne and stopped long enough to chisel his initials in Independence Rock in Wyoming. Riker Sims handled the stagecoach as if he were a solitary horseman, pulling it in and out of ditches, and across rugged mountain territories with ease. To move the coach forward he would shout, "Forward ho!" mainly because it was a habit from his wagon days.

Matt Hackett rode shotgun. He too was a veteran of Indian wars and handled his rifle as skillfully as Sims handled the stagecoach. The two men had driven the southwest line into Texas for ten years. Matt Hackett spent most of his conversational time griping about the railroads, convinced that the trains would eventually eliminate the need for coaches. "They're heading this way, Dakota," he grumbled at the relay station in New Mexico. "Couple more years and the border towns will be scarred by tracks like the rest of the country. There won't be any use for the ol' Concord then."

Riker Sims didn't have much to say about the railroads. In fact, he didn't have much to say about anything. He just nodded thoughtfully and let Matt Hackett speak for him. Folks got like that after a decade of working and living together. I hadn't completed a sentence without Bennie Colsen's help for two years now.

The ol' Concord was indeed an elegant coach. The seats had wire springs to cushion the bounce and soft tapestry coverings to make the ride more comfortable. Velvet curtains with heavy gold brocade and tassels draped thickly across the windows. When the curtains were closed they sheltered us from the dust and sun. They also sheltered us from light, the sky, and fresh air. Against everyone's wishes I pulled open the curtains and growled at anyone who attempted to draw them. A man could stand only so much confinement for so long.

Of course it was Bennie Colsen's fault we were traveling the long, hot southwestern stagecoach line, instead of taking the cooler and quicker eastern railway route to New Jersey. Back at our ranch in Two Rivers, California, Bennie wrongly concluded that since we were going on a cross-country pilgrimage anyway, we might as well dip down into Arizona to visit with his nephew, Danny Colsen, and rest a spell. Danny had learned to form words and ride horses since the last time we had seen him and Bennie felt he was shirking his duties as an uncle. It was impossible to explain to him that you just didn't dip down into the southwest on your way east without experiencing a mighty, mighty long journey. Already we were like two mushrooms that had sprouted from the damp tapestry seat and we were nowhere near New Jersey.

We were near El Paso.

Bennie sat across from me, our knees touching every now and then. It was the only physical contact we had made since Turnpike, Arizona, making the trip seem even longer, and me more irritable. Next to me sat John Edellton. He was a polite man whose only fault was that he was grossly overweight and occupied more than his fair share of the seat. Edellton's fat rested against me heavier than a buffalo coat, and when the stagecoach lurched, which it did often, I'd roll into his stomach and have a hard time getting back out.

"A man would be better off if he got out and walked to New Jersey," I grumbled, peeling my sweat-soaked skin away from John Edellton's sweat-soaked skin.

"Really, Dakota," Bennie laughed.

Edellton cleared his throat with exaggerated nervousness. "Taylor, is it? The gunfighter?"

"That's right," I responded with no small amount of pride. It pleased me to no end that it took only the mention of my first name to set a man's nerves on edge.

"Ex-gunfighter," Bennie volunteered. "He's in the cattle business now."

That drained some of the sap from my blood. It drained completely when Edellton said, "Cattle is a lucrative business," and they went on to discuss the monotonous details of marketing beef, Edellton no longer impressed by the fact that he was riding in a stagecoach with an infamous gunfighter. I stared out the window, wishing the Comanches would hurry up and get here.

Squeezed between John Edellton and the wall panel was a dusty little optometrist who hadn't given his name, though he was friendly enough. He carried a wooden case full of lenses and thin wire frames. Bennie purchased me a pair of spectacles and insisted I try them on for fit right there in front of Riker Sims and Matt Hackett. I promptly pocketed the spectacles with no intention of ever putting the funny-looking things on my face again.

The optometrist had a bad cough and would often spit blood into his neckerchief. His final stop was El Paso. Once there, he planned to re-establish a practice recently vacated by the previous optometrist, who had gotten rip-snorting drunk one night, lost his eyeglasses, and fell down a well. In my opinion, El Paso was a hellish habitat for someone with a consumptive cough, and I almost advised the little fellow to go to California where the salt air from the ocean had healing ways. I'd never met a coast Indian with a cough. But his cough was none of my affair. Besides, even the sincerest conversationalist would have had a hard time edging a word or two between the long-running dialogues of Bennie Colsen and Martha Edellton.

John Edellton's wife, Martha, sat across from the optometrist. She was a gracious lady with high manners and a penchant for conversation, which suited Bennie Colsen just fine. They possessed the mutual talent of remarking on every insignificant thought that crossed their minds from Arizona to Texas. Martha Edellton talked about the Methodist church she and her husband were going to build in San Antonio. Bennie talked about the law office he was going to open in Two Rivers, and about his letter from Walt, as he called him. Me and John Edellton didn't bother to talk. Him being a shopkeeper and me being a gunfighter – well, an ex-gunfighter, now cattle rancher – didn't leave us much to talk about. Nor did anyone bother to converse with the optometrist. The slightest effort to respond to a question threw him into a coughing spell so violent the rest of us winced in pain.

Sandwiched between Martha Edellton and Bennie was the Edellton's daughter, a pretty girl with a straight nose and luminous eyes. When the stage lurched and I rolled into Edellton, the daughter discreetly placed her hand on Bennie's knee to keep from leaning against him. It was a problem that was making her cheeks flush like a rose.

Dressed as he was, all gussied up for traveling and for his visit with his poet, Bennie Colsen was a beauty beyond comparison. The girl derived secret pleasure from sitting next to a fine, educated gentleman who had friends like Walt Whitman.

"Read the letter again!" the girl insisted.

"Of course!" Bennie eagerly obliged. "'My dear Benjamin...'"

I stared out the window. The landscape wobbled and bounced out of focus. Long, yellow flats were cluttered with woodsy sagebrush and dry chaparral. In the distance, rocky hills swelled upwards, breaking into orange-clay mesas. Lifting out of the chaparral, smeared against the horizon until they were almost unrecognizable from streamers of heat waves, jagged-edged buttes stood like thin red fortresses long ago abandoned by some stalwart army.

Miles to the east, an extended ribbon of dust floated lazily against a powdery blue sky. Cattle. Drovers were moving hundreds of head of cattle across the hot, dusty, waterless, colorless Texas plains. The lucky sons-of-bitches. I vaguely wondered how sore Bennie Colsen would have been if I jumped stagecoach and headed north with the cattle drive. Pretty damn sore, I reckoned.

Suspecting a heat rash caused by a scratchy, cotton collar that was too tight, I scratched at my neck. In fact, I itched all over and started to unbutton my shirt. Without looking up from the letter, Bennie nudged me in the shin with his boot, quietly warning me to leave my clothes alone. I had wrinkled my shirt coming out of Tucson and made crooked my tie somewhere in New Mexico. If it were possible for me to look like an intelligent but disheveled man, I did so at that moment. To impress his poet, Bennie had dressed me in a silky black coat, a silver paisley vest, a ruffled shirt, and had even put a gawdamn ribbon around my neck.

At exactly four minutes after twelve, the stagecoach rattled down El Paso Street and stopped in front of the relay station. Riker Sims was four minutes behind schedule and that didn't set well with him. It meant we had four minutes less to unload the optometrist, have supper at an adobe hostelry, and change horses. By one o'clock, we were rattling out of El Paso, minus one sick optometrist, and once again heading east across the flatlands. Once she overcame her initial shyness, the Edellton girl talked nonstop, a talent she apparently inherited from her mother. Her dignity was a little tattered at the hardship of being pressed against Bennie. She took a deep breath, fanned herself against the Texas heat and Bennie's heat, and chattered away like a blue jay. Excited beyond good reason by Whitman's invitation, Bennie shamelessly flirted with her.

"What was your name again?" he asked with an English accent that appeared to be weakening from years spent around my sloppy dialect.

"Caramel," she said.

"Like the candy." If Bennie's smile could make a fool out of a beat-up gunfighter such as myself, one could only imagine the effect it was having on this child.

"Do read the letter again, Mr. Colsen," she said.

"Now, Caramel," said Martha, "perhaps Mr. Colsen..."

"No, I don't mind at all," said Bennie, once again removing the letter from his pocket. After all, it had been over an hour since he'd last read the damn thing. "'My dear Benjamin...'"

Geezus.

Now, I'm not too proud to admit I was a mite jealous of this Whitman fella. Secretly, I wondered if he were a better-looking man than I, but Bennie assured me Whitman was a grandfatherly type with white hair and a white beard, and I relaxed some. Time had added a few more sun lines around my eyes, but I was still brown-haired and hard-bodied, so I stopped worrying, until Bennie added, "Handsome isn't all there is to a man." Well, you could have fooled me.

Not that I was annoyed with Whitman. I wasn't. In fact, I looked forward to shaking the man's hand, him being a Civil War patriot like myself. It was Bennie who was annoying the sap right out of me. Normally, he was delicate when it came to my overbloated pride, but this time, in his excitement, he was stomping my pride right into the ground with hobnailed boots. Once, I attempted to write flowery verse, embarrassed myself, and vowed to never try again. I could flick a gun and shave a man's mustache with a bullet without grazing his skin. I could flick a gun and shoot gnats out of the sky, nary missing a one. But gunplay didn't impress Bennie Colsen. Poetry did.

Bennie was halfway through the letter when the stagecoach abruptly pulled to the side of the road. I swayed into John Edellton. Caramel leaned lightly against Bennie. We stopped in the middle of the sparse flatlands east of El Paso. There were no buildings, no relay stations in sight, just the same sagebrush and chaparral I thought we passed miles ago. The stagecoach sat quietly, unmoving, as the minutes ticked on. Edellton finally stuck his head out the window and shouted up at the driver.

"Is everything all right, Mr. Sims?"

"Yes, sir. We're just waiting on passengers."

"What? Roadrunners?" Edellton said quietly, drawing laughs from all around.

A U.S. jail wagon rolled out of the flatlands, a strange, misshapen apparition moving slowly through the heat waves. Minutes later, the wagon sidled up alongside the stagecoach. Purely interested now, I sat up straight and poked my head out the window to get a good look. There were four men in the back of the wagon, a hostile bunch weighted down with chains. They grasped the iron bars with dirty hands and leered inquisitively at the coach. One of the prisoners, a bulldog with a human body, began to make catcalls at the Edellton women. A big, rugged-looking marshal jumped down from the driver's bench where he'd been riding shotgun, and moved to the back of the wagon. He unlocked the door and threatened the bulldog with death if he didn't mind his manners. Then the marshal pulled a scrawny man out of the wagon and led him to the stagecoach, gently prodding him with his rifle.

"I'm taking him into Broken Wagon Wheel," the marshal said to Riker Sims.

"It's our next stop, Marshal Graves. Find a seat on board," said Matt Hackett.

The jail wagon lurched forward, moving west towards El Paso with the three remaining prisoners. The door of the stagecoach swung open and the marshal shoved his prisoner into the small space next to John Edellton. He took a seat next to Martha.

"Howdy, ma'am," he said, tipping his dust-rimmed hat.

"Marshal," she nodded.

The outlaw wasn't only handcuffed, he was shackled around the ankles, and his chains clanged noisily as he wiggled around on the seat trying to make himself comfortable. We were gawking at him something awful and he sneered at us through broken, black teeth. A real bad guy.

Bennie stopped reading long enough to glance at the man in handcuffs, then stared down at his letter, annoyed that the outlaw had drawn attention away from his poet. Even Caramel momentarily forgot about Bennie and his charcoal eyes and peppery smell and studied the scrawny man with unabashed curiosity.

"Don't stare," whispered Martha, and Caramel turned her attention back to Bennie.

The marshal reclined lazily in his seat, like he had all the room a big man needed, then placed his hat over his face and folded his arms across a barrel-shaped chest to sleep. The marshal's size alone would make most men take care and walk with respect around him. He could crush the skinny outlaw's skull in just one of his hands.

His prisoner had nervous eyes, and they continually darted from his chains to the rifle resting next to the marshal's knee. Desert dust clung to both men's sweat-stained clothes and the coach filled with their odor. It looked as if the outlaw had given the marshal a good run for his pitiful paycheck, and I had to admire the big man's tenacity, even if he was wearing a tin star.

Now, I wouldn't have minded shootin' some bull with the marshal. No doubt he had interesting stories to tell, and I was curious to know what crime his prisoner had committed to put him in double irons. But I was dressed in that ridiculous suit. According to folklore, Pecos Bill laughed himself to death at the sight of a Boston man wearing mail-order cowboy duds. I am inclined to take that for the gospel. The marshal was a hard, trail-battered man. He'd probably get the fatal giggles at the sight of a gunfighter dressed for tea.

Once again, I was thoroughly annoyed with Benjamin Colsen, Jr., and I looked at him hard, forcing him to wonder what he had done to displease me this time. But he was too feather-tickled over his letter to worry about me and my irritations and he beamed at me like a full moon in July.

Riker Sims shouted, "Forward ho!" and the horses pulled onto the road, easily skirting past mesquite and prickly pear. Bennie finished reading his letter out loud, I hoped for the last time.

"'...sincerely, Walt Whitman...'" Then the expressive sigh.

"Walt Whitman?" the outlaw piped up. "Well, I'll be. That's dern important. Dern important."

"What do you know about important, Brooks?" the marshal mumbled from under his hat. "The only important thing you're going to do is hang."

"I've read Walt Whitman. Yes, sir, I have. *'O hotcheeked and blushing! O foolish hectic! O for pity's sake, no one must see me now!'*"

"Oh, for pity's sake, shut up," grumbled the marshal.

Bennie sat there with his mouth hanging open. Then he looked at me smugly, suggesting with that look that even this outlaw, shackled in chains and on his way to a hanging, was a more civilized man than I for knowing how to quote poetry.

"What did he do to deserve a hanging?" Martha finally asked.

Well, hallelujah for her. I'd been busting to know that since they boarded the stagecoach.

"Killed a boy outside of Broken Wagon Wheel and left his body for the coyotes," said the marshal.

"I ain't kilt nobody," the outlaw sulked.

"Yeah, yeah," the marshal drawled. "Convince the hangman."

"There ain't going to be no hanging. Not when Juan Caballe gets hold of this here stagecoach."

If the outlaw expected to put terror in our hearts with his threat, it didn't work. No one on the stagecoach was Texas-born and they had never heard of Juan Caballe. But I had. I knew exactly who Juan Caballe was. All I had to do was close my eyes and I could see the jagged lightning-bolt scar that crossed his cheek, hear his hearty baritone laugh, watch his eyes dance with pleasure when a beautiful woman walked by or the beautiful woman's husband drew on him. Oh, hell, yeah, I knew Juan Caballe. If he had not been so lethal, I would have enjoyed his company.

I had to admit, the sound of his name caused me to blink a couple of times, and I suddenly recognized the marshal's prisoner. Not by sight – I'd never seen the scrawny outlaw before – but by reputation. His name was Judd Brooks, a member of

Caballe's ratty band of horse thieves and bank robbers. Judd was fast with a gun — some say faster than Dakota Taylor, though I chuckled at the notion. Still, Judd Brooks was a mean little man, as wild and unpredictable as a rodent stuck in a trap. Hell and almighty, this stagecoach ride was getting interesting.

"That's right," Brooks goaded the unresponsive passengers. "Y'all be hurtin' when Caballe gets here."

"Brooks, if you don't shut up, I'll hang you from one of them mesquite branches outside," said the marshal.

The outlaw guffawed. "Ya cain't hang a man from a mesquite bush."

"Then I'll shoot you and have it done with."

Bennie leaned close to whisper to keep from riling the outlaw again. "Who's Juan Caballe?"

"Mexican bandit."

"Is he dangerous?" Caramel's bright eyes were made pale from worry.

"Well, ma'am, he can be. But there's no need to worry. Caballe rides southwest of the Rio and makes camp in the foothills of Sierra Madre. I doubt he'll ride this far north."

I said it to calm the girl. The truth was, Caballe was a mad dog who feared no law and knew no boundaries. Most of the border towns of New Mexico and Texas had been terrorized at one time or another by the Caballe gang. Judd Brooks was his right-hand man and his quick draw. Juan Caballe would not let the scrawny outlaw with bad teeth hang. By my estimation, the big marshal was enjoying his final nap before Caballe and his gang tore him apart like a pack of timber wolves.

Shifting in my seat, I felt the friendly bump of a Colt .44 resting against my thigh. For over a decade the two Colts had brought me more comfort than any warm body on a cold night had. And I was glad to feel their warmth strapped against me now. Hunkering down against the tapestry seat, I grinned with cocky confidence at Bennie Colsen. If Juan Caballe was coming, let him come.

2

If someone had taken quick inventory of the passengers aboard the Southern Overland Express, it would have appeared we were sorely lacking in fighting spirit. There was a shopkeeper, a church lady, a young girl, and a pretty fellow who preferred books to bullets. But, upon closer inspection, they would also have found a marshal, a gunfighter, and Matt Hackett standing ready at top. Bennie Colsen could shoot if he had to. He once took a shot at a trespassing horse thief who had it in mind to help himself to my palomino. Bennie didn't harm the fellow any. In fact, he missed by a couple of yards. But he put the thief on the run, without my horse.

So I'd say we were half-lucky. The three of us – Hackett, the marshal, and me – with the help of Bennie's poor aim, might be able, I figured, to hold off a cavalcade of Mexican bandits. I'd say it was about as possible as holding back a raging river.

If the big marshal was worried, he showed it in true Texas style. He snoozed. Sometimes he fell into such a deep sleep, his throat gurgled and a muffled snore crept out from under his hat. The stagecoach hit a bump and the marshal jumped out of his sleep and grabbed his rifle. He blinked at us sheepishly when he realized he'd been jolted by a rut in the road, not by Juan Caballe. Once again, he reclined against the soft tapestry seat and fell into a deep sleep. But I had no doubt the man was ready for anything that came our way.

And then it came. The stagecoach picked up speed gradually, moving smoothly at first, then it began to rumble and roll recklessly. The wheels lifted off the ground and the Concord groaned as if it were about to split apart. Riker Sims took up a shout: "'Ee-haw! 'Ee-haw!" I heard the reins slash the air as he whipped the six-horse team into an all-out gallop. Soon Matt Hackett's rifle sounded above the clatter of the stagecoach.

"Geezus...," I groaned, removing my Colt .44s from their holsters.

"What is it?" asked Bennie.

"Junior," I said, handing him a Colt, "aim that thing straight and shoot to kill. And don't be shy about it."

"Kill what?" He stared at the gun, perplexed.

The marshal was jerked out of his nap and shoved the barrel of his rifle out the window. "You ladies, get down on the floor," he commanded.

Quickly, without asking questions, Martha and Caramel scuttled onto the floorboard. John Edellton closed his arms around his family in an attempt to shield them with his bulk.

"Might as well give 'er up," chuckled Judd Brooks.

I squinted across the flatlands, trying to find movement in the mesquite thickets. Matt Hackett fired a second shot, but I must have been dead blind, because I sure couldn't see what he was shooting at. Maybe a coyote spooked the team. Maybe a snake crossed the road and stampeded the horses. Maybe Matt Hackett had a bad case of snake fright and was taking double shots at it.

The mesquite brush rustled as if a sudden wind had kicked up. It began to twist and bend, becoming a shadowy mass of a dozen horsemen galloping out of the flatlands. Juan Caballe rode at the head, the weight of him bobbing gracefully up and down on his saddle as he pursued us at a dead run. He held his fire until his men were within range, then he lifted his hand and they started shooting simultaneously.

It didn't take them long to gain on us. Their sturdy Mexican-bred horses were accustomed to desert travel, and the grumbling, pitching stagecoach was no match for their speed. I fired at the first man who came near and he tumbled from the saddle. There were more guns aboard the stagecoach than the bandits expected and they split into a V-formation: some of them rode to our right, some to our left, while others trailed behind. Another rider galloped wildly alongside us with his long, heavy poncho flapping and his pistol firing. Doing some fancy riding, he grabbed the rear of the coach, flipped off his horse, and climbed to the roof.

Matt Hackett swiftly stood to meet him, firing point-blank into the bandit's chest. Then Hackett let out a painful holler as a bullet slammed into him. He lost his balance and fell under the hooves of the stampeding horses. The stagecoach momentarily lifted as it rolled over his body.

"Hackett went down," I informed the marshal.

A bullet tore through the side wall panel, ripping into the velvet curtain inches from Bennie's head. In a sudden spurt of anger, Bennie fired blindly out the window. The rider closest to him fell from his horse.

The marshal glanced over his shoulder. "That's fine shootin', son."

The shootin' on our side of the stagecoach was so fine the bandits decided to try their luck on the marshal's side, which was also the driver's side. Juan Caballe knew what he had to do. He had to stop Riker Sims. I stumbled across John Edellton and over Judd Brooks to help the marshal stop an attack on Sims, but I was too late.

"I've been hit!" Riker called. "I can't hold her much longer." Seconds later, the reins slipped from Riker's hands and trailed along the ground.

The Concord swayed and groaned as the horses galloped frantically across the flatland. The Mexicans circled the team in an attempt to stop the stagecoach, but without a driver to direct them, the horses panicked, veered off the wagon trail, and stampeded into the mesquite thickets. The stagecoach tipped dangerously as it rolled over stumps and sand drifts.

"We gotta stop this damn thing," said the marshal.

The thought had just crossed my mind. At this speed, if the coach turned over, none of us would walk away from it alive. "Cover me," I said.

I shoved my Colt into my waistband and squeezed through the window. I heard the boom of the second Colt and a faint yelp as Bennie fired on a bandit that was aiming to take a shot at me. Clutching onto the thin window setting, I hoisted myself out of the coach. Carefully, I balanced my heels on the window ledge, grabbed the top rail, and swung onto the roof. The roof was piled high with trunks, hatboxes, mailbags, and parcels. With the stagecoach tilting and dipping, I didn't have the time or the agility to crawl across the packages. I removed my knife and slashed the ropes holding the luggage in place. The trunks fell into the desert, cracking open on impact and scattering colorful dresses and shirts across the flatlands. Once that was done, I easily crawled across the roof and dropped into the driver's box.

Riker Sims was slumped over, clutching his side. He had taken a hit under the arm and the bench was wet with his blood. He was just conscious enough to be angry about losing control of his rig, and was deliriously cursing himself and Juan Caballe. "I ain't lost one of my coaches yet," he grumbled. "And I don't aim to now."

"Well, you just hang on, old man. We'll get her settled soon enough." Bold words, considering.

I grabbed a rope lying on the seat and secured the wounded driver to the coach to keep him from tumbling into the path of the horses. Then I concentrated on stopping the stagecoach. There had to be a brake somewhere ... somewhere. I found a wooden lever that sort of looked like it should work and put my full weight into it. The horses were big, powerful, and in a run. Even with the brake on, they pulled the coach along as if it were a dainty preacher's carriage. The brake didn't even slow them.

I studied the sweating broad backs of the horses as they swayed through the thorny mesquite. Then I stared down at the reins skipping across the ground. I was trying to decide which course of action would be less likely to get me killed. Should I try to recover the reins? Or should I try to reach the lead horses and bring them to a halt?

A bullet sang past my ear, hastening my decision. I jumped, catching in the harness between the rear horses. Pressed between the two horses, I was pummeled from side to side, and my left leg dropped, tangling in the harness chain. The force of gravity started to pull me under, and I knew if I didn't untangle myself soon, I'd be dragged beneath the stagecoach, suffering the same fate that befell Matt Hackett. I clutched the left horse's mane with my right hand and swung onto its back, kicking my leg loose from the chains. Carefully, I jumped to the middle horses, then across them to the lead horses. Reaching between the two lead animals, I grabbed the bridle.

The larger mare at my left took most of the pull from the bridle and she threw back her head, preparing to give me a good argument, but I pulled harder. Abruptly, without warning, she dug her hooves into the sand and came to a dead stop. Luckily, the other horses followed her lead and did the same. If they hadn't, we would have suffered an ugly pileup. The stagecoach rocked and shuddered for a moment, then finally rested, on all four wheels, among the sand dunes and mesquite.

I didn't have time to consider our luck – constantly changing as it was. The team of horses quickly disappeared in a deep circle of red dust, blinding me, as Juan Caballe and his men surrounded the stagecoach. Their actions once again excited the team, and the lead mare stamped her foot, wishing she could bolt. As I stared down the powder black eye of a dragoon, I kind of shared her sentiments.

It was the biggest damn gun I had ever laid eyes on. Any bigger and it would have been considered a carbine, instead of a pistol. At long range, it was close to worthless; powerful but inaccurate. Short distance, it was both powerful *and* accurate and could make a mess of a man's face. My face was only inches from its power, and after nodding quiet respect to the gun, I let my eyes travel up the arm of the man holding it.

Brown cat eyes peered out from under a wide straw hat. I saw nothing but black hair, a black beard sprinkled with ash, and a scar bolting savagely across a sun-bronzed cheek. Juan Caballe. Handsome as all hell.

"Good afternoon, American," he said, languidly.

"Howdy."

Caballe grinned lazily and slowly moved the dragoon up and down, motioning for me to get off the horse. I disentangled myself from the bridles and jumped to the ground. A short, round man with smooth, coffee-colored skin yanked open the door of the stagecoach. "Throw out your guns," he demanded.

The marshal and Bennie tossed out their guns, then carefully stepped out of the coach with their hands raised. The Edelltons followed after them. Greedily, the round man gathered up the guns.

Clumsy with chains and excitement, Judd Brooks practically fell out of the coach. "What took you so dern long, Frank?"

Frank, whose Spanish name was Francisco, shrugged insolently. "No big hurry."

The round man didn't like Judd Brooks and eyed him with contempt. Just to annoy him, Judd repeatedly called him "Frank," purposely mocking his Spanish name.

"Mebbe not fer you, Frank. I done dirtied my pants fer worry, Frank," he sneered.

Irritated, Francisco moved away from Judd and pretended to busy himself with the horses. Juan Caballe circled the stagecoach on an ugly, shaggy bay mare, then stopped in front of the marshal.

"Marshal Cameron Graves," he said easily. "It is good to see you again. Why do you think we always meet like this? Me with a gun, you with your hands in the air?"

"You're just lucky, I reckon. The luckiest sonofabitch this side of the Rio." Both men were smiling and talking friendly. But the coldness of their smiles and the hatred in their eyes underlined their true feelings for each other.

"I don't think so," said Juan. "I think, perhaps, you are just not very good."

"Oh, I'll track you down again, Caballe. I've done it before, I will do it again."

"Sierra Madre will welcome you." Juan laughed, a robust, playful laugh.

It was a sorry joke. Sierra Madre was a damnable mountain range in Mexico. It welcomed no one but Apache and men as brutally scarred as Caballe. Even the rugged marshal would become as inept as a lost schoolboy against its terrain.

Judd roughly patted the marshal's vest until he found a ring of keys. Anxiously, he unlocked his handcuffs, then went to work on the ankle shackles.

"Pole," said Juan. "Get their money and jewelry."

The man he called Pole was inhumanly tall and thin. His face was ravaged by acne scars, as if someone had taken a tiny knife and repeatedly pricked his skin. He had one white eye and one blue eye, was as gray and lanky as a timber wolf, and looked just as hungry. He was crazy. So far, none of his actions suggested he was crazy – in fact, he was the quietest of the lot. You could just sense it. Pole was more wicked than Caballe's hefty dragoon.

Now, maybe the bandits would be satisfied with robbing us of our money and trinkets and be done with it. If so, I'd be satisfied along with them. I had stolen a couple of dollars and a few cheap brooches in my lifetime. But I was made restless by the fear they might make sport of killing someone; perhaps someone who didn't obey quick enough or who moved the wrong way. I had traveled a long distance with the Edelltons, was more than a little partial to Bennie Colsen, and wouldn't stand for gunning down an unarmed man – even if that man was the law. A damnable mountain range or hell itself wouldn't stop me from hunting Juan Caballe if one of my traveling companions should die without provocation. Carefully, I studied the face of each bandit, letting their images burn into my memory ... just in case I was forced to remember.

The hungry bandit with the white eye promptly freed Edellton of his fat moneybelt. Bennie handed Pole his money without arguing. I could only shrug at the bandit. I didn't carry a moneybelt; putting money in one easy place seemed like a foolish thing to do. I kept my money in my boot, next to my Arkansas toothpick, and that's where it stayed.

A silver bracelet dangled from Caramel's slim wrist. Pole spied the bracelet and reached for it. Caramel pulled away. "It was my grandmother's," she tried to explain. Pole grabbed her arm, twisting slightly.

"Don't hurt her," Bennie snapped.

That was the provocation I was worried about and my muscles tensed as Pole's one good eye flashed at Bennie. My Colt was still in my waistband. I could take Caballe and Pole, and maybe a few more of them, down with one wild sweep of the Colt. No problem. After that, we'd all be slaughtered.

I'll be danged if Pole didn't release Caramel's arm and take a step backwards, amused by Bennie's brashness. He glanced up at Caballe and smiled. A sweet smile for such a horrible-looking man. Calmly, Bennie unlatched the bracelet and dropped it in Pole's sandy palm.

"Gracias," he muttered, still amused.

Juan Caballe leaned across his ugly bay and once again pointed the dragoon at my chest. "Brooks," he said, "unbutton his coat."

"Why?" the nervous outlaw whined. "Let's get outta here." Judd was free of his chains, but was still jittery, and there was fear in his voice. Double irons and the shadow of a noose will do that to a man.

"This one is good. He can remove the eye from a humming-bird while it's in flight. There's a gun bigger than a cannon under his coat. Do you want to turn your back on him? I don't."

Skepticism flashed across Brooks's ferret face. "Frank got all the guns."

"Unbutton his coat," Juan demanded quietly.

Judd unbuttoned my coat and found the last Colt. He removed the gun and held it up to the sunlight to admire it. "Ain't it purty? Where's the other one? There were two of 'em."

"It's mine," said Francisco, quickly shoving the Colt I had given Bennie into his pants.

"Gimme it."

"To hell with you. I found it first."

Judd Brooks shot him. Just flat-out shot him. The round man crumpled at Martha's feet without so much as a whisper of complaint.

"That's got a boom to it!" Judd laughed. He leaned over Francisco's body and gathered up the second Colt, then squinted up at Caballe. "He should have given me the gun."

Juan looked down from his horse at his men as if they were incorrigible, mischievous children instead of brutal killers. He didn't know if he should scold Brooks for shooting Francisco or let him have his fun. "You are one *loco hombre,*" he finally said.

They were all *loco.* And you couldn't trust one *loco hombre,* let alone a wolf pack of them. "You got what you wanted," I said, coolly. "Why don't you take your boys and ride on now?"

There was the hint of a challenge in my words and Caballe recognized it. He studied me for a second, trying to decide if he should meet that challenge. "Get on your horses," he said to his men.

"What about Francisco?" asked Pole.

"Leave him. But bring his horse." Juan turned his shaggy bay, then glanced over his shoulder at me. "That's a nice suit you are wearing, Dakota."

3

I don't believe Juan Caballe really appreciated my suit. He just wanted to let me know he knew who I was – by name, not just reputation. I wasn't sure if that was good or bad, though I reckoned it bordered on bad. My previous encounters with Caballe were always brief, not personal. On the few occasions that I sat across a smoke-filled saloon from him, I watched with slight detachment as his men drank, boasted, and caused general mischief. But I never sat at a table with Caballe, never played a hand of cards with him, or drank a round of whiskey. My instincts warned me we were a deadly combination. Now there was a good possibility I had made an enemy of Juan Caballe, and, as I scrambled up the side of the stagecoach to tend to Riker Sims, I knew in my gut that Caballe had made an enemy of Dakota Taylor. The thought would give a weaker man the shivers.

The Mexicans' horses were retreating specks on the horizon when I lowered Riker from the box into the marshal's waiting arms. "He took a mean hit," I said. "He's bleeding mightily."

The marshal laid Riker out on the ground, pulled open his shirt, and inspected his wounds. Riker swatted at him, either from pain or irritation.

"Where's Matt?" the old man demanded, lifting himself off the ground and pushing the marshal away.

"We lost Matt in the run," said Cameron. "Now, Sims, hold still and let me put something on this wound before you bleed to death."

"Lord Almighty..." The fight went out of him and he allowed the marshal to plug his wound with a bandana.

"Help me lift him into the stagecoach," said Cameron as I dropped down from the driver's box. "There's a sawbones in Broken Wagon Wheel."

"Is that where we're going, Marshal?" asked John Edellton. The shopkeeper feared he would never get his family safely to San Antonio.

"Yes, sir. You folks can reach your destination from there. Right now this man needs a doctor and Broken Wagon Wheel is the closest town."

"Of course." Edellton ushered his family back into the stagecoach. Bennie got in, then Cameron and I gently slid the wounded driver across the seat, where he rested his head on Bennie's knee. Riker Sims was about as comfortable as a man with a bullet in him could be.

"Careful not to crush that package," said Riker, still feisty despite a serious loss of blood. "It's got mountain bluebells in it. Too fragile to ride on top."

Bennie picked up the package and peered through the airholes before putting it off to the side. "Bluebells ... in south Texas?"

Riker chuckled. His head lolled tiredly in Bennie's lap. "For Richard Mecum, the finest horticulturist there ever was. He could grow a Christmas tree in the middle of the Sahara."

"He would have to," muttered Bennie.

Riker coughed, grimaced, coughed again, then shouted, "Dammit, Marshal Graves, we'll be a year behind schedule if you don't get this coach moving."

The marshal quickly secured the door. Together we wrapped the dead bandit in a canvas and heaved his body upon the roof for the undertaker. When that was done the two of us stood staring at the Concord.

"Can you handle this rig?" asked Cameron.

"You bet." Actually, I had never operated a stagecoach before, but it was an interesting prospect, and at least I knew where the brake was located. We were in good shape.

It was tricky leading the horses out of the mesquite thickets, but once we were on the wagon trail I smoothly swung the coach around and headed back to retrieve Matt Hackett's broken body. There wasn't time to gather up the clothes or packages and I left them in the desert. Comanches would no doubt stumble upon them and put them to use. But Matt Hackett was a decent man who deserved a proper burial. I wasn't going to leave him for the Comanches or the coyotes, even if it meant another delay. We found him in the road, looking peaceful, and bundled him up in a canvas and placed him on the roof alongside the dead bandit. Then I led the horses east and they happily trotted towards town.

"You're Dakota Taylor," said the marshal after we had ridden an hour in silence. It was a statement, not a question.

I didn't respond right away. This man was wearing a big star on his big chest. "I might be."

He chuckled softly. "I'm Cameron Graves. Town marshal of Broken Wagon Wheel."

"I picked up on your name. And your occupation."

The marshal studied me carefully out of the corner of one eye. "As far as I know, you're not wanted in the state of Texas."

"Is that right?" The news surprised me some. The last time I had been in Texas, I was forced to hightail it across the border into Mexico, then follow the river back into New Mexico. At a cantina in Del Rio, a Texas Ranger had drunk too much and boasted too long and wasn't as fast as his liquor or his boasts led him to believe. "I thought I killed a Ranger round these parts."

"Wild Wes Fossey. I know the man. He can drink a keg of whiskey, but he can't hit the broad side of a barn standing sober."

"Then I got lucky. He drank a keg of whiskey and missed me by a couple of miles. The trouble is I didn't miss him, and folks in Texas don't take kindly to sharpshooters killing their Rangers."

"Son, you damaged him some, but you didn't kill him. There were a dozen witnesses who said Wes drew on you first, though you did encourage him to do so. You'd know that if you hadn't run for the river like a man on fire."

"I don't stick around after putting a bullet in a lawman." I tapped my head. "Not smart."

"Welp, Wes is still grumbling about it, and he's walking with a gimp now. I'd stay far out of his way if I were you."

Wes Fossey was one of those men who carried a chip on his shoulder because he was short. Barely five-two in heels. After a few drinks he took his shortcomings out on taller men just to prove he was tough. Maybe he was tough. Maybe he could have given me a decent beating if I'd given him a chance. But tough doesn't make you fast with a gun. Wes Fossey's failing was that he didn't understand that Dakota Taylor, the gunfighter, doesn't care to prolong arguments. Either a man had better draw his iron or shut up, go away, and leave me alone. I wasn't going to be rolling around in the sawdust because someone was bothered about his height. The news that Fossey was still alive, and the ire in my stomach reserved for Juan Caballe, just convinced me more that Texas was not the state for me to linger in.

"Is New Jersey far enough?" I asked.

"Is that where you're heading?"

"Yep."

The marshal glanced at me sharply. "What are you doing in Texas?"

"A small detour," I mumbled.

"I reckon." Cameron sucked in his breath. He was tired, the depth of his exhaustion demonstrated in the hard way he breathed. "If you're interested in sticking around for a while, I'd offer you a job."

"Doing what?"

"I could use a deputy. One good with a gun."

I darn near laughed. In fact, I would have laughed if I hadn't been so sore about losing Matt Hackett and my precious Colts. All I could do was manage a grunt. "I ain't interested in sticking around."

"I've spent six months tracking Judd Brooks. I caught him, I brought him to trial, got a conviction..." He breathed deeply again. "It took less than ten minutes to lose him."

If he was trying to get my sympathy it wasn't going to work. I shook my head violently. "It ain't my concern. Why don't you deputize some of your boys in Broken Whatever-it-is."

"Oh, hell, they're scared senseless of Juan Caballe. A scared man is a useless man. Before the citizens of Broken Wagon

Wheel hired me, Caballe and his men were treating themselves to all the money, supplies, and livestock they could steal. But I can't keep them out on my own."

"Call in the Rangers."

"They're here. So is the army. They have the Comanches under control, but Juh is keeping them mighty busy."

"Juh? The Apache?"

"Chiricahua Apache."

I whistled through my teeth. "Geezus. God didn't make 'em any meaner than that."

"Juh slips into Arizona, New Mexico, Texas, with his raiding parties, then slips back into Mexico without leaving a shadow behind. No one has ever seen him, that's how slippery he is. Juan Caballe is more visible than the afternoon sun in comparison. But I'm only one marshal against him and his two dozen merry men. The Southern Pacific is fixing to bring a railroad through the pass. They want the Indians and the bandits cleared out of here before they will start laying tracks."

"Them railroad boys are a delicate bunch, aren't they?"

"The Rangers and the army are keeping their side of the street swept clean. Broken Wagon Wheel is my town. That makes Juan Caballe my problem."

"You're not afraid of Caballe?"

Cameron grunted. "Should I be?"

"Sure, you should. He collects more badges than he does livestock. And he lives to brag about it."

"I still have mine." Cameron tapped his round chest, then looked down at my side. "Appears to me he collected your guns instead. An empty holster is a useless holster. Son, you might as well throw that gunbelt away."

That was the solemn truth. Some weasely eyed, black-toothed, low-life outlaw stole my Colts and it was a source of pure irritation. I wasn't in the mood to even admit it, let alone be ridiculed. I stayed quiet.

"Now, it seems to me," Cameron continued, "that Dakota Taylor would not let a man strip him of his guns and walk away."

My face flushed, either with anger or embarrassment. Hard to tell which. "Since you think you got me figured, Marshal, you should know I don't travel on your side of the law. I've collected a few badges myself. I'll take care of Judd Brooks and Juan Caballe should either of them be foolish enough to cross my trail again."

"Judd Brooks killed a boy. He wasn't even twenty yet. He hit him in the head, strangled him, then threw his body down a gully. Just threw him away like he was an old shoe."

"He's a cruel sonofabitch. You have your work cut out for you."

"You ain't scared of Juan Caballe, are you?" Again, he peered at me out of the corner of one eye.

I ain't dumb. I knew what the marshal was trying to do. He was trying to shame me into becoming his deputy marshal. What the marshal didn't know was that Dakota Taylor felt no shame, on no occasion. Shame is a waste of time.

"You know the fellow who was driving us crazy by reading that letter from his poet friend over and over again?"

"The boy you're traveling with?"

I nodded. "His name is Benjamin Colsen, Jr. I'm more scared of him than I am of Juan Caballe. And he's hell-bent on getting to New Jersey."

The sun seemed to rest two feet above the horizon and was dropping fast when we rolled into Broken Wagon Wheel. Its eerie, weakening glow cast upon the town tarnished orange shadows that highlighted the anterior of the buildings. Squat, sun-baked adobes lined most of the streets, but there were a few plank buildings. Two-story board buildings with fake facades, drooping awnings, and sloping porches stood grandly next to low, square adobes. Their paint had been chipped and discolored through the years by sun and sandstorms. The town was small, as most border towns were, but it was well populated, and rambled on past the main street to form alleyways and back roads where more low adobes sat side by side. The roads were wide, dusty, and deeply rutted. The land around Broken Wagon Wheel was so flat you could see a rider coming from a hundred miles.

Wagons and fancy buggies rested outside of a two-story hostelry. Saddled horses stood impatiently at hitching rails, stamping their feet, swishing their tails, waiting for their riders to emerge drunkenly from one of the two saloons. As soon as the stagecoach rumbled down Main Street, a large group of people filled the boardwalks and walked towards the depot. It seemed to me there were far more people than there were buildings to shelter them all.

"You got a busy little city here," I said to Cameron.

He nodded grimly. "They came to see a hanging. Laredo, San Antonio, El Paso ... Folks from south Texas traveled hundreds of miles to watch the outlaw Judd Brooks swing in the wind."

"They're bound to be disappointed."

I guided the stagecoach past a recently constructed gallows, then stopped in front of Pappy's Livery as instructed. The stagecoach was quickly surrounded by people, which wasn't out of the ordinary. The mail, sometimes a relative, came in on the stage and it was customary for townsfolk to make a special occasion out of its arrival. But, even by an arriving stagecoach's standard, this was a large swarm of people. Nearly everybody in town, including visitors from Laredo, San Antone, and El Paso, stood in front of Pappy's humble livery. Judd Brooks was supposed to be on board and they had come to take one fearless look at the condemned man.

But when they saw Cameron Graves riding shotgun and a stranger holding the reins, idle conversation turned into excitable questions. Where was Riker Sims? Matt Hackett? Judd Brooks? And why was this dandy in a ruffled shirt driving the coach?

An old man with bowed legs and a bent back shuffled out of the stables and wordlessly took control of the gathering even as he looked upon me with suspicion.

"Where's Sims?" he demanded.

"He's been hurt, Pappy," said Cameron. "Send Lucky to fetch the doctor."

"Lucky!" Pappy shouted up at the hayloft. "Fetch the doc. Hurry it up now."

A little girl who was dressed like a boy swung out of the hayloft on a rope, dropped into a haystack, then ran fleet of foot down the boardwalk.

John Edellton threw open the door and, with Bennie's help, unloaded Riker Sims. The driver was still cantankerous and insisted he didn't need a doctor. Two burly men hoisted him across their shoulders and hauled him away despite his protests.

"Take care of my horses, Pappy!" Riker shouted over their shoulders. "And don't forget to sign the manifest."

"Was it Juan Caballe?" Pappy whispered in a gravelly voice.

Cameron nodded, then dropped out of the box. "Tell Mayor Bagley to call a meeting at the Crow. We have some things to discuss. And find Josh Reynolds. I want him there." The marshal started towards his office, away from the townsfolk and their persistent questions, had second thoughts, and turned to me. "If you change your mind, I'll be at the Crow."

"Change your mind about what?" asked Bennie.

I jumped down from the coach. "Nothing, Junior."

Once the marshal had barricaded himself in his office, the crowd began to quietly return to their homes and hotel rooms, gathering in small pockets here and there to exchange what little information they managed to find out among themselves.

Bennie wiped sweat from his neck with a white linen neckerchief and looked around him. "Good Lord, where are we?"

I squinted down Main Street. Sun and plains and chaparral and mesquite stretched for miles, a painful sight to behold. But, unless my tired eyes were playing tricks on me, in the center of town was a spot of green and blue ... and palm trees. A mirage.

"If we're not in Texas, I'd have to say we're in Florida."

Bennie noticed the flowery oasis and said, "What a strange sight." Then his dark eyes flashed with recognition. "Ah, Richard Mecum, the horticulturist."

"The what?"

He reached inside the coach, took out the package, and rattled it in front of my face. "Bluebells."

It was the only parcel that had survived Juan Caballe's attack. Everything else was lost in the desert. I was especially concerned for the Edelltons. Their money had been stolen, their belongings tossed in the desert like garbage. They were left with nothing but big dreams and their lives, which, I suppose, was more than most folks had after a violent encounter with Juan Caballe. Cameron assured me the Christianly people of Broken Wagon Wheel would see to the Edelltons' needs while they were in town.

As for me, I still had a thick wad of money in my boot. The first thing I was going to do — well, the *second* thing, the first being to wet my dusty throat at the nearest saloon — was to buy me a change of clothes. I wasn't going to spend an extra day in this gambler's costume.

"We'd better see that Pappy gets that package," I said. At least he would know that *something* came in on the stagecoach that day.

A rotund woman, dressed in a dazzling, yellow-checkered smock, suddenly accosted Bennie. I had noticed her standing among the crowd. In that dress, and with a two-foot straw hat covered with large satin sunflowers, she was hard not to notice. She grabbed Bennie by the arm and refused to let go even when he instinctively recoiled at the sudden closeness of her.

"Is it true? Did Juan Caballe really attack the stage?" Her face was as sweet as the moon, though it was pinched with concern.

"I'm afraid it's true," Bennie answered solemnly. Gently, he placed his hand on her hand in a discreet attempt to get her to release her grip on his arm.

But she dug in her fingernails as she emphasized each question. "And Judd Brooks escaped?"

Another solemn nod from Bennie. "I'm afraid so."

"And Matt Hackett and Riker Sims were killed?"

"Well, that's only half..."

"See, Elizabeth?" She suddenly released his arm and turned to a diminutive woman standing silently at her side. "Didn't I tell you that's what happened? Didn't I tell you it *would* happen?"

The larger, moon-faced woman turned back to Bennie and stuck out a small, pudgy hand. "I'm Hattie Liverpool and this is Elizabeth Ratcliff. We're from the Ladies' Welcoming Committee. If we can be of assistance..."

Bennie Colsen nearly jumped for joy. The boy had a fine appreciation for welcoming committees and had tried on several occasions to organize a committee in Two Rivers. Bennie's central goal in life was to establish a certain amount of decorum in a town that was nothing more – and didn't want to be anything more – than a rowdy mining center. Ninety-nine percent of Two Rivers' population were hard-drinking, fast-playing, goatish men; men who broke their guts laughing over Bennie's proposal to start a welcoming committee. Working under the assumption that women equaled decorum, he set out on a campaign to bring more women into Two Rivers. He had, in fact, advertised for a woman law partner to join his law firm, knowing that very few women came equipped with a law degree – an injustice that set him off on another campaign. Before he became distracted by Walt Whitman's invitation, Bennie was on a letter-writing crusade, demanding that Harvard and Yale open their courses to women. Of course they ignored him, which just irritated him further, so he joined a women's suffrage movement in Sacramento. And all because he wanted a simple welcoming committee in Two Rivers. Personally, I was satisfied with a town full of goatish men.

His immediate respect for Hattie Liverpool was almost gushing. "Yes, you can assist us," he said happily. "Where can we find a place to eat?"

"The Wagon Wheel Eatery is two blocks down, on Elm Street," said Hattie.

"Elm Street?" I looked around for an elm tree.

"And there's the Crow," said Elizabeth.

"Don't tell them about the Crow!" Hattie snapped. "No one with an ordinary stomach wants to eat at the Crow."

"We also need a place to stay, and a barber and a bath. It's been a terribly long journey," said Bennie.

"The Wagon Wheel Inn is located right next to the restaurant. They offer baths for an extra ten cents. Course, with the hanging and all, they may not have a vacancy."

"But you might find a room at the Crow," said Elizabeth.

Hattie nudged the smaller woman. "Pay no mind to Elizabeth. Only gamblers and harlots and people of low morals stay at the Crow. Catherine Waters is a fine woman, but she's unmarried and in need of hard currency, if you know what I mean. Take my advice and go to the Wagon Wheel Inn. I'm sure they'll make room." Hattie took Elizabeth by the arm and led her down the street. "I swear, Elizabeth, if you keep directing folks to the Crow we'll never get a better class of people in Broken Wagon Wheel, now will we?"

"But the Crow is fun!" Elizabeth scoffed.

"Apparently, she thinks we have high morals," I said. "It must be the clothes."

"Dakota, I don't think a woman as astute as Hattie Liverpool would be fooled by your clothes."

I chuckled and looked towards the Crow. In that den of iniquity was cool, wet beer and, I hoped, a friendly card game.

At the moment, it was packed full of men. There were so many men, they spilled out the doors and into the street, straining their necks to get a look inside. Cameron Graves lumbered down the boardwalk and pushed through the crowd, looking as if he had just swallowed a bottle of bitters. A loud uproar followed his entrance.

"Let's try the Wagon Wheel Eatery," said Bennie.

"Let's try the Crow," I said, walking towards the rumble of men.

We squeezed through the crowd outside to find only standing room inside. It was hot and stuffy, filled with other men's breath and sour whiskey. I elbowed my way through the men outside, drawing angry, impatient looks, but trying to maneuver to the bar looked nearly impossible. It was lined three men deep.

From what I could see, and I could see plenty since I was standing taller than most of the men in the saloon, the tables were covered by red-checkered tablecloths − made from the same material as Hattie Liverpool's dress, only a different color. A small decorative lamp sat on each table. The bar was short and built from worm-eaten, heavily weathered planks. A man could get slivers in his elbows leaning on such a bar. Dark amber bottles and smoke-blue mirrors lined the back of the bar. A mural of a bosomy, half-clothed harlot, reclining lazily on a velvet settee, looking warm and content, was partially concealed by a staircase that disappeared upstairs. A kitchen, which looked as if it had been hastily attached to the saloon, stood off to itself in a far corner. A fat man with a greasy apron was firing up the stove. Whenever one of the men from the saloon spilled into the kitchen, the fat man would whack him with a spatula and chase him back out.

"Well, hell, Cookie," said one such unfortunate man, "I got shoved."

"Outta my kitchen," Cookie growled ominously.

I didn't know what Hattie Liverpool was talking about − this joint had plenty of class.

But not according to Bennie Colsen. Our travels had taken a toll on the boy. He was red-faced, sweaty, and weary. He was in no mood for hot, sweaty, jostling cowboys. I was. "This is tiresome," he sighed. "Let's go to the Wagon Wheel Eatery."

Cameron stood on the third step of the short flight of stairs. He let out a holler, trying to quiet the angry citizens of Broken Wagon Wheel, but his demand was met only with another surge of shouts.

"Listen to me," he shouted. "Now y'all calm down and listen to me." They didn't listen to him a bit.

Finally, a tall, stately woman with thick auburn hair falling all over her face and shoulders stepped up next to Cameron. "Shut up! All of you!" The room immediately fell silent. "Let the marshal speak, for chrissake."

Cameron turned as timid as a whipped pup. "Thank you, Miz Waters," he said. Then he stood and stared at her, seeming to forget where he was and what he was doing there.

"Well, Marshal!" someone shouted. "Speak up."

He quickly yanked his eyes off Catherine Waters and cleared his throat. "I was saying, we're not going to get anywhere shouting over each other. If you have something to say, do it one at a time."

"What if Caballe and his gang ride into Broken Wagon Wheel?" a slender, white-haired man said.

"He ain't going to come back, Richard. He's probably halfway to Sierra Madre by now," Cameron replied.

Bennie tapped my shoulder. "That must be Richard Mecum, the horticulturist."

"The what?"

"That's what you said when he stole Clem's wife," said a man named Sam Bradford. Sam was a filthy fellow. He was so dirty you couldn't see what he looked like under all the grime.

His brother, Clem Bradford, sat at a corner table, sulking and drinking heavily. He was muscular, with long dirty hair and a matted beard. At the mention of his wife, he lowered his head in his hands and sobbed. Everyone ignored him. They were used to his whiskey tears.

"And before he came back and robbed the bank," said Richard Mecum.

The saloon door banged against the adobe wall, sending chips of plaster falling to the floor, and a burly, rough-looking cowboy slammed into the room.

"And stole half my herd!" the cowboy shouted. It was Josh Reynolds.

"I'm sorry about your wife, Clem. Sorry about your cattle, Josh. But I have no jurisdiction to go into Mexico," said Cameron.

"Then find someone who does," bellowed Josh Reynolds. "You can't just let a bandit ride in and steal the womenfolk."

"Now, everybody calm down." Noticing that everyone was getting hotheaded again, Joseph Bagley, the portly, shrill-voiced mayor of Broken Wagon Wheel, stood next to Cameron and waved his arms. "I've wired the governor and asked for a warrant to go after Jennifer Bradford in Mexico. I'm still waiting to hear from him."

"And you'll be waitin' till Christmas. We don't need the gawdamn governor's permission to hang our outlaws. That's what we hired the marshal here for," said Josh.

"Dang it, I need you boys' help. I can't do it by myself," said Cameron.

If he wanted to silence an angry mob, that was the way to do it. The men shook their heads and mumbled among themselves.

"Our help?" said Richard Mecum, incredulously. "Why, I'm only a banker."

"You can shoot a gun, can't you?" asked Catherine Waters. She was still standing next to Cameron, scowling fiercely at the men on the bottom floor.

"All Mecum knows how to do is grow flowers," said Josh. That drew general laughter from all around, and Richard Mecum turned red and got flustered.

"The marshal gets paid for catching dangerous outlaws, not me," said Richard.

"Richard's right," said one fellow who looked too old to chase outlaws, dangerous or not. "We're mostly farmers."

"And we have families to look after," said another fellow.

"Look, I can't bring in the Caballe gang on my own. I've tried and I admit I've failed. I'm willing to deputize some men. I need volunteers."

Again, the room fell silent. The men began to twitch and scratch at their chins as if someone had dumped itching powder all over them. They were too uncomfortable, maybe too ashamed to look at each other for fear their cowardice would show, but they were not stupid. Cameron attempted to sound as if he were offering them an honorable position when in fact he was asking them to die unmercifully at the hands of a crazy gang of bandits. They weren't fooled. They stayed quiet. No one volunteered.

"I can't believe you people," muttered Catherine Waters before she stepped off the makeshift podium and started mopping up her splintery bar.

Cameron didn't give up as easily. "Sam? Clem? You want Jennie back, don't you?"

"Hell, Marshal," Sam said miserably. "Clem ain't no good fer nothing since Jennie been gone. And I got them hides to tan..."

"What about you, Reynolds?"

The rough-looking cowboy rubbed his stubbly jaw and said, almost apologetically, "I'm taking a herd up to Abilene in a couple of days."

"Suit yourselves." Pretending to be unperturbed, Cameron stepped lightly off the steps and put on his hat.

I had kept my mouth shut through the entire proceedings. Juan Caballe and the folks in Broken Wagon Wheel were none of my affair, and I never made a habit of meddling in other folks' business. I was just waiting for the meeting to be over so I could sidle on up to the bar and buy a beer and sit at one of the pretty red-checkered tables and eat a plate of whatever the greasy cook was cooking. That's all I wanted.

But, as if I had no control over my own tongue, I found myself uttering, "I'll help you out, Marshal." Then I quickly looked around to see who had said it.

Bennie's hand tightened around my arm. "What are you doing?" he whispered loudly.

"I want my guns back, Junior."

"Your guns?" His jaw was clenched so tight the word "guns" sounded like "geens." "We'll buy more guns in New Jersey."

"New Jersey is on the other side of the continent. Too far to travel without armament."

"We'll buy guns in San Antonio."

I reckoned he would say that, make it sound so simple. Bennie never had fully understood the importance of my guns, and he didn't understand now. It wasn't any ol' New Jersey or San Antonio gun I wanted. I wanted two Colt .44s, circa 1860, with ivory handles, gold inlaid initials, and deadly filed-down triggers. Dakota Taylor's guns.

"I've had them for fifteen years. I can't just let some bandit — scholar that he was — pluck them off me. He might go off bragging."

Cameron pushed through the crowd of dumbfounded men and stood hulking next to me. "If I heard you correctly, then I sure do appreciate it."

"You heard me correctly."

"Well, what do you know..." Catherine rolled her eyes skyward. "A man among us."

"Buy this stranger a beer!" hollered Mayor Joseph Bagley in his pip-squeaky voice.

"Cookie, bring him a plate of sowbelly," said Catherine.

And in that moment, I became the most popular man in Texas. That night I didn't have to pay for my drinks or for my supper or for the cramped little room above the kitchen. Yep, I was the darlin' of Broken Wagon Wheel. I was everybody's buddy. Everybody's pal. Everybody loved me. Except Bennie Colsen.

5

I didn't have to pay for my new clothes, either. The shopkeeper had gotten out of bed at dawn and opened his shop to accommodate me. Then he followed me around the store in his nightclothes, slapping me on the back and insisting, "Take anything you like. Anything at all." He was a wiry little man with a whole bunch of teeth. I couldn't tell if he was smiling or if his mouth was just too small to hold all his teeth in. The smile was perpetual and he was a cheerful fellow, though I had rousted him out of bed at that evil hour. I picked out some sturdy riding jeans, a light cotton shirt, a vest, leather chaps to protect my legs from mesquite thorns, and a wide-brimmed hat that would hold more dust than a funeral urn. When I put my bundle on the counter and held out my money, the shopkeeper pulled his hands away and said, "No, siree, I wouldn't take a red cent from you. No siree, wouldn't think of it." I kind of liked this little town called Broken Wagon Wheel.

So there I was in the saddle, feeling comfortable in my new clothes, skirting easily past mesquite thorns, and listening to the wild calls of desert animals. When the chaparral closed around me, and the dew released the smell of sage so pungent it tickled my nostrils and made me sneeze, I thanked Lady Luck I was tracking a dangerous outlaw instead of brooding over tea in New

Jersey. I sneaked a sideways glance at my riding partner, Marshal Cameron Graves, and felt so grateful to him for losing Judd Brooks and involving me in his problems, I wanted to give him a hug.

He looked my way and I grinned. He grinned. And we kept riding. Despite the tin star, the man was cut out of the same cookie batter I was. He, too, was grateful to be there, riding the flatlands, out of town, away from the crowds, away from the pressures of his job. The only difference between us was he was a man of the law. I was a man of the lawbreakers.

We approached the south side of Dead Horse Canyon just as the sun painted the canyon walls with soft morning scarlets and burgundy hues. We traveled a rock-littered trail into the cliffs. The sun had not completely ascended the eastern peaks, but I could already feel a hint of what promised to be another scorching day. The cool of morning was only fleeting; the mist that curled along the canyon floor was a mere apparition. It would soon disintegrate when the sun finished climbing over the peaks. Morning was a graceful moment; vague and delicate, a temporary reprieve before Cameron and I were tossed into the volcanic heat of another south Texas day.

By midmorning I took off my vest and tied it behind the cantle of my saddle. I unbuttoned my shirt, removed my canteen, and saturated my neck and chest with water. My skin stayed wet for maybe two seconds. The marshal rode on fully clothed, seemingly oblivious to the fire that burned inside the belly of the canyon.

Cameron rested his mare at the edge of a cliff and stared across the flatlands below us. "Down there," he said, leaning forward in the saddle, the leather creaking and groaning under his weight. "That's where the boy's body was found."

Six months had passed since the body had been discovered by a passing muleskinner. All evidence that a crime had been committed was long gone. Still, the marshal seemed compelled to ride to the barren spot. After we reached the gully, we stayed on our horses and stared into an empty hole.

"His name was Clay James," said Cameron. "He'd been in Broken Wagon Wheel only a few months. No one knew him, no one knew where he came from. Hell, I don't even know if he had family."

"A drifter?"

Cameron wagged his head slowly. "He was of a higher caliber than that. He came in on the stage, rented a room above the Crow, and pretty much kept to himself. He was a good-looking boy; wore expensive, tailored clothes. He had an air about him. Sort of like that friend of yours."

"He ain't my friend anymore."

Bennie Colsen hadn't strung one polite sentence together since midnight of the night before. He was one peeved boy. I couldn't remember when I had last seen him this unforgiving ... Unless it was the time I stored his crates of books in the barn and it rained for forty days and forty nights before I got around to repairing the barn's roof. His books were swimming in water, their pages glued together, before I remembered where I'd left them and rescued them. Bennie tried to dry them by the fire, but they were ruined, and I went ahead and used them for firewood.

Bennie was mighty riled then, but it was nothing compared to now. By the end of the afternoon, Bennie Colsen would be on a stagecoach bound for San Antonio without even a fond fare-thee-well.

"Now, the way I figure it," said Cameron, "Judd Brooks met Clay James at the Crow the night he was killed. James wasn't happy about being in Broken Wagon Wheel. Sometimes he took to drinking and started flashing around an expensive pocket watch. I warned him over and over again that he was only inviting trouble, that someone was going to steal that watch from him. Judd Brooks saw the watch, followed the boy to his room, cracked him over the head, then finished him off by strangling him."

"For a watch?"

"You've seen what an ornery sonofabitch Brooks is. Look at what he did to his own *compadre* over a gun."

"He shot him."

"Right. Over a gun."

"I mean, he shot him."

"Right," the marshal repeated, still not understanding my meaning.

"Judd Brooks is a gunfighter."

"I know that."

"Doesn't it seem peculiar that a gunfighter would kill a man by strangling him?"

Cameron lifted his heavy shoulders to shrug. "He didn't want to make noise. Didn't want to draw attention to his crime."

"That ain't the way a gunfighter operates. Drawing attention is half the fun. If they want something bad enough, most gunfighters will take it in the light of day with a crowd around them. That's part of the excitement, that's how they make a name for themselves. Gunfighters don't sneak around in the dark, whacking people over the head. It doesn't make sense."

"I reckon you're more schooled in the ways of a gunfighter than I am. But we're talking about the Caballe gang. Nothing they do makes sense. Like kidnapping Jennifer Bradford. Now, why would they do something like that?"

"I don't know. But I'll bet a couple of free beers they took her when everyone was looking."

"No bet. It was demoralizing. There was nothing I could do to stop them. I was outgunned twelve to one." Cameron reined his horse slightly to the left and pointed at the ground. "Brooks was riding a chestnut gelding that was missing a shoe on its hind foot. The tracks we found were left by a three-legged horse. When I caught up with him he was still riding the horse. And he still had the watch on him."

"Marshal, there aren't any tracks left. In fact, there's nothing important left here at all. Shouldn't we be riding south?"

As if to answer me, Cameron turned his horse and started north. "If they went south they'd be in Mexico by now."

"So? We'll ride into Mexico after them."

I watched the marshal's wide back lift in a deep-throated laugh. "We play by the rules, Deputy Taylor. A lawman can't go into Mexico and drag patriots out."

Deputy Taylor ... geezus. The tin star burned hot against my chest and flashed gaily in the sun as if it were taunting me. Now, I didn't mind the complimentary drinks and food that went along with the job, but I sure didn't need an announcement pinned to my shirt. The tin star could draw looks of confusion, maybe even looks of contempt from old friends of mine. Still more shameful than the star and the title was the toy revolver Cameron had loaned me. I'd be lucky if I could drop a mad dog at ten feet with the little peashooter.

"It still doesn't make sense riding north," I said.

"We're riding north because of Gypsies," he replied.

"Gypsies?" Now I was really confused. Cameron had a bad habit of talking in riddles. He never said anything directly. Everything he said was slow and vague, almost dreamlike, and I found myself responding to most of his statements with questions.

"There's a small caravan of Gypsies camped south of the Pecos River. It's just an old granddad and grandma, a couple of sons and daughters, and children. Sometimes they go into Pecos and steal a few chickens and some candy for the kids, but most of the time they're content to sit and spin tales around the campfire and take your picture for a gold coin."

"That's the Gypsy way," I said.

"They say they can look at the stars and predict your future, or look at the palm of your hand and tell you how long you'll live. I think it's a pile of horseshit, myself."

"I dunno. The Gypsies have some kind of magic."

Cameron chuckled. "Yep, they have the magic of parting a fool from his money."

"So we're going to give them a couple of gold coins and they're going to predict whether or not we're going to get killed by Judd Brooks. Is that the plan?"

"Don't rightly think so." Cameron grinned.

"Then," I said, patiently, "why are we riding to Pecos? It's a long stretch from here."

"Lala Rudshika. She's the most beautiful woman God decided to create. Except for Catherine Waters, that is."

"Catherine?" I glanced at the marshal.

He nodded solemnly. "Catherine Waters is the most beautiful woman on earth."

Geezus, was he serious? Catherine Waters was handsome enough, I suppose. She was big-boned, lean, and muscular, and had enough hair to weave a couple of winter coats with. I especially admired her ability to grab a rowdy cowboy by the scruff of the neck and pitch him out the door without argument. I found those traits attractive in a woman. Most women were so frail you'd be scared to cough next to them. Catherine Waters was not frail by a long shot, but was she the most beautiful woman on earth? I sure didn't think so. But eyes don't see accurately when you're in love, and it was plainer than the southwest sun that Cameron Graves was in love. Pitifully so.

"She isn't overly fond of me," he continued. "She thinks I'm a useless loafer with a star on my chest."

"Why is that?" Cameron didn't seem like a loafer to me. Slow, maybe, but certainly not a man who would shirk hard work.

"Welp, she thinks I'm ignorant. Catherine prefers educated men; the brainy type who sit at a desk all day and count money. Men like ... Richard Mecum." He said Richard Mecum's name with such contempt, it was obvious the two men were competing for Catherine Waters's affections.

"Cameron," I said, and I said it nicely, because I genuinely knew how the poor man felt. There was nothing worse than loving someone who thought so badly of you. "Are you telling me we're going to ride seventy miles in this heat to look at a beautiful Gypsy woman?"

"Nope." He shook Catherine Waters and Richard Mecum out of his mind and got back to the business at hand. "But Judd Brooks will. Lala Rudshika is his wife. Well, kind of his wife. It was one of them Gypsy ceremonies. Lala will cut out our tongues protecting the ugly critter. Now, the way I see it" — he shifted his weight in the saddle — "Brooks has been cooling his acorns in jail for a couple of months. If you've been locked away that long and suddenly found yourself free from the hangman's noose and you had a beautiful wife waiting for you, wouldn't you ride a horse into the ground trying to reach her?"

"It ain't likely." But I got the marshal's meaning. Give me a Gypsy man and no horse would be safe. I rode quietly alongside Cameron, studying his slouching shoulders and flat, ruddy profile. Catherine Waters was wrong. The big marshal was smarter than she thought.

"Look up there." Cameron pointed east. "Them birds are the desert's greatest trackers."

East of us, buzzards swirled like a darkened whirlpool against the pale Texas sky. We reined our horses around and trotted towards the scavengers. Cameron was certain of what he would find and it didn't take us long to find it. Lying among the mesquite was a dead horse. It had been ridden until it dropped from under its rider. Cameron dismounted and inspected the animal.

"It's been dead for hours." He wiped sweat from his upper lip and squinted at the sun. "It belonged to Judd Brooks, all right."

"That means he's on foot." From my horse, I studied the ground and the surrounding brush for signs. Brooks had taken his riding gear with him. A man burdened with a saddle wouldn't travel far in this heat. "He's heading northeast towards that ridge. How far is the Gypsy camp from here?"

"Too far. We're likely to lose our own horses if we continue. There's an old stagecoach station a few miles over the ridge. It used to be an active spot before the stageline bypassed Dead Horse Canyon. Gray Ritter is still there manning the ovens. He's become a lunatic from lack of company, but he still cooks a good pot of beans and keeps a few horses around. Brooks can get a fresh mount there."

"We'd better get moving, then. Maybe we'll catch him before he gets another horse."

Cameron slowly shook his head and looked at the fallen horse. "I hate to see a horse go down like that. Poor bastard. I've seen many a dead man in my lifetime, but I sure hate the sight of a dead horse."

"Well, hell, you wanna bury it?"

"Nope. No purpose. The Bradford brothers can use what's left of the hide at the tannery." He put his foot in the stirrup and pulled his bulk up. "I don't want to be burying my horse either. We'll spend the night at Gray's and get an early start come morning."

"Brooks will be long gone by then," I protested.

"He ain't going nowhere, son. He'll spend the next few nights with Lala Rudshika. Maybe we'll catch him with his pants down."

Marshal Cameron Graves didn't know it, but I didn't have all the time in the world to outthink a lovesick outlaw. I reckoned it would be wiser to catch Judd Brooks, take back my guns, drink another round of free beer with the grateful folks in town, then hightail it to New Jersey before Bennie decided life with a poet was less troublesome than life with a gunfighter.

We climbed to the top of a sharp-edged ridge when I quickly reined my horse to a standstill. "Did you hear that?"

"Nope." Cameron stopped to listen.

"There it is again." My eyesight wasn't so good, but I could hear a snake crawl across a marble floor. The noise sounded like a whelp pup crying; a small, desperate cry in the desolate countryside. "It's coming from that ravine."

Before I finished the sentence, another cry, louder this time, pierced the air. It was a clearly a call for help. A man's voice. A man in pain. We galloped to the edge of the ridge where we could see the bottom of the ravine. A young man was tied spread-eagled on the desert floor. His arms and legs were roped to sturdy stumps of mesquite bushes. He pulled on the ropes and the bushes shook, but neither the boy nor the bushes were going anywhere. When he saw our shadows outlined against the sun, he stopped squirming.

"Down here!" he shouted. "I'm down here!"

"I'll be damned...," said the marshal. "That looks like young Billy Waters."

The wall of the ravine was too steep to take the horses down, so we circled until we found a flat trail in, then raced to the boy's side.

"Is that you, young Billy?" said Cameron.

"Marshal Graves?" The kid's voice was heavy with relief, and hoarse from shouting for so long and hard. "Boy-howdy, am I glad to see you."

Cameron swung off his mare, unsheathed his knife, and swiftly cut the ropes. "What the hell are you doing out here?"

"Water. You got water?"

"Sure, Billy, sure."

I threw my canteen to Cameron. His hands trembled as he removed the cap and handed the canteen to Billy. The marshal was scrambling to save the boy's life. But I'd say, besides being painfully sunburned and mightily thirsty, he appeared to be in good shape. Greedily, he lunged at the water and poured it down his raw throat.

"What the hell are you doing out here?" Cameron repeated.

"Pecos...," Billy stuttered between taking large gulps of water. "I went to Pecos to pick up a couple of steers..." He guzzled more water. "...for Catty." Guzzle.

"Take it easy, son," said Cameron, pulling the canteen away from him. "You'll get belly-bloat."

Billy let the marshal cap the canteen, then wiped his mouth and chin with his sleeve. "I was ambushed coming over the ridge."

"By Comanches?" asked Cameron. Tying a man in the scorching sun, then riding off and leaving him to die was a time-honored sport of the Comanches. And that was only if they were in a playful mood.

"No, sir. It was Judd Brooks. I know he's supposed to hang right about now, but I swear it was Judd Brooks."

Cameron glanced up at me, then back to Billy Waters. "Was he alone? Or was Juan Caballe with him?"

"My heart would have stopped beating if Juan Caballe had been with him. Far as I could tell, he was alone. He fired above my horse's head. She spooked and threw me. Brooks came out of the brush holding two six-shooters longer than my arms."

"Ivory handles?" I asked.

"Yes, sir, and fancy etching. Believe me, I got a good gander at them guns."

"It was Brooks, all right," Cameron muttered.

The kid dropped his head between his knees. "He took my horse and he took the steers. Catty's going to kill me. Them animals cost three months' earnings."

"Your sister ain't going to kill you," Cameron consoled him. "She'll be damn happy you're alive."

"No, sir. She'd rather have me dead than to lose them two steers and that old Appaloosa. In fact, she said it loud and clear: 'If you don't bring them steers home, then you best not bother coming home at all.'" Billy did a good job of mocking his sister's big voice and I had to laugh, even if he did look miserable.

"Well, hell..." Cameron looped an arm under the boy's armpit and pulled him to his feet. "I reckon she didn't mean it. Judd Brooks doesn't leave most folks alive after stealing their horses. You're a fortunate lad."

"Catty won't see it that way."

Young Billy Waters found his hat under a sage bush, dusted it off, and plopped it down on a mess of brown curls. He looked up at me with a wide grin. His cheeks were scratched fiery red from the sun. He had freckles, a blistered nose, and big, red-rimmed ears. Cute kid.

"Howdy," he said.

"Howdy."

"That there is my deputy, Dakota Taylor," said Cameron.

"In which direction did Brooks go?" I asked.

"Best deputy I ever had. Hellion on horseback." Cameron climbed into the saddle, then held out his hand and pulled Billy up behind him.

I was not a good deputy. I was a man who was impatient to have his Colts back safely in their holsters. "Which way?" I said, ignoring the marshal.

"I don't rightly know which way he went, Deputy Taylor," said Billy. "I was too busy staring at the sun."

6

Now we had Billy Waters to worry about and Cameron worried in silence. We were at midpoint; halfway between Pecos and Broken Wagon Wheel. With Juan Caballe in the area, we couldn't send the kid back to town on his own. It was too chancy. Cameron considered dropping Billy off at Gray Ritter's place, but the former depot man had become reclusive, almost unsociable, and Cameron didn't trust him to care for Billy. Then there was the problem of Catherine Waters. If her baby brother didn't make it home soon, she would come looking for him, and that would only add to his problem. After giving it a lot of slow thought, Cameron decided to escort Billy back to Broken Wagon Wheel. If we should collide with Juan Caballe or Judd Brooks, Cameron didn't want a sunburned kid tagging along.

Billy wasn't eager to return to town. Despite his near-fatal meeting with Judd Brooks, Billy was an enthusiastic boy who would rather suffer an attack by Mexican bandits than suffer a scolding from a big sister.

"Marshal Graves," said Billy as we left the rocky canyon behind and retraced our steps across the dusty flats, "I'd be right proud if you would deputize me. I'll ride with you and Deputy Taylor."

"That's mighty brave of you, young Billy. But I reckon I need my deputies a bit older and more experienced."

"I can shoot straight. And Gray Ritter has an extra horse. I saw a half-dozen of them when I stopped by the old depot with the steers."

"If it were solely up to me I would bring you along. But we're tracking a dangerous outlaw and if there's some shooting to be done, Miz Waters ain't going to take kindly to you being in the middle."

"Hell, Marshal, Catty don't take kindly to anything I do."

"That's a fact." Cameron grinned and kept riding towards Broken Wagon Wheel. "She don't take kindly to anything I do, either. Don't let it worry you none."

Billy was visibly disappointed, but he dropped the argument. A boy his age was used to disappointments. Billy Waters was no longer a boy, yet he wasn't a man, either. He was too old to play or to take life lightly, but he was too young to fight or to be taken seriously by adults. In another year or two his upper body would grow to complement his arms and legs; his head would grow to complement his ears, and he would be a man to reckon with. But, for now, he was a long-limbed, freckled-faced child wiggling around on the back of a horse.

It was late afternoon when we reached Four-Mile Waterhole. Why it was called Four-Mile was open to speculation. There wasn't anything or anybody remotely near the dirty pool of water. Broken Wagon Wheel was the closest township and it was still twenty miles south. We dismounted, loosened our saddles, and let the horses drink, then ate a dry meal of corn pone.

"I'm hotter than Cookie's kitchen," said Billy. "Think I'll soak in that pool of water for a spell."

"Suit yourself," said Cameron. He took out a pouch of tobacco and rolled a cigarette.

Billy removed his boots and outer garments. Dressed in faded red, long underwear that sagged at the rear, he tiptoed to the water's edge. He let out a loud groan when he submerged his scorched skin in the murky water.

"Why can't he ride with us?" I asked. "We could use an extra gun."

Cameron handed me the cigarette. "Do you want to spend the next few days baby-sitting a kid?"

"It would save time."

"We got plenty of time. Brooks ain't going nowhere."

"So you keep saying."

"Trust me, Deputy Taylor." Cameron grinned. "Judd Brooks is probably rolling around in the arms of Lala Rudshika while we lie here sweating like a couple of pigs. Don't seem fair, does it?"

The horses noisily sucked at the water, drinking so deeply I thought they would drain the pool. "You ain't doing Billy any favors by protecting him, or by sending him back to his sister for a whupping. He's gotta grow up sometime."

"Try telling that to Catherine Waters. I'd like to see how fast you can run. She thinks Billy is still five years old." Billy let his feet float to the surface of the water, then wiggled his toes and laughed. "I'll be damned if he don't act it."

"Where's his folks?"

"Dead. Both of them. They were killed in a Comanche raid when Billy was a baby. Catherine was only a young girl herself, but she raised him without complaint, and did a fine job of it, in my opinion. She would have Clem Bradford tan both our hides if we took him with us."

"Well, he's her affair."

Reclining flat on his back in the warm sand, Cameron folded an arm under his head, and crossed his legs at the ankles. Quietly, he studied the cloudless sky, smoked his cigarette, and thought his thoughts. I rested my back against a hot sandstone, stared at the cloudless sky, smoked my cigarette, and thought my thoughts.

My thoughts were of Bennie Colsen. Right about now he would be on his way to San Antonio with the Edelltons. After the meeting at the Crow had broken up the night before, Catherine escorted us to our room above the kitchen. The cramped little room was the only vacancy left in town. Long after the sun went down and the rest of the world began to cool, our room stayed hot and airless and Bennie refused to let me touch him, blaming it on the heat, though I'm sure it had something to do with New Jersey.

I wasn't having second thoughts about my decision to stay. The truth was, I was glad to be sitting there baking in the sun, but the other truth was I was going to miss Bennie something awful. I didn't know how deep his anger was. Bennie's anger had always been hard to figure. There were times when he seemed so angry I thought he was going to shoot me, but five seconds later he would be kissing on my neck. Then there were times when he didn't seem angry at all, just cool and quiet, but he wouldn't have anything to do with me for days. Weeks. I had to admit, I was concerned about his anger this time. It ran so cool, so quiet, I thought he'd been struck deaf and mute in the middle of the night.

My old buddy, Ryder McCloud, warned me once that a man such as I should never marry. Matrimony would dull my wits and make me indecisive. It would pull me apart until I became two separate individuals: the settled married man and the foot-loose gunfighter. By all accounts, I'd been married for nearly five years, and I'll be damned if my wits weren't duller than a preacher's sermon, my indecisiveness almost hazardous, and I found myself wishing, on more than one occasion, there were two of me. One of me to sit next to this stagnant pool of water under a scorching Texas sun. One of me to bed down with Bennie Colsen in New Jersey. Ryder McCloud was a pain in the ass.

Nor was I sorry Bennie had left. In fact, I would have been downright sorrier if he missed his engagement with his poet on account of me and my guns. There wasn't one good reason why Bennie should stay in a dirty border town while I chased a gunnapping criminal up and down the Rio Grande. Nope, I was glad Bennie was gone. It was the way he left that worried me.

Folks shouldn't leave when they're angry. Not in this kind of country. Death could be standing around the bend or hiding in the thickets. Mexican bandits, Comanches, poisonous snakes and centipedes ... any one of them could strike a man dead before he had a chance to look into the face of his killer. What if Juan Caballe and his vicious pack of timber wolves came shooting out of the chaparral while we were lying there smoking and relaxing and butchered us all? What would Bennie Colsen think about that? He would be forever saddled with grief, forever haunted by the final memory of denying me one last night of pleasure.

Actually, the thought brought me some comfort. It's a shame a man has to wish himself dead to get a little sympathy.

Cameron groaned and took a long pull off his cigarette. No doubt he was thinking about Catherine Waters and how he was going to explain the loss of her steers and Appaloosa without looking like a loafer with a star on his chest. What a pathetic team we made. Real professionals. If Caballe did sweep out of the chaparral, the merciful thing to do was to unbutton our shirts and expose our hearts. Put it right there, son. Put the bullet right there.

"The harder I try to win her favors the more she treats me with contempt," Cameron said in a low, rambling voice.

"Are you talking to me or to yourself?"

"Both. If you're listening."

I flicked my ash and watched Billy dunk his head under the water and blow bubbles through his nose. "Maybe you should stop trying so hard."

Cameron lifted up on his elbows with some effort, then rested his back against a sandstone. "Do you think so?"

"Geezus, Graves, I don't even know you, but I would find you annoying if you were wooing me."

"How so?"

"Out here, in the desert, you're a capable man. Sure of yourself, sure of your skills as a marshal. But when you're around Catherine Waters you turn into an idiot. Last night, after she closed down the Crow and asked you to pick up the glasses, you fell over a chair and broke them all."

"I looked like a fool." Cameron groaned again.

"You did." I laughed at the memory, then stopped when I saw the pitiful look on the big man's face. "Look," I said, trying to be helpful. "If you want to win someone's favors you shouldn't let them know how you're feeling. Not right away, anyway. Behave the opposite of the way you truly feel. It will confuse them."

"I want Catherine to be confused?"

"It helps."

"I don't know..." There was serious doubt in his voice.

"The last thing you want to do is act like some lovesick jackass. Don't stand there twisting your hat and shuffling your feet and talking with a little boy's voice. Stop bleeding all over the floor like you do. It ain't flattering."

"But I am a lovesick jackass."

"I didn't say you couldn't be. I'm just saying you ain't supposed to show it, for chrissake. If you want someone to notice you, ignore them. It keeps them guessing. That's my advice."

"It works for you?"

"You bet." I grinned.

"Welp, I ain't never met a woman who likes to be ignored."

I glanced at him. "Hell, I never met anybody who likes to be ignored. That's the point."

✦

The last twenty miles into Broken Wagon Wheel were uneventful. It now occurred to me that Cameron had done the right thing by taking the boy back to town. Billy could outtalk Bennie Colsen and Martha Edellton combined.

We trotted into town at dark. The moon lingered over Pappy's livery stable, gently illuminating the horses milling in the corrals. Catherine Waters stood on the drooping porch in front of the Crow. A shawl was wrapped around her shoulders and she hugged it tight against her body, not for warmth, but for worry. She waited on the top step, staring apprehensively down the street. When she saw us crossing Main Street with Billy dangling off the back of Cameron's saddle, her face relaxed, turned soft for a second, then pinched up with anger. She stepped off the porch and stomped up the street to meet us.

"Boy-howdy," Billy sighed as he watched her coming. "I sure wish I had them steers and that old Appaloosa."

"Where have you been?" Catherine demanded, her voice as tense as her shoulders. "And where's Apple?"

Apple, I assumed, was the horse.

Billy slid off the back of Cameron's horse. "It's a long, hard story, Catty."

"Where are the steers I sent you after?"

"It's a long, hard story."

She looked to Cameron for an explanation, but he turned into a jellyfish on horseback. "Welp," he stammered. And that was all he was capable of saying. When she didn't get an answer from him, she wanted one from me.

"Apaches," I said. An anxious silence filled the night air as the dreaded word echoed down Main Street. "Worse than Apaches. It was *the* Apache, Juh."

Lies instantly leap from my mouth when I sense conflict. Sometimes, to avoid trouble, a person has to exaggerate their hardships and turn their opponents into sympathizers. To have told the truth – that Billy was ambushed by Judd Brooks – would only make the marshal look more inept. Half the town already wanted his badge for letting Brooks escape. If Brooks was torturing young boys and stealing their horses, the townsfolk would gladly hang the blame on the big marshal, holding him responsible. But Apaches ... Hell, Apaches were God's fault. And the Apache, Juh, was the Devil's fault.

"Apaches?" said Catherine fearfully.

"Yes, ma'am. They stole the steers and horse. Then they used four mesquite bushes for jerky sticks and left Billy to dry in the sun."

"I thought the army had chased Juh back into Arizona." She had her moment of doubt, but ultimately she believed me, and her anger dissolved into pity. She touched Billy's blistered cheeks. "Come on, Billy, let me put some lemon balm on them burns."

"Thanks, Deputy Taylor," said Billy, smiling all the way into the Crow.

"Where did you learn to fib like that?" asked Cameron.

"I don't know. I think I was born with the skill." I was momentarily pleased with myself, but then I quickly turned on the marshal. "Graves, you are one sorry coward. Why didn't you just tell her the truth?"

Cameron shuddered. "It's my fault Judd Brooks escaped and stole her critters."

"I was there when Brooks escaped. It didn't look to me like you had much choice in the matter."

"I'm the town marshal. It's my job to protect these people. I ain't doing my job if I let a bunch of bandits run free and steal their livestock. If young Billy had been killed..." He let his words drift down the street, not wanting to consider what would have happened if young Billy had been killed.

"You're just one man. There's only so much one man can do."

I dropped off my horse and looked up at the windows on the second floor of the Crow. A light burned in Catherine's room. Then one came to life in Billy's room. My room was at the far side of the saloon, facing an alley, with a view of the north end of town and the gallows. I couldn't see the window from where I stood.

Cameron took the reins from my hand. "I'll take the horses over to Pappy's. You go on ahead and get some sleep. We'll head out again at sunrise."

"I'll let you do that." Wearily, I entered the saloon, inwardly dreading the lonely night that lay ahead of me without Bennie Colsen. I'd become accustomed to him being in my bed, and the thought of lying in one alone made me so uncomfortable I considered taking my bedroll and bunking down with the horses at Pappy's.

Catherine was in the kitchen smearing grease all over Billy's cheeks. He waved cheerfully as I climbed the short flight of stairs to my room. The first thing I noticed when I stepped into the hall was a thin streak of light shining from under the door of my room. The room was supposed to be empty.

Gunfighters are naturally suspicious; it's inbred in them. The Colts and I had bullied our way from one town to another and made plenty of enemies along the way. Every year or so one of those enemies hunted me down and attempted to even the score. Who knows? Maybe the Texas Ranger, Wes Fossey, heard I was in Texas and was waiting behind the door with a loaded revolver.

Caution was as much a part of my nature as suspicion. Unholstering the peashooter, I crept silently down the carpeted hall. Standing with my back to the wall, I took a deep breath, slowly turned the knob, then swung and kicked open the door. I whirled into the room, peashooter aimed, ready to kill any shadow that moved.

Bennie sat at a cluttered writing table, composing a letter to Walt Whitman. Although he knew I had a gun trained on his back, he didn't look up from the desk. He wasn't even startled by my busting into the room like I did. Bennie was as accustomed to me as I was to him.

"You're back early," he said, calmly. "I wasn't expecting you for a week."

I holstered the peashooter and casually flung my hat on the bed. "How ya doing, Junior?" I said as cool as mornings in Montana.

T he problem with Bennie Colsen was that he didn't make love like most men. Which is to say, he wasn't in a hurry to get the job done. Bennie could spend hours kissing and stroking, exploring, until my every nerve was on edge. Then, when I was about to explode like a vial of nitroglycerin, he'd roll away and say something that made me squint. Something unnecessary like: "Are you happy, Dakota?"

Well, heck, yes.

But that was a short answer and Bennie wasn't looking for short answers. He was looking for words. Important words. He wanted promises and guarantees and reassurances; wanted to know how things would stand tomorrow. As if I knew. All I knew was tomorrow I would wake up and be the same man I was today. Bennie would be the same man. Broken Wagon Wheel would be hot and Texas would be big and dry. Surefire guarantees. What was the point of wasting time best spent mussing up a bed to discuss happiness and guarantees? Philosophical discussions were best saved for long, monotonous trails, not the bedroom.

When Bennie posed one of his questions it had to be answered as wisely as King Solomon would answer. In Bennie's mind there was only one correct answer, and if I answered wrong he was likely to grab a blanket and sleep in a chair, leaving the bubbling vial of nitro unexploded. When Bennie asked, "Are you happy, Dakota?" I responded by saying, "Yeah, Junior, I was a wretched lowlife until you came along. Now my days are as warm and peaceful as summer evenings." Which was pretty much the truth, but who wants to be forced to admit it every night? After I correctly answered the question, Bennie would roll back against me and once again start stroking and kissing for hours. Making love to Bennie usually meant a night of frustration combined with deep pleasure.

Tonight Bennie was full of questions. "Are you glad I stayed?" he asked. He stroked my chest lightly with his fingertips.

The correct answer was, "Yep, it would have been pure lonely if you hadn't." And that was the truth.

Then he asked, "Were you surprised when you came in and found me here?" His fingers were now trailing down my thigh, making it difficult to concentrate on the questions.

"Yep, I darn near shot you," I responded.

He didn't quite know how to take that answer. His fingers stopped traveling for a second as he considered it, then, satisfied, started their journey again. Finally, he ran out of questions and went about the business of satisfying me.

The mattress was stuffed loosely with straw; plain old barn straw. It crinkled under our weight and jabbed at us like wasps. The bedsprings squeaked and squawked, and the iron headboard slammed against the wall like a mallet. I thought we might go through the floor and end up in Cookie's kitchen. The oven in the kitchen had been shut down for hours, but the heat continued to permeate the floor planks and I pushed Bennie aside now and then just to draw a breath of air.

Sweat ran down Bennie's neck, his stomach, his back, and his legs, and the sheets were so damp you would have thought we were rolling in a puddle of water. Bennie arched his back, let out a holler, then collapsed underneath me. Exhausted, scarcely breathing, he looked as if he were dead.

"Junior?" I whispered, just in case he might be.

"Good Lord, it's hot," he mumbled.

He was alive. I reached for a bottle of whiskey sitting on the night table. Like the room, the whiskey was a gift from Catherine

Waters. The bottle was warm to the touch, but the liquid inside was still cool and I guzzled it. Bennie came to life just long enough to lift up off the mattress and drop across my chest. He lay sprawled there as if I were a river raft and he was floating lazily down the Mississippi. I pulled deeply from the bottle again, then handed it down to him.

He made an ugly face and pushed the bottle away. "It'll rot your brain."

I studied the label for a second, said, "Hell, this is good whiskey," and took another long drink, as if my brain would notice the difference. After placing the bottle on the night table, I picked up my badge.

"Junior, if I'd known lawmen were treated this cordially I would have stolen myself one of these things a long time ago."

"I don't see anything cordial about being shot at by every outlaw in Texas."

"Not every outlaw. Just Juan Caballe and his Mexican army." I turned the badge over, feeling its coolness in the palm of my hand. "It ain't uncommon for a gunfighter to become a lawman. I heard Wyatt Earp is deputy marshal up in Wichita. I reckon if it's good enough for Wyatt, it's good enough for Dakota Taylor."

"*Ex*-gunfighter," corrected Bennie. "You're not a gunfighter any longer, remember?"

"That's what I said: ex-gunfighter."

He was about to argue over the preciseness of my words, but was interrupted by a light tap on the door. Bennie leaped off me, grabbed a sheet that was draping on the floor, and pulled it up around his neck. "Who could that be?" he whispered, fearfully.

"Maybe it's Marshal Cameron Graves come to arrest us both for abusing this here bed," I said.

"You shouldn't joke. These walls are thin."

I laughed and slipped into my pants. As an afterthought, I reached for my gunbelt and strapped it on sloppily. A man couldn't be too careful. The walls were thin. They were made out of chicken wire and crumbling plaster. Catherine's room bordered ours, and Bennie had an arousing habit of shouting when he was excited. Arousing, that is, when we were in a cabin in the middle of nowhere. But his noises were somewhat worrisome when there were neighbors on the other side of the chicken wire, and I damned near held a hand over his mouth when he reached the height of his excitement.

Of course I had no intention of using the peashooter on Catherine Waters, but if the law had come to see what all the noise was about, I'd be damned if I'd be dragged off to the gallows without a fight. After going through the trouble of building a gallows, the people of Broken Wagon Wheel were itching for a hanging. Stringing up a couple of sodomites would probably be as satisfying a spectacle as hanging Judd Brooks.

When I opened the door, I was greeted cheerfully by the heavyset woman we met the first day in Broken Wagon Wheel, Hattie Liverpool. Her miniature sidekick, Elizabeth, stood quietly behind her. All I could see was the top of Elizabeth's head, which was covered by a red gingham bonnet.

"Good evening, gentlemen," said Hattie. "We're from the Ladies' Welcoming Committee. We were introduced yesterday. I hope we didn't wake you, but we saw your lamp shining in the alley. We baked you a pie. Actually, Elizabeth baked it. She tends to be better at that sort of thing. I'm a seamstress by trade. I do the sewing, Elizabeth does the cooking." Hattie shoved the pie at me, then peered over my shoulder at Bennie.

"That was very nice of you," said Bennie from the bed.

I lifted the corner of the cheesecloth covering the pie. "Thanks," I said.

"It's persimmon," said Elizabeth.

"We apologize for the room," said Hattie. "But with the hanging and all it was the only room available."

"The room's fine," I said and started to close the door. "It was mighty kind of you..."

"No one will rent this room after what happened to the last fellow who occupied it," said Hattie.

"What happened to him?" asked Bennie, letting the sheet drop from his chest, and preparing himself for what promised to be intriguing gossip.

"He was murdered," said Elizabeth.

"Why, this is the room Judd Brooks killed that boy in," said Hattie, annoyed that Elizabeth gave away the heart of the story so abruptly. "Some say he was strangled right in that bed as he slept." She pointed at the bed.

"Really?" said Bennie. He looked down at the mattress as if he expected to see the body still lying there.

"The room is fine by us," I repeated. I had a pretty good idea where this was leading. By the time Hattie finished her ghost story, Bennie would be so spooked we'd end up sleeping in one of Pappy's horse stalls. "Thanks again for the pie."

Hattie started to say something else, but I closed the door before she could, then listened as they quietly shuffled back down the hall.

"That was rude," Bennie mildly scolded me and took the pie from my hands.

I nodded. "They were snooping."

"They're curious about their new deputy. They have every right to be."

I stretched across the bed, wrapped my arms around his waist, and bit him above the shoulder blade. "They can be curious tomorrow. Tonight their deputy has more important things to tend to."

Bennie grinned, licked sugar from his fingers, and said, "Want some pie?"

"Nah, it won't mix with the whiskey."

"Oh," said Bennie, quickly setting the pie on the night table. "There's something I want to show you."

"I'm eager to see it."

He had only to crawl to the foot of the bed to reach the bureau. The top of the bureau was crowded with a water pitcher, some combs and brushes, and old perfume bottles. He pushed it all aside and picked up a bundle of envelopes tied together with a yellow string.

"They're love letters," he said.

"Are they yours?"

"Good Lord, I don't keep old love letters."

"That's probably smart of you because I don't recall writing any, and if you kept letters from your old beaus — all tied up in pretty ribbons — I suppose I'd have to go through the trouble of pretending I was jealous."

"Pretending," Bennie scoffed. "Fool yourself, Dakota, but you can't fool me. You would be jealous. Be man enough to admit it." He repeatedly coaxed me with the ball of his foot. "Go on,

admit it. Before I invite Hattie Liverpool back for pie and tea."

"I would be jealous." His threats were truly sadistic.

Laughing lightly, he retracted back under the sheet. The bed groaned and a piece of straw poked him. "I don't have any former beaus."

"I find that hard to believe. What about when you were in Boston? Didn't you have a man to play with then?"

"No," he said uncomfortably.

"Well, hell, is there something wrong with the men in Boston?"

"No, they're just discreet, a concept which you are not familiar with. I've met men whom I suspected were interested in me, but we only had the nerve to stare at each other across a room, both of us afraid to make the first move, so no one did."

"That sounds like a spry hoedown. Sorry I missed it."

Bennie whacked me with the envelopes. "Besides, you're not supposed to read another person's love letters. They're private."

"How do you know they're love letters if you didn't read them?"

"I glanced. I mean, just to see what they were. I found them when I was putting away my clothes. They were tucked away in the back of the bottom drawer. I don't think he wanted anyone to find them."

"Who didn't?"

"Clay James. The boy who was strangled in this bed."

"No kidding?" I sat up. Now I was interested in the letters. "Junior, I consider it my professional duty to know the contents of these letters. Read them."

"Do you think it's proper?"

"Proper be damned. It'll be a hoot."

"Well, all right." Slowly, he untied the string. When Bennie Colsen was curious he could be persuaded into all sorts of improprieties, especially if duty was involved.

Bennie breezed through the handwriting in the first letter, then moved on to the second one. They were love letters, all right, but they weren't written by a woman. They were written by a man. Written by one man to another man. Well, geezus, I couldn't believe my good fortune. It was a rare day in hell when you stumbled upon love letters written between men.

The letters were written by a fellow by the name of Timothy Addams. Not only was Addams badly smitten with Clay James, he was obviously one lonely bastard. The letters were rife with sexual descriptions; they were explicit and made an enjoyable read. I found myself getting aroused again and wondered if Bennie had the gumption to go at it again.

"Geezus," I mumbled after one particularly detailed phrase describing a part of Clay's apparently ample anatomy. "I thought you said men in Boston were discreet."

"These letters aren't from Boston, dear." He turned an envelope over and looked at the postmark. "They're from Washington, D.C. I don't know what men in Washington are like, although I've heard rumors. Clay James was — as you western men so gallantly put it — a soiled dove."

"A whore?"

"Obviously."

"Are there any pictures?"

Bennie pulled the letter away from me. Already, he was becoming protective of Clay James and his letters. "You shouldn't make fun."

"Who's making fun?"

"Well, just try to be a little more respectful."

"I'll do my best. Finish reading them."

Timothy went on to inquire about the gifts he sent to Clay. He mentioned a gold pocket watch that sang — the watch that Judd Brooks had in his possession when he was apprehended — and a gold locket inscribed with an intimate message. Did Clay receive the gifts? Timothy wanted to know. Did he enjoy the gifts?

"'There are so many things I want to give you, dear love,'" Bennie quietly read, "'but until I can see you again I can only give you these small favors, which mean nothing. My only hope is they will remind you of me ... Yours in love, Timothy Addams.'"

Bennie sighed and methodically placed each letter in its proper envelope. "How sad."

In the postscripts, Timothy pleaded with Clay to destroy each letter after reading them. The reason was plain. Timothy was an important man — a congressional aide or something — in Washington, D.C., and he feared the letters might fall into the wrong hands. Clay did not destroy the letters, and Timothy Addams was damn lucky they were now in the respectful hands of Bennie Colsen.

Had Clay James kept the letters out of loneliness? Had he kept them to pore over again and again as he sat in this dirty little room in this dirty little town? Or had he kept them for more sinister reasons? Clay James made his living by bedding down with important men in Washington, then extorting money from them. Was Timothy Addams to be his next victim?

Bennie finished tying a bow around the envelopes, then said, "Do you think Timothy knows Clay was murdered? Do you think anyone notified him?"

"I don't know, Junior. But I do know Timothy Addams won't be happy to learn there's a whole stack of his letters left behind in an underwear drawer. Even I'd be nervous."

"I doubt that." Bennie smiled. "Timothy doesn't have anything to worry about. I'll destroy them."

"Not just yet, Junior."

"Why not?"

"I don't know," I said, shrugging. Truthfully, I didn't know why I made such a request. It was just a feeling. One of them irritating gut feelings. Maybe it was just a coincidence that Judd Brooks happened to kill a young prostitute who happened to be blackmailing powerful men in Washington, D.C. Maybe it was just one of them rare quirks that an infamous gunman − a gunman who reveled in the attention his quick draws and awesome accuracy with a pistol received − sneaked into this very room and strangled the same young man for a pocket watch. Maybe ... but I wasn't so sure.

"Why?" Bennie repeated. "What's so important about the letters?"

"Nothing, Junior," I said. I took the letters from him and dropped them on the floor. "You got the gumption to go at it again?"

8

At sunup I stood under the sagging awning of As the Crow Flies Saloon and waited for Cameron. Broken Wagon Wheel was quiet and peaceful at the break of dawn, a stillness washing over it now that the visitors who had come to watch a hanging had returned to their respective towns. The wide, sweeping streets were deserted, abandoned, and it was a lonely looking town. At intervals, I heard the muffled noises of people moving around in their houses, preparing breakfast, preparing to get on with the day. I heard the unhappy complaints of a child, the yipping of a dog that was probably tied and was displeased about it. A horse whinnied and a donkey brayed in return, and then the town fell into silence again.

A shy warmth brushed the air. When the sun finished slipping down the Rio Grande, the shyness would turn bold and brutal. But at this moment even the gallows seemed as harmless as a giant, wooden toy. The noose swayed gently in a breeze that fluttered down Main Street and halfheartedly lifted bits of paper and sand.

I hadn't made up my mind yet if I should tell Cameron about the letters, though Bennie thought it was hellfire important. I made the mistake of mentioning my concerns – as vague as they were – over the death of Clay James to Bennie and he eagerly leaped on the idea, blowing a mere suggestion completely out of proportion. Bennie spent the rest of the evening speculating wildly about why Clay James was killed, who killed him, and where he was killed. By the time I fell asleep, he had President Grant involved in the conspiracy. I thought Bennie was bored. I thought Bennie should maybe give up the idea of being a lawyer and write dime novels instead. That way he could put all of his imaginings down on paper and stop pestering me. My only question was why a gunfighter – gunfighters being renowned for their lazy indifference when it came to fighting – would go through the trouble of strangling a man when all he had to do was shoot him. I didn't think President Grant or the government had anything to do with it.

Now Bennie was demanding that I bring Cameron into his dime novel. But when I saw the big marshal lumbering down the boardwalk, still wobbly from sleep, I quickly decided against it. Love between men was a dangerous subject for conversation – you never knew how a person might react. Hell, weapons could be drawn. If I had no reason to bring up the subject, then I wasn't about to. I already had Hattie Liverpool peeping into my sleeping quarters; I sure didn't want the law stumbling around there. I came to the conclusion that I was not in Broken Wagon Wheel to discover who killed Clay James or why. A jury had already settled that. I was here to capture the outlaw, Judd Brooks, and reclaim my Colt .44s. That's all. If Bennie wanted to play detective in his spare time that was fine by me. After all, the poor kid would have a lot of spare time to play in.

Cameron strolled sleepily across the street towards the saloon, his untidy hair poking out from under his hat, badly in need of a proper combing. He tripped over a dozing dog lying in his path – a dog even a man with bad eyesight could plainly see. I turned my head so he couldn't see me laughing. The marshal had enough folks snickering at him without his deputy doing the same.

"Mornin'," said Cameron. He pulled a leathery palm over his leathery face, scratching the tiredness away.

"I already outfitted the horses," I said. Two horses were hitched to a rail across the street, geared for traveling.

"I see that. You're a useful man to have around." Cameron paused to light a cigarette. "Is she up?"

"Who?"

He jerked his head towards the Crow. "Miz Waters."

"I didn't see her."

"Maybe we should go in for coffee before we leave."

"Well, if you don't mind being overly eager, I suppose we could."

The marshal stared at me dumbly. "Oh, yeah, I'm supposed to ignore her, right?"

"That's right." I nodded. "And she'll start wondering where you've been." Cameron followed my advice and stepped off the boardwalk. The window of the Crow slid open and Catherine poked out her head.

"If you boys want some coffee and biscuits before you leave, you had better come on in. I ain't going to be hand-feeding them to you out the window." Just as suddenly the window slid shut.

"See there?" I said, cocksure of myself.

Daunted by the prospect of spending the morning next to Catherine Waters, the marshal quickly took off his hat and raked his fingers through his hair in a sorry attempt to comb it. "Do you have a comb?"

I smirked at him. "Got a curry comb in my saddlebags."

He smirked back, pushed past me, and disappeared into the Crow. The saloon was empty and we had our choice of the four tables. We sat near the open door to let the cool breeze tickle our backs and to keep a lawful eye on the street, though it remained deserted of both citizens and potential lawbreakers. Catherine dropped a bowl of biscuits in front of us.

"Thanks for rescuing my baby brother," she said.

"Welp, that's what we're here for, ma'am," said Cameron. "We'll bring back your horse and steers when we get the chance."

"Don't you be tangling with Apaches over a couple of cows. You have better things to do. Like bringing in Judd Brooks."

"Yes, ma'am." Cameron glanced at me irritably. The lie was harmless enough when I first dreamed it up. Now Cameron seemed convinced it would only tarnish him further in the eyes of Catherine Waters. When we caught Judd Brooks, which we were hell-bound to do, he would probably still have the steers and horse in his possession, and how would Cameron explain that without dreaming up yet another lie?

Catherine moved to the back of the bar, picked up a broom, and started sweeping the bare, plank floor. It was about as pointless as sweeping the street. I nearly broke a front tooth biting into a biscuit. Just for fun, I knocked the wooden biscuit on the wooden tabletop. Catherine threw me an unfriendly look from behind the bar.

"I suppose you think because I own this establishment I can bake a biscuit. Cookie has the morning off. Eat them or starve. Your choice."

"Yes, ma'am," said Cameron. He nudged me under the table, once again annoyed that I had started trouble with the woman he loved.

Obediently, I ate the small rocks and attempted to stir coffee that had the consistency of buttermilk. "She is a mite humorless," I said, quietly.

Cameron numbly wagged his head. The big man was going nowhere awfully fast, and, if I were him, I would start looking for affection somewhere else. I'd bet my miserly deputy's wages he wasn't going to get any from Catherine Waters. Not only did she seem uninterested, she seemed downright irritated by him. And irritated with me because I was sitting next to him. I planned on discussing this with him when we were out on the trail.

"Billy Waters!" Cameron and I nearly jumped out of our chairs. Catherine stepped out on the back porch and hollered for her kid brother. "Billy, where are you?"

She waited for an answer. When one wasn't forthcoming she came back into the saloon. "I swear," she said, "that boy disappears quicker than money."

"Would you like me to find him for you?" asked Cameron.

She dropped into a chair next to us and poured a cup of coffee. "He's probably hiding out at Pappy's. He was supposed to hook up a hand pump in the kitchen today. It would be a hell of a lot easier than toting buckets of water in every night. But whenever there's a chore to be done Billy is nowhere to be found."

"My deputy and I will hook up the hand pump for you, ma'am. You just show us where you want it."

I stared grimly at Cameron. The marshal's brain was dripping all over Catherine's feet. On any other day I wouldn't mind doing a long list of chores for this woman. She treated Bennie and me like kin, and didn't say a word about our headboard slamming against her bedroom wall last night, didn't even cast me a curious glance. But I was not in Broken Wagon Wheel to install a hand pump. I was here to apprehend a dangerous outlaw. An outlaw who could be crossing the Canadian border before Marshal Cameron Graves even put a foot in the stirrup.

Catherine pulled her mass of auburn hair on top of her head, twisted it, and attempted to hold it all there with a single hairpin. It collapsed all over her face and shoulders. "That's kind of you, Marshal, but it's Billy's job. If you should see him, tell him to get his skinny ass home." She pushed her cup away. "Gawd, that coffee is awful."

"You should try the biscuits," I said.

Cameron looked riled enough to take away my badge.

With the biscuits knocking against our stomachs, we rode down Main Street and turned left on Sycamore Street. It was just another fancy name. A sycamore wouldn't grow on Sycamore Street if God himself – or Richard Mecum, for that matter – planted it there, but there was plenty of chaparral and more square adobe buildings.

"How come you folks don't give your streets more appropriate names like Chaparral Street or Mesquite Street? Sycamore Street, Elm Street, Oak Street ... they just don't make sense."

Cameron chuckled. "Welp, it was the idea of the Ladies' Welcoming Committee. They like to think Broken Wagon Wheel is more important than it is. The street names look good on the stagecoach manifest."

At the end of Sycamore Street stood the hard reality of what Broken Wagon Wheel really was. The Bradford Bros. Tallow and Tannery was a small, crumbling building. A crooked chimney stack poked through a loosely thatched roof. The roof was covered with an inch of black soot. The place stank. It smelled of death.

There were no windows in the shed, and the only light filtered through the open door. The walls were lined with small animal skins and tanning tools. Mounds of cow and buffalo hides covered the floor. A vat of rank-smelling lime sat next to a potbelly stove. A grimy man with a long, tangled beard worked in a corner at the back of the shed, tanning a hide. When we stepped into the room, he squinted through the dim light, grunted, then returned to his work.

"Mornin', Clem," Cameron bellowed cheerfully.

"What do ya want?" was the cool reply. "Ain't you supposed to be lookin' fer my wife 'bout now?"

"There's a dead horse in the canyon. I thought you might be interested in salvaging the hide. It will ruin before too long."

Clem kept his back to the marshal. "Ain't interested."

"That's a shame," said Cameron, his voice losing its friendliness. "It's better put to use."

"Then skin it yerself."

Cameron suddenly grabbed the tanner by the beard and spun him around. Yanking hard on the beard, Cameron shoved the barrel of his six-shooter against Clem's nose. Clem let out a painful howl. I winced for him.

"Now, listen here, you mangy dog," Cameron growled. "It's nobody's fault but your own that Jennie ran off with Caballe. You stink like an animal and you live like one too."

"She didn't run off!" Despite his painful situation, Clem remained defiant and glared at the marshal with hatred. "Caballe took her while you was sittin' on yer fat ass." The tanner spit in Cameron's face, the spittle slowly trailing down his cheek. Moving quicker than I'd anticipated, Cameron snapped the butt of his gun against Clem's head. Clem fell to the floor in a heap. It was hard to separate him from the cow and buffalo hides.

I heard the cock of a rifle behind me. "Uh ... Graves," I muttered.

Clem's burly brother, Sam, stood behind us. He balanced a short-barreled carbine against his hip. Sam had puffy, black circles under his bulging eyes. They made him look as scared as a trapped coon.

"Lissen, Marshal," he said quietly. "Ya cain't jist come in here and beat on Clem like that."

Cameron holstered his six-shooter. "He was asking for a cuff alongside the head." The marshal's voice was low and soothing once again. "Maybe it'll knock some sense into him."

"Ya cain't jist walk into a man's home and treat 'im wrongly," Sam insisted.

"All right...," Cameron conceded. He leaned over to help Clem to his feet. "I was just trying to give him a dead horse, for chrissake."

Clem Bradford swayed slightly, but stayed upright. Blood dribbled like a ruby teardrop down the lobe of his ear. He pressed his filthy shirtsleeve against the gash on the side of his head. "He insulted Jennifer. Said she ran off with the Mex'can." The grimy tanner began to cry, just started blubbering without warning. His despair appeared as quickly as Cameron's temper tantrum had.

"Now, Clem..." Sam lowered the rifle and patted his brother's shoulder, then turned to me and sheepishly explained, "Clem ain't been right in the head since Jennie been stole."

"No one in this hell-town will do anything to bring her back. They jist lissen to that old hen, Hattie Liverpool." Clem sniffled and swiped the dirty and now bloody sleeve across his nose. "She didn't run off with no Mex'can."

Cameron sighed heavily. Morning had hardly cast its light upon the horizon and already he had one more problem to solve, as if the capture of Judd Brooks and the unsuccessful wooing of Catherine Waters weren't enough. "My deputy and I are riding to the Pecos River to bring in Judd Brooks. No doubt Juan Caballe will be somewhere nearby. If we find Jennifer we'll bring her back."

Clem stopped crying and shook a skinning knife at the marshal. "Bring back that dirty dog, Caballe, while yer at it. I'll make a coat outta his hide."

"One miracle at a time," Cameron muttered. He gave Sam directions to the fallen horse, then we eagerly left the depressing tanning shed, mounted our horses, and headed back down Sycamore Street towards the livery stable.

"Junior would call that place odoriferous," I said.

"Jennie called it hell. That bastard would start drinking and blacken her eye for the sport of it. I've had to stop the townsfolk from lynching him on several occasions." Cameron sighed again. "I suspect that Jennie left with Caballe on her own. And it ain't just Hattie Liverpool who says so."

"I take it we're not going to bring her back, then. This is still a free country. If she left on her own, then we got no business tracking her."

Cameron mulled over the legalities and the morality of his decision before he answered. "Welp, the trouble is no one really knows for sure. She might be waiting for someone to come and help her, especially if Caballe took her into the Sierra Madre. That's hard country. Life with Juan Caballe may not be any better than life with Clem Bradford."

I twisted my torso in the saddle and looked back at the filthy tanning shed belching black smoke from the crooked chimney. I pictured Clem Bradford's yellow, tobacco-stained teeth and greasy beard. Then I pictured Juan Caballe's flashing cat eyes and dashing grin.

"I doubt that," I said.

We stopped our horses in front of the livery stable. Pappy was sitting on a sorghum barrel braiding a rope. He mumbled a greeting, but didn't look up from the rope.

"Have you seen Billy Waters around?" asked Cameron.

"He lit out of here early this morning with Lucky in tow like he had chores to do or something. They took their shotguns. They'll probably be bringing home quail for supper."

"Welp, when he gets back tell him his sister is looking for him."

The marshal's duties in town were finally done and we turned our horses back down Main Street, riding north. We rode past sun-rusted palm trees, past a murky pool of water lined with colorful flowers and ferns.

"That sure is an unusual sight," I said.

Cameron grunted. "Richard Mecum, the banker. How can I compete with a man who can grow gawdamn flowers in the middle of the gawdamn desert?" His chest swelled with anger again and Cameron kicked his horse into a trot. We trotted past Richard Mecum's pool and past the gallows at the edge of town. The noose pivoted playfully in the breeze and the floorboards creaked in the heat. It, like everyone else, was waiting patiently for us to bring in Judd Brooks.

9

Gray Ritter's abandoned stage depot was forty miles south of the Pecos River, deeply embedded in the heart of Dead Horse Canyon. It once served as a resting station for soldiers. Later, it was used by the Southern Overland Express stageline until they engineered a faster, more convenient route, and bypassed the canyon. Now it was a midway point for haggard cowboys, lone Indians, and other lost souls who wandered too deep into Dead Horse Canyon. Gray Ritter offered overnight lodging – if you didn't mind throwing your blanket next to his mule in the stall; a home-cooked meal – of mostly fried chili peppers and sinewy steak; and a horse – provided you were able to ride a half-lame nag. But what Gray Ritter possessed that had endless value to those who traveled in and out of the canyon was a standing well. And that meant water. A day's ride through the canyon quickly reminded a man of the sacredness of water.

Our canteens were almost empty and our horses were limping when we rode over a crescent-shaped ridge that led to the old stage depot. There wasn't much left standing below. A low rock-and-mud structure leaned dangerously to one side. The corral was constructed of uneven, broken poles, and they were leaning over, held in place only by boulders stacked around the posts. The corral was barely capable of holding six horses, but six gaunt horses it held. The horses stayed in the flimsy corral because there was nowhere for them to forage. They depended on Gray Ritter for their food and water. Just like we did.

Skinny pullets scratched at the leftover feed in the corral. A full-grown boar rooted around the stone well, probably wishing he could break into the water and make himself a fine mud hole. There was no sign of Gray Ritter.

"We'll get some grub and fresh horses before going on to Pecos," said Cameron as our horses limped tiredly up to the shack.

"Sounds good to me," I said. Especially the grub. Catherine's biscuits had filled my belly with lead.

Gray Ritter slipped quietly out of a teetering doorway. Though he stood partially hidden in shadows, I easily recognized the double eyes of a shotgun. It was staring right at us.

"You men, get! Get, I say!" Ritter shouted.

"Gray? Is that you?" Cameron queried uncertainly, squinting into the shadows. "I'm Marshal Cameron Graves from Broken Wagon Wheel."

"You don't have to introduce yourself. I know who you are and I don't give a spit. You just turn them horses around and skedaddle."

Cameron calmly shifted his bulk in the saddle and let his reins rest loosely in his hands. I didn't know what to make of the old man's unfriendly greeting, but Cameron didn't seem bothered. Maybe Gray Ritter greeted all his guests in this manner and you just had to suffer through the formalities before getting supper. Or maybe he had become more of a lunatic since the last time Cameron visited the depot.

"We've ridden darn near fifty miles through the canyon. It's been a long haul. You don't have to invite us for supper, but we'll need fresh horses and water," said Cameron.

"You can take the water. I ain't never denied a man a drink of water and I never will. But I'll pepper you with buckshot if you touch them horses."

"We're willing to pay." Cameron pulled gold coins out of his pocket and pitched them at Gray. The coins rolled under his worn old boots. "That's double of what any one of them horses is worth."

"I said I don't have no horses, for sale or otherwise. I ain't interested in your money. Now, get!" He shook the shotgun at us like it was a feather duster.

Wordlessly, I turned towards the corral. Gray's shotgun nervously followed my back.

"Where's he going? Tell him to stay away from them horses or I'll shoot."

I dismounted at the corral and uncinched my saddle. "Old man," I hollered over my shoulder, "I've ridden this horse through. Now you put that gun away before Marshal Graves yanks your beard and slaps them irons on you."

Cameron waited a heartbeat before he said evenly, "You heard Deputy Taylor."

Gray jumped as if he'd just been stung by a bee and lowered the shotgun. "Dakota Taylor, is it?" He squinted at me, recognition making his eyes burn with madness. "Christ Almighty! It's bad enough we have outlaws crawling through this canyon like red ants. Now they're wearing tin stars and riding with the law and stealing a man's horses."

"No, sir. Them horses have been paid for," said Cameron quickly, lest it be known that Marshal Cameron Graves was a horse thief.

The old man reluctantly settled himself in a three-legged chair leaning against the wall of the mud hut and scratched his crotch. He laid the shotgun across his lap and watched closely as I gathered up two horses, but he didn't make any moves to stop me. Cameron joined me at the corral.

"I've got a bad feeling about this," he said, glancing over at the depot man. "Gray's never been real sociable, but he's never denied a man a fresh horse or a meal."

"Something's got him spooked," I said.

"He's a tough old cuss. He don't spook easily."

"Caballe's been here," I said. It wasn't just a lucky guess. I had roped a shaggy little bay from the corral and tethered it to a rail. The mare could belong to only one man.

"Gray would know for sure," said Cameron. "He'd know how many men were riding with Caballe, which way they were riding, and how long ago they left." Again, Cameron glanced at Ritter and wondered if it would do any good to try and shake information out of him.

"Well, I don't want to light no fire under the old man's feet. I can tell you what you need to know."

Cameron grinned doubtfully. "Is that right?"

"There were six of them. They're riding north, and they left the depot two days ago. Three at the most." Without waiting for his reaction, I walked to the well, dropped the bucket, and scooped up the water. Then I filled our canteens.

"Son, that's amazing," said Cameron, following close behind me. "Where did you learn to read signs like that?"

"It don't take a Harvard graduate to figure it. Those are Mexican horses in the corral. They're ganted from hard riding, but they've had a few days' rest. See that ugly little mare?"

Cameron studied the horse for a second before he recognized it. "It's the horse Caballe was riding when he ambushed the stagecoach."

I nodded. "He wouldn't have left his mount here if he was riding into Mexico. That little horse is a desert horse. All of them are. If Caballe and his men are going to make it back to Sierra Madre, they'll need those horses to do it. Gray Ritter's old nags might take them to the Pecos, but they sure won't carry them across Mexico."

"Can you pick up their trail?"

"Oh, hell, yeah. They're riding towards the Gypsy camp. Just like Judd Brooks is." I grinned. "Just like we are."

"Welp, ain't that the lot of a man who was born penniless and luckless."

"Now, you ain't getting spooked on me, are you?" I handed Cameron his canteen.

"All I want is Judd Brooks," the big man sighed. "I want to put handcuffs on him, haul him back to town, and hang him. Is that too much to ask?"

"I reckon it is."

"It's a damn shame I have to fight the entire Caballe gang just to hang one scrawny outlaw." Cameron swung onto a thin horse that still had a touch of spryness left in it despite its exhaustion. Just to annoy Caballe, I took his shaggy bay. Then I leaned over, pulled open the gate, and chased the remaining horses from the corral. They scattered into the canyon. If Caballe wanted his horses back, it would take him a few days to track and gather them. They would probably head for Mexico on their own.

I gave Gray Ritter a high salute and we started back up the ridge. Ritter didn't return the salute. He just sat in his three-legged chair and watched us leave, a slight madness still burning in his narrow eyes. "You got hell a-coming for taking them horses!" he hollered as we ascended the ridge.

No doubt.

We rode out of the bowl of the canyon and began another climb up a steep wall of broken rock. The trail was slick, but the Mexican horses were unshod and they pulled our weight up the sloping trail without slipping. The passage through the rocky mountain suddenly became so narrow we had to lift our legs from the stirrups to keep our knees from skinning on the boulders. After riding nearly a mile through the narrow pass, we came out on a wide trail that was once again sparsely decorated with sage and chaparral.

I spotted movement ahead of us and quickly reined in. Two hundred yards ahead of us, picking their way slowly down a northern slope, were a band of horsemen a half-dozen strong. The horsemen noticed us at the same time we noticed them. They stopped. We stopped.

"Geezus," I muttered.

"Is it...?"

"You bet."

"Sonofabitch."

"Juan Caballe."

The question that entered each man's mind on both sides of the trail was: Should we run? Or should we hold ground and fight? It was easier for Caballe to make up his mind. He had us outgunned three to one. Suddenly his men let out a battle cry and charged. That was what a Mexican soldier was bound to do. I could almost hear the wail of a trumpet as they galloped down the slope towards us.

Our horses stood stolid, without flinching, but Cameron and I were mighty nervous. We had no choice but to retrace our steps through the narrow pass and find cover in the rocks. Wildly we swung our mounts around and turned them loose across the wide flat. Caballe and his men were riding Gray Ritter's sorry horses and we lost them in a plume of dust. But that was only temporary. Once we were in the narrow pass we slowed to a near stop to keep from breaking our legs.

"Let's get up in them rocks," Cameron shouted. We jumped from the horses and scrambled up the face of the ridge wall. I grabbed my Winchester before jumping from the horse and balanced it on an outcrop of rocks. As soon as Caballe entered the narrow pass, I opened fire. One of the bandits was jerked from his saddle when a bullet tore into him. Caballe quickly did a fancy back-dance out of the pass. When they reached the wide flat below us they fell from their horses and spread out through the brush.

The sun was now over the canyon and the Mexicans were blurry shadows moving through the chaparral. They fired on us in spurts, some of the bullets coming from the left, others hitting on our right. They chunked into the rocks in front of us, missing their mark by yards. The gunfire stopped and I cautiously peered over the ridge and squinted into the flat, cursing myself for not bringing along the spectacles Bennie insisted I buy from the traveling optometrist.

"Can you see anything?" Cameron breathed heavily. With the sun in his eyes, he wasn't much better off than I was.

"Nope, I'm just shooting to keep them jumping." I continued to fire the Winchester until I emptied it, then I crouched low and reloaded. I expected Cameron to open fire while I was reloading, but he kept peering over the ridge.

"I don't see Judd Brooks or Jennifer Bradford. Do you?"

"I don't see anything." Despite that, I leaped back up and started firing again. The Mexicans didn't return fire.

"Son," said Cameron, "they're out of range."

Which would explain why they weren't returning my fire. I let the last of my gunfire echo through the canyon, then I listened. I heard the blowing of a horse, heard the rustling of dry brush as the men moved to surround us. Slipping gracefully up a slope to my left was a tall, skinny man. It was Pole, the one-eyed bandit. I swung my rifle and shot at him. He quickly dropped to the ground and rolled into some thickets, unharmed. Reconsidering the futility of a frontal approach, Pole tried to crawl on his elbows and belly back down the slope.

I wasn't going to let him go. I had one, and only one, man in my sights and I stubbornly held him there with a wall of bullets, blocking his only means of escape. Pole found shelter beneath a clump of chaparral and stayed there.

"Are you gonna help me out here?" I snapped at the marshal. He was leaning against the rock, watching thoughtfully, his rifle snuggled in the crook of his arm.

"I told you, they're out of range. You're just wasting ammunition."

"They're trying to surround us."

Cameron studied the wall of rock that rose sharply behind us. "Welp, they might try, but they won't succeed. In order to reach the back of this wall, they'll have to move back into our sights and you'll pick them off if they do."

Juan Caballe boldly stepped out of the brush. He was a large, rotund man and was dressed in a long, colorful Indian poncho. He made an awesome target. With the sun blazing at his back, illuminating his profile, he almost looked like God. In full view of us, he sat on a flat rock, uncapped his canteen, and took a long, leisurely drink. Then, unperturbed, he took off a boot and dumped out the sand.

"Geezus," I mumbled, "look at that bastard."

Cameron chuckled. "He's toying with us."

I slapped the lever of my rifle back and shot at him. The bullet hit the dirt a good ten feet from where he sat. Caballe looked at where the bullet hit, laughed, then took off his other boot. Cameron laid his paw on the barrel of my rifle and lowered it for me.

"It's like spitting on a forest fire. No point. Caballe will have his fun, then move on."

I let the rifle rest. "What makes you so sure?"

"Have you ever played chess?"

"Is it anything like five-card stud?"

"It's a game of kings. When both kings are cornered and can't make a move, it's called a stalemate. That's what we have here. A couple of kings that can't make a move. Caballe can't come into the pass without us firing on him. We can't get onto the flats without him firing on us. If we don't call the game, hell, we'll all sit here and fry in the sun."

Pole was still lying flat in the brush. He couldn't go any farther without endangering himself. "Maybe I can reach him. Cover me."

The marshal had no intention of covering me. He sat like one of the rocks, studying me carefully, grinning oddly. "You got a fire burning in your belly that's likely to get us both killed. I'm not going to die. Not here. Not now. Not until I win Miz Waters."

"Would you kindly forget about Miz Waters?" I said, impatiently. "I don't want to hurt your feelings none, Marshal, but that woman can hardly stand the sight of you."

"She can stand the likes of Richard Mecum," he snorted. "She talks sweet to him."

Suddenly swinging the Winchester, I took a shot at Pole. The bandit slinked farther into the underbrush. Out on the flatlands, Juan Caballe's big belly shook with laughter.

"Did you see how fast that one-eyed bandit can move?" I looked at the marshal and grinned.

"You're wasting bullets, son."

"I got plenty."

"If these jackals get us cornered, you'll wish you hadn't. We're going to pull back and let them go. Judd Brooks isn't with them. Neither is Jennie. They're the ones we want, remember?"

I stared at the marshal in disbelief. "I ain't going anywhere," I said.

"Suit yourself." He shrugged.

And so we waited.

"The Pecos River is still five hours from here," he reminded me.

I knew that. But I ignored him and waited some more. Caballe lit a cheroot and began to banter with his men, who were still crouched in a defensive stance in the brush. I couldn't hear what he said to them; all I could hear was his laughter.

"A man has to compromise sometimes," said Cameron.

Well, I ignored that, too. Compromising was a yellow-belly way to end an argument. Cameron gave up trying to persuade me and rested against a boulder. He placed his dusty hat over his dusty face and dozed, his rifle still resting in the crook of his arm.

Pole was now sitting cross-legged in the underbrush, sharpening his hunting knife.

And we waited some more. The sun was high, brutal. It would be hours before it softened, melted into the dark. I drank from the canteen, then handed it to Cameron.

And we waited.

"*Amigos!*" Caballe shouted. "My men grow restless. You cannot win. We cannot win. There is cold wine and soft beds in Mexico. You let us go, we let you go."

"All we want is Brooks," Cameron shouted.

"All we want is passage," said Juan.

"Turn Brooks over to us and you and your men can go your way."

I nudged Cameron. "Ask him about Jennifer Bradford."

"And Jennifer Bradford. I want Miz Bradford returned to us safely."

"The little criminal is not with us," said Juan. "There is only me and what's left of my men. I do not know this Jennifer Bradford. You make a mistake. Is the *gringo*, Dakota, with you?"

"He's here."

Caballe took off his wide leather hat and bowed grandly. "It's an honor to be shot at by such a *pistolero.*"

"Move up ten feet," I shouted, "and I'll oblige you some more!"

His perpetual laugh was hearty, cheerful, echoing through the narrow pass. "It's an honor to be shot at by you, not shot by you."

Just for the hell of it, I fired off another round. The bullet disappeared and Caballe laughed again.

"Caballe," shouted Cameron, "we're pulling out. I'll give you five minutes to get through the pass."

"Am I supposed to trust this? With the *pistolero* up there?" said Juan.

"I give you my word. We'll hold our fire. Both of us."

Caballe said something to his men and they apparently agreed, for they began to move slowly, warily, out of the brush. Cameron got to his feet and dusted off his pants. "Come on, let's find our horses."

"We're going to let them go?" I shook my head.

"Unless you want to sit here all week."

"Geezus, this is the second time we've let them just ride away."

"Son, this is the hundredth time I've let them ride away. Someday he won't be so lucky."

The Mexicans mounted their horses and began the slow crawl into the pass. They came within range and we held our fire. Soon they moved below us, easy targets. My finger moved restlessly on the trigger of my rifle.

"I gave them my word," Cameron reminded me.

"I know that," I said, angrily. "I ain't going to shoot a man who ain't fighting me."

Not that Caballe wasn't prepared for us to break our word at any moment. His men moved past us nervously, their eyes skimming along the ridge, their fingers also resting heavily on the triggers of their guns. When they were through the pass, Caballe tipped his hat, then rounded the bend and was out of sight.

"Let's find Judd Brooks," said Cameron, patting me on the back. "You'll get another crack at Caballe. Don't you worry none."

10

Once again, we were moving north towards the Pecos River and the Gypsy camp, leaving the brief gun battle with Juan Caballe behind like one leaves a bad memory or an unfriendly locale. My blood was pumping; the excitement itched at me like a heat rash and I couldn't say whether that was good or bad. Cameron was right. I had an unholy fire burning in me. A fire that five years of gentle living couldn't squelch. A fire that sparked and burst into flames at the simplest opportunity. Normal men would feel fear, then relief, after encountering and surviving a gun battle. I felt excitement. What did that say for me except that I was not a normal man?

Cameron didn't like these chancy meetings with death. He rode alongside me quietly, sullenly, deep in thought. Perhaps he was thinking about his own mortality, that every time someone pulled the trigger he was only inches away from death. Or, maybe he was thinking he should have been a man of the gospel instead of a lawman, because he eventually said, "Preachers don't get shot at. Bankers don't get shot at. I picked the wrong profession." Then he slumped back into his solemn mood. Cameron Graves didn't like to brush the shoulder of death and was glad to have Juan Caballe far behind him. As for me, I wanted to turn the shaggy bay and continue the fight with Caballe until one of us was declared victor. It wasn't a death wish. I had no more desire to die than the slow-moving marshal did. But I sure didn't like the idea of being a stalemated king. I wanted to be the conquering king.

Which was why Bennie Colsen was useful to have around. When I was with Bennie I didn't particularly care about being the fastest or the best or the winner. I was content to sit on the porch, smoke a cigarette, and listen to him talk. But out here, set loose in wild country, even the most civilized man became something he wouldn't be within the confines of a township. Survival became his predominant consideration, and every shadow, real or imagined, threatened that survival. Educated men migrated west and into the Deep South convinced that they and others like them could bring civility to the Territories. But, once here, they fought renegade Indians, sadistic outlaws, savage animals, drought, and dust storms so violent they made a man's eyes bleed. It was only a matter of time before these men learned to sleep with their boots on, their rifles within easy reach, a look of stony panic carved on their toughened features. They had not tamed this wild country. This wild country had untamed them.

I was mulling all this over as we carefully entered a thicket of low mesquite. One thing I appreciated about Cameron Graves was he didn't talk much, even when he was in a jolly mood. Whatever he said was said only after he'd put great thought into it. He didn't talk for entertainment or out of boredom. An idea rolled inside his head like a wave, and when it became calm, then, and only then, would the marshal speak. Because of it, his riding partner had a lot of time to silently question why educated men would want to leave their safe homes and migrate west in the first place.

"Son," said Cameron after we had ridden five miles in silence. "Someone's trailing us."

The news surprised me. I was putting so much thought into why I had the urge to ride back and shoot at Juan Caballe some more, I wasn't paying attention to our back trail.

"Which way are they coming?"

"From the southwest. They're traveling along that knoll up yonder."

"How many are there?"

"Two."

Whoever was following us, they weren't very good trackers, nor were they careful about not being seen. In fact, they were more noticeable than the thorns on the mesquite. The two riders were following us along a small knoll off to our right. The long shadows of their horses were so visible it was almost laughable. They weren't Indians, that's for sure. Indians had a spooky, silent way of tracking you. They were smooth predators; most of the time you didn't know an Indian had the jump on you until he was jumping. These folks were just meandering along, obviously following us, but not caring whether or not we spotted them doing so. They were so intent on watching us, one of the fellows let his horse step in a rabbit hole and almost fell. He reined up sharply at the last second and avoided a spill down the knoll.

Cameron turned to me and grinned. "Should we circle around and give them a good scare?"

"Well, hell, yeah. It's rude to follow someone when you haven't been invited to."

We suddenly kicked our horses into a run and dropped into a gorge where we couldn't be seen from the knoll. The mesquite was thicker in the gorge and Cameron's horse didn't like it and tried to shy its way out of the brush, away from the thorns, but the shaggy-coated mare kept traveling like she was a buffalo instead of a horse. The next time I saw Juan Caballe and we weren't shooting at each other, I would tell him that she was a damn fine horse.

Circling the hill, we gaited up behind the riders. They were standing in their stirrups, shielding their eyes from the sun, as they overlooked the flats in an attempt to find us.

One of the riders was small, real small. He had on a long, baggy overcoat and a hat so large it covered his ears and half his face. Cameron lifted his rifle and scoped the slightly larger man's head in his sights.

"Careful," I whispered. "They're kids."

"You there!" Cameron shouted. "Keep your hands where I can see them."

The larger rider's hands leaped in the air, then dropped on top of his hat. The smaller one held still, very still. A buffalo gun was strapped onto his saddle.

"Don't shoot!" said the larger one. "It's just me, Marshal Graves!"

Cameron quickly lowered the rifle and squinted at their backs. I couldn't help but laugh. Two kids had ridden through the waterless Dead Horse Canyon, had ridden past Juan Caballe and his bandits while two *pistoleros* barely made it out of the chute alive.

"It's that young Billy Waters again," Cameron grumbled. "Billy, is Lucky with you?"

Smiling widely, Billy loped over to us. Lucky followed behind. If Lucky was smiling I couldn't tell: the hat was covering the little one's face.

"Howdy, Marshal. Howdy, Deputy," said Billy.

"What the devil are you two doing here?" Cameron shouted. Billy reined back his mare, kicking up dust and causing our horses to fidget. He stared at us stupidly, as if he had just pulled off some great feat, but had no idea what it was. "We want to ride with you. I owe it to Catty to bring back her steers and horse."

"How did you get past Juan Caballe?" I asked.

A small voice responded from under the hat. According to the voice, the smaller rider, Lucky, was a girl, not a boy as I'd first assumed. But it was darn hard to tell.

"Hell, it was easy," Lucky scoffed. "Nobody saw us for the longest time. The only reason you spotted us was because we wanted you to."

"Billy, this isn't a game. We're closing in on Judd Brooks and he isn't going to come along peacefully. This is no place for children," said Cameron.

"I ain't a child no longer. I had a birthday last month. And Lucky's never been a child."

"Holy Mother...," Cameron cursed. "When I was your age, my pappy was just teaching me to use a gun." Cameron looked at me, hoping I could help convince Billy that his age should be held against him. The only way I could help him was by keeping my mouth shut. By the time I was as tall as Billy, I'd already killed one sorry fellow who deserved killing, drank a riverful of whiskey, and bedded down with enough men to populate a small town. I stared across the mesquite flats, drumming my fingers on the pommel of my saddle.

"We ain't going back," said Billy. "Me and Lucky will get the steers back on our own if we have to, but we ain't going back."

"I guess you'll do what you're told to do," said Cameron. Again, the marshal looked to me for support.

I said, "It's going to be dark soon and Caballe ain't in Mexico yet. If we send them back now, there's a good chance they'll run them down and make sport of them. We'll worry about it come morning."

Billy's grin spread from ear to ear. "Thanks, Deputy Taylor."

"Just until morning," Cameron warned him.

We rode on until we found a clearing and made camp.

✦

Despite Cameron's threats, Billy stayed cheerful. He'd won a temporary reprieve, and he was certain he'd found an ally in me. Perhaps he would have – I've never put much stock in the common opinion that a kid couldn't take care of himself in a tight situation. Billy and Lucky carried guns, and though they weren't sharpshooters, they knew how to aim and pull. But Billy talked too much. And the talk consisted mainly of topics young folks liked to talk about because their lives weren't yet filled with interesting adventures. At least when Bennie talked, he had real stories to tell. Billy had only kid talk, peppered with unabashed enthusiasm because he imagined himself to be a deputy marshal tracking a dangerous outlaw. Cameron and I endured, grunting when it was appropriate, chuckling when it was polite.

Lucky, on the other hand, said very little. And it wasn't because she was shy. It was because she'd already learned that the sounds of the night were more important than hearing her own voice. Now, I wouldn't have minded bringing Lucky and her buffalo gun along. There was no doubt in my mind that she knew how to use it, even if the power of it would knock her out of the saddle.

"Why, Danny Haberson joined the Texas Rangers when he was sixteen," Billy was saying. "And Gregory Milo was a soldier in the U.S. Army when he was barely fourteen – course, he lied about his age, but that didn't make him any less fit for fighting." Billy babbled while he was putting together the campfire. He babbled while Cameron heated coffee and set a pot of beans in the fire to warm them.

"I swear, Billy," said Cameron as he slowly stirred the beans. "I don't see why you're in such an all-fire hurry to get yourself killed."

"What difference does it make?" Billy shrugged and filled his mouth with corn pone made soggy with beans. "Nobody would notice anyhow. It's a dang sight better to die a hero than to die unknown and unappreciated."

I chuckled. In different variations I had mouthed those same words when I was a youngster. To die a hero. To die a hard-riding, feared, respected gunfighter. What more could a young man want?

"That sister of yours sure would notice. And she would hold me responsible besides," said Cameron.

Billy also ate like I did when I was a kid. His mouth was so full he had to guzzle hot coffee to push the food down his throat before he could speak. "She'd only notice she didn't have someone to yap at all day or do her chores for her."

"If I were to get you killed she'd have me to yap at all day. And she wouldn't stop until the day I died. And rightfully so." Cameron paused and offered Lucky another cup of coffee. She took it and another helping of beans. "Speaking of chores, you were supposed to hook up a hand pump today."

"I don't want to spend the rest of my life hooking up hand pumps or thatching roofs or gathering chicken eggs or sweeping floors and making beds. I want to be a deputy marshal, dang it."

"Welp, someday you might be. But not today."

Evenings in the canyon were long, but not much cooler. The moon had to fight for its rightful place in the sky. It was a dim moon, faded by the sun's stubborn refusal to go to bed. We didn't need the campfire for light or heat and after supper we let it burn low, leaving just enough coals to keep the coffee warm.

After filling my belly, I sat upright on a boulder that was still warm from the sun and rolled a cigarette. Carefully I tapped a thin line of tobacco onto the paper. It was a serious operation and I tilted the paper at the faded moon for better light.

"Catty's trying to hitch me up with Sally Reynolds," said Billy. His mouth hung open with disgust. *"Sally Reynolds!"*

Lucky snorted. "She's a witch."

"What's so wrong with Sally Reynolds?" Cameron protested. "She's pert and pretty. She comes from good family, and any fool can see she has eyes for you."

Lucky was rolling on the ground, giggling hysterically. Billy swatted at her. He was not amused.

"Her pappy, Josh, owns a big spread north of Broken Wagon Wheel. You could do worse." Cameron tried to continue with serious talk.

I had to agree with Lucky. I'd seen Sally Reynolds coming out of the haberdashery on the arm of her barrel-chested father, Josh Reynolds. She was not pert or pretty. She was short and squat and as barrel-chested as her father. I shook my head. I was now convinced Cameron was more dim-sighted than I was. No wonder the two of us weren't able to shoot more than one Mexican bandit out of a half-dozen of them running straight at us. It was a scary thought.

"Well, I ain't interested," said Billy. "And I wish Catty would stop hounding me about her. 'Sally Reynolds this, Sally Reynolds that...' If I ain't old enough to be your deputy, I sure ain't old enough to be marrying Sally Reynolds." Billy shook his entire body as if he were shaking Sally Reynolds off his back. Slowly I licked the cigarette paper, watching the boy carefully. "Why, I'd rather marry Lucky here."

"I would slit my throat first," said Lucky, who was once again sitting straight and staring at the coals in the fire.

"Who said anything about marrying?" said Cameron. "Your sister just wants you to ask Sally to the picnic this Sunday after church. There's no harm in that. It's a damn sight better than hanging around Richard Mecum."

"Why, Richard's a good friend," said Billy, surprised that Cameron noticed the time they spent together. "He's a worldly man. He knows everything there is to know about horaculter."

"That's horticulture, and I don't see why flowers should interest you. You should have friends your own age."

"I do. I have Lucky here."

Lucky made a sour face. "And I'm a damn sight younger."

"Richard's generous, too," Billy continued. "Look at what he gave me for my birthday." Billy pulled a gold locket dangling from a thin chain from under his shirt collar. "It's genuine gold. And it came all the way from Washington, D.C. That's where the president lives."

"Washington, D.C." Cameron snorted. "The town of shysters and thieves. Maybe I should deputize you."

"Can I see that?" I asked Billy.

Billy unlatched the locket and dropped it in my hand. It was gold, all right. I turned it over. There was an inscription on the back: "To my dearest friend..." The rest of the letters were carefully scratched out. Didn't Timothy Addams send Clay James a locket similar to this one? A locket from Washington, D.C.? How the hell did Billy — or Richard Mecum, for that matter — end up with it? I handed it back to Billy, a little puzzled.

Lucky took a pouch of Bull Durham from her pocket and stuffed a wad of it between her lower lip. "Want some?" She offered me the pouch.

"No, thanks. This smoke will suit me fine." I never picked up the habit of chewing tobacco mainly because I could never find a convenient place to spit. Bennie would go into convulsions if I spit around the house.

"What's that? Chaw?" Cameron demanded. "Girl, you put that away."

"Pappy lets me chew." Lucky shrugged and spit a neat stream of juice onto the coals. She was a professional at it.

"Hell and almighty, I don't know what's wrong with youngsters today. Here we have a girl chewing tobacco and packing a buffalo gun, and here we have a boy taking presents from old men. Pretty soon girls will be wearing pants and boys will be wearing skirts."

Billy got a good laugh out of that one. "Boys wearing skirts. I swear."

"Richard is sweet on Billy, that's why he buys him presents," said Lucky.

"You mean he's sweet on Billy's sister," Cameron corrected.

"If you say so." Lucky grinned nasty.

"You shouldn't be taking presents from old men. You should be giving presents to young ladies. Ladies like Sally Reynolds. Billy, you got it all half-assed backwards," said Cameron.

"Ah, forget it," said Billy miserably. "You're always on Catty's side."

Billy threw down a reed he had been absentmindedly shredding, picked up his saddle, and stomped towards his horse as if he were going to saddle up and ride away in a fit.

"Now he's going to pout," said Lucky. "What a crybaby."

Cameron shook his head. "Sally Reynolds is a fine girl. Pretty as a pistol and as sweet as fresh honeycomb. By God, there's something wrong with that boy."

"No doubt." I lit my cigarette, cupping the match between my hands. "But you'd better not let him ride off mad. He's likely to run into Caballe ... Billy! Watch out!"

Quickly, I dropped the cigarette and reached for my peashooter. What appeared to be a stick lying beneath low shrub suddenly came to life. Within seconds the stick had a domed head and a mouthful of fangs. We could hear the singing of the rattles.

Billy tried to jump away from the rattler, but the snake moved swiftly, burying its fangs in Billy's leg just above his boot.

"Criminey!" Billy screamed. Violently, he shook his leg while the rattler released its venom. "Get it off me!"

I tried to level a shot, but Billy was leaping around in a panic, making it impossible for me to get a good bead on the snake. Cameron and Lucky reached the boy at the same time and Cameron beat the snake off with Lucky's buffalo gun. After knocking it loose, I put a bullet into its head.

Billy fell to the ground and struggled to pull off his boot. Already his foot began to swell. I whipped out my Bowie knife and cut away his pant leg. While Cameron held the boy down, I cut an incision across the fang marks and quickly sucked out the poison. I sucked, then spit the blood on the ground.

The venom was moving fast. I'd learned the hard way the only way a man could survive the bite of a poisonous snake was to remain calm. If you panicked and started breathing hard, making your heart beat faster, it would push the poison through your blood and into your vitals like a stream of water. But Billy Waters was not a man. He was a terrified boy, and he thrashed around and fought for air, ignoring all my demands for him to settle down.

Finally, it was the venom that settled him. His cries faded and he became strangely red and feverish. His breath was labored, coming in short, noisy spurts. Within minutes, he lay limp in Cameron's arms.

"This boy is going to die," I said.

Cameron's pale eyes filled with water as he wrapped his arms around the kid's thin chest. "Sonofabitch, young Billy, you should have done what you were told and stayed home."

Lucky looked down at the lifeless red face and said, "I shouldn't have called him a crybaby."

"How far is the Gypsy camp from here?" I asked.

"It's about ten miles downriver."

I lifted Billy's limp body onto the shaggy mare. With no time to saddle or bridle the horse, I climbed on bareback, using the hitching rope for a rein.

"I've gotta move fast. You two catch up with me later." I spurred the Mexican horse around and we galloped for the Pecos River.

The night had turned from feathery gray to obsidian black. The moon was at its peak, the stubborn sun long settled behind the canyon. The sky was so clear the stars cast a million tiny candle flames off the Pecos River. The river whispered softly, and I didn't realize I'd reached its banks until I saw the stars reflecting on the surface.

Everything was calm around me – the swaying river, the clear night, the flickering stars – while my own heart chugged like a worn steam engine. I was scared. That I had to admit. Boys with foolish grins and brave hearts have died in my arms before, and I swore it would never happen again. Even if I wasn't to blame this time.

If I reached the Gypsy camp in time, there still may not be time enough to save young Billy Waters. Gypsies had magic, of that I was certain. They possessed more magic than the partially pick-led medical doctors I've encountered in the past. But I was bringing them a boy who was already close to death, a boy with the poison of a rattlesnake running through his veins for nearly an hour. Even Gypsy magic had its limits.

I considered prayer. Maybe just a little "How 'bout some help here?" type prayer. But I reasoned that God made the venomous snake in the first place and if He didn't want folks dying of snakebite, He wouldn't have bothered. Nope, until we reached the Gypsy camp, me and young Billy were on our own.

Despite good reasoning, I mumbled a quick thanks that we'd reached the river and Billy was still alive. He let out a low moan, like that of a sick calf, and thrashed around in a sudden fit, making it difficult to keep him on the horse. I held onto his britches and spurred the shaggy bay up the banks of the river, running blind. The mare was a rough rider, but she was sure of her footing, sure she could reach our destination without light.

"You just hold on, kid," I said. Billy stopped thrashing and slipped into a world where he could no longer hear, but I kept talking to him anyway. Sometimes words could interrupt death, if only for a few minutes, and a few more minutes was all I needed.

Scattered pinpoints of light burned up ahead and the silhouettes of four wagons came into view. The wagons were arranged in a crescent-moon position twenty feet off the banks of the river. A large bonfire burned in a clearing in front of the wagons. The flames from the fire leaped so high, sparks danced against the sky like firebugs. Softer lights burned in the windows of the wagons.

As I approached the camp, the wagons came into clear view. They had thin, high wheels and shuttered windows. The panels of each wagon were gaily painted. Heavy cloth curtains covered the doors. The evening was warm and the shutters were open. The largest of the four wagons had a tin chimney sticking out a side window. I could see people moving inside the wagons, and, even from the distance of the river, I could hear the angry wail of an infant.

Two steers ambled along the shores of the Pecos. A small herd of thick-coated mules were hobbled near a cottonwood tree. Among them was an Appaloosa mare. I told Billy that I found his horse and steers, hoping the news would cheer him enough to keep his heart pumping a little longer.

An iron caldron hung from a tripod over the open flames of the bonfire. An old man with a heavy mustache and thick salt-and-pepper hair covered by a light wool cap sat near the fire, poking at the coals with a long stick. He stood when he saw me galloping up the banks of the river, but made no aggressive moves. He silently drank from a burlap-covered flask made sweet with Manzanilla wine.

I galloped into the Gypsy camp without fear. Now, if it had been an Indian camp, I would have slowed to a cautious walk and politely asked for their assistance. But Gypsies weren't normally hostile. They were suspicious of strangers, but their childlike curiosity usually got the best of them. Once they understood you meant them no harm, the Gypsy people were a gay and social bunch who welcomed company. Although I galloped into his camp like a wild man, the Gypsy elder stayed calm and passive.

"I've got a sick boy," I said. "He's been snake-bit."

The old man moved to the side of my horse and I lowered Billy into his arms. "Sitka!" he shouted. "Bring medicine."

The curtains to the largest wagon — the one with the chimney — were pulled open and an old woman who wore yesterday's beauty as elegantly as she wore her colorful, multilayered skirt stepped out. Necklaces and earrings and bracelets dangled from her neck and ears and arms, and she made music when she walked. Like the old man she was calm and unhurried, but she spoke with crusty, authoritative confidence.

"Put him down," she said.

We laid Billy out flat in front of the bonfire. The old man waved a lantern across Billy's face. The boy was a sight. He was bloated with poison, his face pale and his lips blue. Billy Waters looked as if he were dead, and had been for a while. The low moaning had stopped a mile down the river. After taking one quick look at Billy in the lamplight, I was convinced I'd delivered to the Gypsies a dead boy.

"It got him in the leg," I said. "Just below the knee."

The elderly woman, Sitka, inspected the tiny wounds on Billy's leg. The leg was horribly swollen and discolored. In case Billy was still alive, I readied myself for an amputation and hoped the Gypsies had something other than a Bowie knife to perform the surgery with. Fortunately, Billy was wandering in a world without pain. If we needed to remove the leg we needed to do it quickly, before he regained consciousness.

"He's not breathing," said the man.

"He hasn't been breathing for a couple of minutes," I said.

The dull padding of horse's hooves, as Cameron and Lucky galloped up the banks of the river, sounded faint against the heavy pounding of my heart. I had some bad news for the big marshal. Bad news for the little girl. In turn, Cameron had bad news for the woman he loved. He had done his best to protect the boy by chasing him back to his sister, where life was safe and there were no snakes hiding under bushes. His best hadn't been good enough.

I couldn't shake the feeling that I was somehow responsible for the death of Billy Waters. I could have been more firm about sending the boy home, but — if the truth be told — I'd felt a bit heroic knowing that he would choose to follow us, that he wanted to emulate us. Feeling responsible for the misfortune of others was a habit of mine, and I carried blame around like a comfortable old saddle. And, if I felt this responsible for the kid's death, I could only imagine the size of the saddle Cameron would be carrying from now on.

From the corner of my eye, I watched Cameron trot into camp and swing off his horse. Lucky stayed in the saddle. She wouldn't look at Billy.

"How is he?" Cameron breathed.

"He's dead," I said.

Sitka lowered her head to the boy's chest, then looked at her husband. "Tito," she whispered in a hoarse voice, "he isn't dead."

She placed her mouth over Billy's mouth as if she were kissing him. Maybe she was. Maybe she was kissing him good-bye. Maybe it was some sort of Gypsy death ritual.

"What's she doing?" said Cameron.

The woman kept her mouth over Billy's. Then she briefly lifted her head, took a deep breath, and kissed Billy again.

"She is breathing life back into him," said Tito.

Cameron glanced at me. I shrugged. I didn't understand it any more than he did. The Gypsy people looked at the lines on the palm of your hand and told your future. They based their actions on the stars and the moon, claiming they had some kind of influence over you. I dunno ... maybe it wasn't such a good idea bringing Billy to the Gypsies, but you either believed they had magic or you didn't.

Billy suddenly coughed, choking on his own spittle. Sitka looked up at the marshal. "There is breath," she said, placing her withered hand on Billy's chest.

"Sonofabitch," said Lucky, for the first time looking down at Billy.

"Tito, hurry, there is snakeweed in the wagon," said Sitka. Tito hurried to the wagon to prepare the snakeweed. "You men, bring the boy inside."

Again, Cameron glanced at me. Billy's chest was rising slightly. He was breathing. If I hadn't seen it with my own eyes, I would scoff mightily at anyone telling the story of an old Gypsy woman breathing life into a dead boy. But she had done it. Billy was breathing again, raised from the dead. Maybe the Gypsies did have magic.

Before we could hoist Billy off the ground, the curtain to another wagon parted and a woman dropped from the tail plank. Her wild black hair lashed at her rouged cheeks and her brown eyes sparked with danger. Lala Rudshika, I assumed, because that time Cameron was right. She was without argument the most beautiful woman on earth.

"Send them away!" she demanded.

The old woman looked bewildered, but said nothing.

"Lala...," said Tito, returning from the wagon. "What is it you are saying?"

"Can you not see the stars on their vests? They are *shandola,* the law. They will bring us nothing but grief."

"But the boy will die," said Tito.

Lala spit on the ground. "He is nothing to me. It is my husband and child I care for. Kalei!"

I heard the cock of a rifle. A young man stepped around a wagon holding an old Spencer. He had olive-colored skin and a mass of black curls falling over his forehead. A turquoise kerchief was knotted around his neck and his white shirt was unbuttoned to the navel. I'm sure Cameron would disagree with me, but through my weathered eyes, this boy was even more stunning than his sister, Lala.

"Get on your horses," Kalei said nervously. He wasn't used to holding such a big weapon.

"What about Billy?" Cameron demanded. The rare temper began to swell in the marshal's chest. I could almost hear it rumbling.

The elder Gypsies looked down at Billy with pity. "The law has never been good to us," said Tito. "Why should we defy our daughter to help him?"

The sorry truth was I could take down the boy with the radiant skin and dark curls with a flick of my calloused hand. But these people standing around the bonfire were just an old man and woman, a young man, and a woman more deadly than the rattler that had felled Billy. They were an innocent people, a harmless people, and we had not been invited.

Still, Cameron could not let Billy die without a fight. Coolly he pulled out his six-shooter and placed it against Tito's head.

"Uh ... Graves," I said uncertainly.

"You're gonna help this boy," Cameron said in a flat, emotionless voice. "If Billy dies, this old man dies."

Kalei looked at his sister, uncertain of what to do next. The weapon he held in his hand just kept getting heavier and heavier. Convinced the big marshal was only bluffing, Lala remained defiant. Me? I wasn't so sure he was bluffing.

"Go ahead, *gajo,* pull the trigger. Kill a harmless old man," she demanded.

"Ma'am," Cameron said in the same flat voice, "I don't want to kill anyone. But this boy is like a son to me."

"Enough of this," said Sitka impatiently. "Kalei, put down that gun and help put the boy in the wagon. He'll die as we argue."

Kalei's shoulders drooped with relief and he quickly leaned the Spencer against the wagon wheel and helped us lift Billy. Lala angrily whirled around and returned to her wagon. The baby abruptly stopped crying. From inside the wagon, I heard a man's voice gently soothe the child.

We placed Billy on a pallet in the wagon. It smelled of garlic, kerosene, and smoke from a mesquite branch burning in a potbelly stove. Billy began to shiver violently and Sitka covered him with furs while Tito stoked the stove with more branches, though it was hotter than Cookie's kitchen inside the wagon.

Small apothecary bottles lined a shelf in the wagon. Sitka uncapped a rank-looking bottle and sniffed at its contents. "This will do," she mumbled. "It is oil from the plantain plant." I'd never heard of the plantain plant, though I reckon I've been stepping on it most of my life. Temple Taylor, my step-pa, was a traveling medicine man, but his remedies consisted mainly of whiskey and sugar. The only good his medicines ever did was make a sick man drunk and an ailing woman have a sweet tooth. I respected Sitka's remedies a mite more and started to back out of the wagon to give her more room. Whatever chance Billy had at life rested in the gnarled, tobacco-stained hands of the old Gypsy.

"Marshal?" Billy began to mumble. "Marshal Graves?"

The marshal knelt next to the pallet and took Billy's hand. "I'm here, Billy."

"Marshal," Billy mumbled fitfully, "promise me..."

"What is it, son?"

"Promise ... you won't make me take Sally Reynolds to the church picnic."

The poor kid was delirious.

Lucky was still perched on her horse, staring into the bonfire as if she were in a trance. Lucky was a hard one – even at her tender age – but she couldn't quite absorb the fact that she'd nearly lost her only friend. So she sat on the horse, stared into the fire, and pretended it hadn't happened. When Cameron and I left the Gypsy wagon, she didn't look away from the fire. Unnerved by the thought of almost losing one child, the big marshal wrapped his arm around Lucky's thin waist and said, "Come on, kid, let's bunk down for the night," then sort of half lifted and half dragged her to a clearing under the cottonwood. He wanted her nearby, in case any snakes might be lurking about.

The cottonwood was fifty feet from the Gypsy camp and we built a smaller version of the huge bonfire burning among the wagons. Tito invited us to throw our bedrolls next to his fire, but I was convinced Lala had a ruby-handled dagger in her possession and wouldn't hesitate using it if Ma and Pa weren't around to discourage her. Lucky bundled up in a bedroll and promptly fell asleep. Her thin, slight body was nearly invisible under the heavy canvas blanket. Cameron and I sat facing the wagons, keeping a watchful eye out.

"It's ironic, isn't it?" said Cameron. "Judd Brooks is fifty feet away from us and we still can't get to him."

"This is the wrong place and the wrong time for a shoot-out," I said.

"There never seems to be a right place or a right time. He's the luckiest sonofabitch born to woman."

"He's got the luck of the Gypsies on his side," I said.

Cameron grinned. "You don't really believe all that malarkey, do you?"

My face flushed. Yeah, I did believe it. Wholeheartedly. But it sounded pretty silly to admit. "You saw what they did for Billy. I swear, Graves, that boy was dead."

"Maybe he just looked dead," he said quietly. But it was enough to give him thought.

A slight wind swept into our camp and the cottonwood shivered and whispered. "Would you have shot that old man?" I asked.

"Of course not," Cameron answered indignantly. "What kind of man do you take me for?"

"I don't know. You're mighty fond of Billy."

"That I am, son, that I am."

Tito's shadowy figure left the bonfire and moved towards us, Kalei's shadow following close behind him. They approached our campfire and Tito offered us a drink from the wine flask.

"He is resting now," said Tito of Billy. "Sitka says he will live. He is out of danger. Sitka is never wrong about these things."

"We appreciate what you're doing for him," said Cameron, then quickly added as an apology, "I never would have pulled that trigger."

Tito only shrugged. "I would do the same for my son, no?"

"You would." Cameron nodded, took a drink from the flask, and passed it on to me. Tito and Kalei crouched next to our fire, waiting for the wine to come back around. "Where are you folks from?"

"From far away," said Tito, enigmatically. "From across the seas. We are travelers. We are a people without a home." Like gunfighters, Gypsies were not comfortable answering questions about themselves and Tito's reply purposely lacked detail. "From across the seas" sounded mysterious, exotic, and guaranteed his safety. He could have just as easily have come from New York, wanted by the law there.

"America is your home now," said Cameron. Now that the Gypsies had saved young Billy's life, Cameron's slight contempt for them turned to affection and respect, and he offered them his country with arm-sweeping generosity.

"Maybe so," said Tito, not missing the generosity of Cameron's offer. "But in the hearts of most *gajo* we are not welcome here."

"Tomorrow," said Kalei excitedly, "we will go to Mexico." As soon as he said it, his face dropped, knowing he had said too much.

Tito didn't scold the boy or act as if he had said anything wrong. He simply remarked, "Maybe. Maybe we go to Mexico. Maybe not." Then he drained the last of the wine and got to his feet. "Gentlemen, it is late, no? Come, Kalei, let them sleep."

Throwing a sheepish glance our way, Kalei followed his father back to their camp. Kalei made his bed under one of the wagons while Tito went inside to Sitka. The lamp in the big wagon went out.

"Mexico," Cameron muttered.

"Geezus," I said. "Brooks is going to take the whole troop with him."

"And use them for shields."

"I want to go to Mexico," said Lucky from under her blankets.

Cameron patted the small bundle. "Nobody's going to Mexico. Not you. Not me. Least of all, not Judd Brooks."

"Go ahead and get some sleep," I said. "I'll keep an eye on Brooks."

The marshal stretched out on the ground and put his floppy hat over his face. Seconds later, he was snoring. Hours passed. The bonfire burned low, our campfire went out completely. An owl roosting in the cottonwood sang a low, solemn song. From Lala's wagon, a woman laughed and a man hushed her. After that, I accidently dozed off.

I was awakened by the sound of a horse blowing, and the clumsy footsteps of a man trying too hard to be quiet. I laid the palm of my hand on my gun and sneaked to where the mules and Appaloosa were hitched. Crouching behind a chaparral bush, I watched as Judd Brooks hushed the Appy in the same gentle voice he had hushed Lala. Then he quietly led the horse away from camp.

Judd Brooks made his second mistake – the first mistake being he stole my guns. Now he had separated himself from the protection of the Gypsies. Why he did it, I didn't know. Maybe he wanted to distance himself from his family, in case there was some fighting to be done. Maybe he figured he could make it to Mexico faster without them. Whatever his reasons were, it was a foolish thing to do. Nothing stood between us now. Not the Gypsies. Not Juan Caballe. It was down to a solitary battle, with Cameron Graves and Dakota Taylor on one side, and the scrawny outlaw, Judd Brooks, on the other. And Judd Brooks, fast as he might be, mean as he might be, didn't stand a chance.

12

The sharp smell of garlic and wild leeks frying in lard rousted me from my sleep. I opened my eyes to find Sitka's slight figure moving languidly around the iron caldron. She stoked the coals under the caldron, humming softly to herself, then stirred whatever she was cooking in the large pot. Men and women from the other wagons joined her at the campfire. There were two couples: young, handsome offspring of Tito and Sitka, with their mates. There were no *gajo* among them. They were all olive-skinned with dark hair.

Three children ran up from the river, where they had just dipped themselves in the water, taking their morning baths. A puppy, wet and shivering, trailed behind them. The children did a sloppy job of washing up. They surrounded the cookpot, chattering wildly, their wet hair standing on end, impatiently waiting for breakfast to be served. Sitka eventually grew weary of their chatter and shooed them away from the caldron. Unperturbed, they screeched and chased the puppy back down to the river.

I grinned and closed my eyes. It was comfortable in my blanket on the ground and I wanted to enjoy the smells, the laughter from the children, and the warmth of my blanket for a few minutes more. Kalei walked over to our camp and tapped me on the shoulder.

"Come and have breakfast, *shandola,*" he said, smiling pleasantly. "Before my sister arises."

"How's Billy?" I asked, purposely avoiding the young man's brown eyes.

"I wasn't asked to bury him. I guess that means he is still alive."

Kalei's smile, his closeness – I could smell the river water on him from his morning bath – was becoming dangerously hard to ignore, so I rolled over and nudged Cameron out of his sleep. Waking the marshal was like waking a gentle, brown bear. He stretched and yawned and roared and scratched his chest with his huge paw. Lucky was already on her feet, pulling on her long overcoat and placing her hat over her stringy, unkempt hair. Now that we were all dressed for breakfast, we followed Kalei to the campfire's edge.

"The boy is no longer in danger," said Sitka before Cameron had a chance to ask. "He will live. But he is too weak to ride. Leave him here until he gathers strength. You men, however, must go. Have your breakfast, then go. The girl can stay."

Sitka wasn't being unfriendly. In fact, her instructions were delivered with soft kindness. The old Gypsy woman was no fool. She knew why the marshal and I were sitting in her camp, and it wasn't just because we had a sick kid. We had come for her son-in-law, Judd Brooks. Wild-eyed Lala had not been mistaken when she accused us of being bearers of grief. Grief would be in the hearts of every one of the Gypsies when the hangman's noose tightened around Judd's neck. To most law-abiding citizens, Judd was a scoundrel, and few would argue that he didn't deserve to hang. But the outlaw fed the Gypsies, protected them from hostile townsmen, and guided their wagons to safety. Wise old Sitka knew what Judd's unhappy ending was to be as assuredly as she knew what medicines she needed to heal Billy's snakebite.

Lala stepped out of the wagon before we finished breakfast and I braced myself for another round of her anger, but none was forthcoming. She held a tiny, bundled-up baby next to her breast and seemed almost happy. Ignoring the marshal and me, she swayed around the campfire as if she were doing a slow dance. Then she caught my eye and smiled a faint, creepy smile.

Yep, Lala Rudshika was one pleased woman. Her outlaw husband had sneaked out of camp and into the darkness under the watchful eye of the *shandola*. They'd really pulled one over on us. But Lala wasn't as wise as her mother: she didn't understand that her happiness was only temporary. Judd's hours were winding down like a broken clock. I knew the bandit had headed for Dead Horse Canyon, and I knew how long it would take for us to bring him in.

Still, Lala's intense stare and creepy smile gave me the shivers. Gypsy magic worked two ways: it could help you, or it could hurt you, and it suddenly occurred to me that the slow-dancing woman was putting a curse on us and I danged near gagged on my stew. She was humming, but it wasn't a cheerful song like her mother's morning song. It was a long, eerie chant. Cameron and I had enough troubles without packing a Gypsy curse around with us.

"Well," I said, just as suddenly losing my appetite. "You're right, Miz Rudshika. We'd best be on our way. We'll return for Lucky and Billy in a few days."

"I'm not finished with my breakfast," said Cameron.

"Yeah, you are." I emptied his plate for him and practically dragged him to the horses. I saddled mine quickly, then pushed the slow-moving marshal out of the way and saddled his.

"Hell almighty," said Cameron. "What's gotten into you?"

"A curse."

"Pardon me?"

I nodded towards Lala. "That woman is putting a curse on us."

Cameron let out a deep-throated laugh that made his chest rumble. Then he doubled over and held his stomach as if he were in pain. Tears came to his eyes and he didn't respond, he was having so much fun.

Go ahead and laugh. But we were in a heap of trouble. I'd bet any bad fortune on it.

✦

There were sections of Dead Horse Canyon that stretched uninterrupted for miles, with only a few rock formations breaking the monotony of the vast canyon. Most of the rock formations couldn't rightly be called mountains, although they were large enough to conceal a small army and their horses. We had ridden across the canyon floor for three days, making camp during the heat of the afternoon and traveling into the night by the light of the cool moon. The canyon narrowed and shifted into twisting, turning passages lodged between mountains so high you had to look straight up to see the sun. Then we rode out onto brutally scarred plateaus that offered no shelter, no protection from the sun. If a man wanted to get lost in Dead Horse Canyon, he could be lost for years, and Judd Brooks had done a damn good job of getting lost.

He could be hiding behind one of the giant slabs of sandstone only a few feet ahead of us, or he could be hunkered down on one of the broken ridges miles behind us, waiting for us to give up the search. We were certain of only one thing: the outlaw was not heading for Mexico. Judd was leading us on a chase through the canyon, taking us forward, then causing us to rein up and reconsider the route we had just taken. A few times Cameron and I stopped to argue over which direction to go next.

"You mean you haven't picked up his tracks yet?" asked Cameron irritably.

"Geezus, Graves, I ain't an Apache. I can't read signs on hard rock," I answered just as irritably. The heat and the endless tunnels of the canyon were wearing us both down, making us edgy. Feigning confidence, I nudged the shaggy bay into a trot and disappeared into a narrow passage. I didn't have the slightest idea where I was going or why I was going there. I just wanted to lope away from Cameron and his grumbling.

Truthfully, I was more irritated by the heat than I was with Cameron, though I was mighty annoyed with him. The canyon floor was made of hard granite that left no tracks behind. The best tracker — and, all modesty aside, I was one hell of a tracker — could not read signs on granite.

The canyon seemed to hold the sun in its arms, embracing it as if it were a cool, goosefeather pillow, or a sweet-scented lover instead of a fiery mass of rage. Riding straight into it, like Cameron and I were doing, offered us no shelter. There was some shade to be found, but only in the airy hollows of the cliffs, or behind jagged precipices that hung dangerously from the walls, or in the cool weather-beaten caves. Shade, like water, had to be doggedly pursued, and once you found it, you had to sit and soak it in, like Judd Brooks was undoubtedly doing.

Heat swelled from the canyon floor as if the core of the earth were only inches below our feet. In some places the heat was visible, swirling like a blue, hellish fog along the trails. Hell is what Cameron tiredly called our surroundings once he caught up with me in the pass. We were treading heavily through Hell, playing cat and mouse with the Devil's son.

We rode across ancient riverbeds, through mesquite as brown as sand, momentarily through cool shadows, then once again along blistering plateaus. Our eyes constantly followed the rims of the cliffs, the heat waves obscuring anything or anybody that might be hidden behind them.

My eyes would never become accustomed to the blazing orange cliffs or to the heat generating from their terraced floors. My eyes were sensitive to the greens of thick California forests and to the blues of the Pacific coastline.

Judd chose a formidable maze in which to play his game and I began to appreciate the outlaw's skill, his cunning. He was a man who was aware of every move he made, who was capable of outthinking us and leading us around like a couple of calves on a rope. He knew we would eventually give up our search and leave Dead Horse Canyon or we would die.

Cameron and I were arguing over just that — whether or not to leave Dead Horse Canyon and return later with a posse — when we stumbled upon our first sign. It was a clue as simple as a broken branch on a mesquite bush. A few feet ahead of the broken branch, I found horsehair clinging to the side of a smooth sandstone wall. The trail took us up a steep embankment barely wide enough for our horses to pass safely. A gray piece of cloth, torn from a man's shirt, was draped over another bush. I picked up the cloth.

"Didn't this become as convenient as all hell?" I said. "Broken branches, horsehair, and a gawdamn shirt." The signs were too easy. We had traveled for three days without finding anything as revealing as a stone that had been chipped by a horse's hoof. Now, all of a sudden, we were finding pieces of the outlaw's clothes.

"What's he up to?" said Cameron.

"He's trying to lead us into an ambush."

"Welp" – Cameron nudged his horse ahead – "the only way to find out is to walk into it, I reckon."

I didn't always agree with the marshal's plans and now was one of those times. We were plainly out in the open. Judd could be safely sheltered behind a fortress of rocks anywhere along the trail. Giving him something easy to shoot at didn't seem like such a smart idea, but I followed the marshal anyway. The fact was, I didn't know where else to go, and I sure didn't want to spend another three days in the fiery belly of this canyon. I'd rather Judd put a bullet in me.

Cautiously, we continued our journey up the embankment, riding for an hour before we reached the spiraling top. Once we were at the top, Judd's carefully arranged tracks led us back down again. We had come full circle. Our horses stopped to rest at the spot we had left hours earlier.

"That sonofabitch," Cameron growled. He removed his hat and angrily swiped at the sweat trickling into his eyes and down his ruddy cheeks. "He's going around in circles."

"You mean he's leading us around in circles."

In three days, we had combed every inch of the canyon and now Judd was leading us back over it again. "To tell you the truth, Marshal, I'm getting mighty tired of chasing this joker in circles or in straight lines."

"Welp, we could go back to Broken Wagon Wheel and put together a posse."

"We've been over that. You haven't had much luck putting together posses. It's a waste of time." I circled until I had the shaggy bay riding north, back towards Pecos.

"Where are you going?" Cameron shouted.

"Back to the Gypsy camp. He's probably heading home to pretty Lala and that caterwauling baby of his."

So north it was. North, south, west, east, it didn't really matter anymore. Judd Brooks had us under his thumb. The bastard. And if he was riding north, we would ride north. If he rode south, well, we would be sure to follow. I imagined for a second Judd would take us all the way to New Jersey and I chuckled, though I was certain Bennie Colsen wouldn't find it very amusing.

"There's nothing funny 'bout the situation," Cameron grumbled.

I didn't realize I had laughed out loud, but Cameron looked so sorry, I laughed louder. Then he laughed. And there we were, sitting on horses that were walking out of pure horse instinct, laughing at nothing, like a couple of fools.

Then Judd Brooks made his third mistake – the first being he stole my Colt .44s, the second being his leaving the Gypsy camp, and third ... The third mistake was that he took a shot at us. If he'd succeeded in hitting one of us, it would not have been a mistake. But he missed. Not by much, but a miss was still a miss. Whether you miss a man by inches or by yards, the results are the same. Judd Brooks gambled and Judd Brooks lost the whole game.

Before the echo of gunfire died down, we dropped from our horses and ran alongside them, using their bodies as shields. When we reached a wall of boulders, we slapped the horses away and rolled behind the rocks.

"Where did the shot come from?" asked Cameron, crouching down behind the wall.

"Up there." I indicated a shadowy cliff directly in front of us. "He's behind that ridge."

"Judd Brooks!" Cameron shouted. "This is Marshal Cameron Graves. You are under arrest for the murder of Clay James. Throw out your weapons and..."

Another shot interrupted Cameron's decorum. His floppy hat leaped from his head and landed in the sand behind him. There was a bullet hole dead center in the crown of the hat.

"Good shot," I chuckled. "Lucky for you he left some hair behind."

"You are a dark-humored man, Deputy Taylor," said Cameron, inspecting the hole in his hat. "This is the only hat I own."

"Seems to me if a man can only afford one hat he needs a better-paying job."

"Seems to me I need a less dangerous job."

Judd took another shot at us. It blew a piece of our hideout away. "I'm telling you for the last time, Marshal, I ain't kilt nobody. Now you get off my tail and leave me be!" Judd's angry voice resounded through the tunnels of the cliffs.

Two more shots followed his protest. One of the bullets slammed into a boulder off to our left, almost splitting it in half. I recognized the bellow of those guns as assuredly as a mother recognizes the cry of her child. Them were my guns. My precious Colt .44s. I was damn happy to hear them, even if they were sounding my way.

A slippery trail led behind the ridge where Judd was hiding. Small outcrops of broken rock offered some protection, but not much. "I'm going up that way," I said. "Cover me."

The marshal fired a few rounds at Judd while I quickly scrambled up the trail. Once again, I heard the roar of my Colts and the ground broke in front of me. I dropped behind a boulder. Cameron shuffled up behind me.

"Do you see him?" asked Cameron.

"No, but he's there." I swiftly ran forward, dropped to my knees behind another boulder, waited a few seconds, then ran to the next boulder. The gunfire ceased momentarily. Unsure of our whereabouts, Judd peered over the edge of the ridge. He was unable to get a bead on me so Judd continued his assault on Cameron, pinning him behind rocks fifty feet behind me. I needed the marshal by my side. To keep Judd occupied, I fired three quick shots towards the ridge and he ducked down, then he sprang back up and unleashed the Colts on me. It gave Cameron the opportunity to skip from boulder to boulder until he fell in beside me.

"It ain't no use, Marshal," Brooks hollered. "You get any closer and I'll leave yer dern brains sittin' on the canyon floor." His threat was followed by another boom from the Colts.

In all, I had counted twelve shots. If I had counted correctly, then Judd had emptied both guns and needed to reload. It isn't something you notice when you're leisurely loading a gun, but if you're in a hurry it can take a painfully long time to fill a cylinder to its capacity. And, if you're nervous, you're likely to fumble with the bullets and waste even more time. I reckoned Judd was plenty nervous.

I motioned for Cameron to follow me, then I sprinted up the last of the trail until I reached the top of the ridge. I stumbled in a shallow furrow, sending a small, but noisy avalanche down the side of the cliff. Judd turned quickly, but, as I had guessed, he was still fumbling with bullets, trying to get them loaded into the guns. My peashooter was pointed at him and Cameron leveled his rifle. The outlaw was cornered.

"Drop 'em," Cameron demanded. The Colts swayed nervously in Judd's hands as he considered the marshal's demand. "You heard me," Cameron warned. "Drop 'em."

"No, wait...," I shouted.

The scrawny outlaw hesitated for another second before he pitched the Colts to the ground. They skidded in loose shale and slipped towards the edge of the cliff. Dropping to my knees, then diving flat-bellied across the ground, I scrambled to retrieve them. The Colts flowed over the edge, cracking against the rocks hundreds of feet below us. They shattered into pieces, then disappeared into a bottomless crevice.

"Geezus...," I groaned. I lay on my stomach at the edge of the cliff, staring into the dark crevice.

"Dern sorry 'bout that," said Brooks.

I was on my feet. Roughly, I grabbed him by the shirt collar, lifted him off the ground, and dangled him over the edge of the cliff.

"I said I were sorry!" He screamed and kicked at me. "Marshal ... Marshal..."

Cameron fired a shot in the air. "Deputy Taylor," he said, coolly. "We can't be throwing prisoners off cliffs."

13

"Sonofabitch!" said Billy, about as chipper as a boy who had just escaped death could say. "Is that really the outlaw, Judd Brooks?"

"Son, who gave you permission to swear like that?" said Cameron.

"Lucky swears all the time," said Billy.

"Welp, Lucky is..." Cameron considered his words carefully. "...not like most folks."

Lucky stayed quiet, but her bony chest swelled with pride at the compliment.

"I'll say this, young Billy," Cameron added. "We couldn't have caught him without your help."

And that made Billy's bony chest swell even bigger than Lucky's.

"Dern it," said Judd. "You're going to hang an innocent man."

Judd never said another word after that. He rode in silence, contemplating all the wrong moves he had made and questioning his decision not to cross the border into Mexico. Juan Caballe was probably drinking cool wine in the foothills of Sierra Madre, while Judd was being led, roped and tied, to his death. I reckoned Judd was wishing he had followed his captain into Mexico instead of staying in Texas to play with his wife and child.

We had reached our rendezvous point on the southern outskirts of Dead Horse Canyon and were plodding slowly towards Four-Mile Waterhole. Cameron had escorted Judd through the canyon, while I was given the chore of riding back to the Gypsy camp to fetch the kids. Not wanting to face the spooky Lala, or the kindness of the Rudshikas, I preferred the job of escorting Judd, but Cameron was the head honcho here, and I was only his lowly deputy.

Taking Brooks in to hang made me feel a little guilty, and I was sure the guilt showed in my eyes when I faced Sitka for the last time. The Rudshikas had treated us good, and I wanted to give them a present. Gypsies liked presents. All I had on me was a pocket watch Bennie Colsen had given me – it had belonged to his grandfather or something – so I gave it to Sitka. The watched pleased her, and she fastened it to her skirt, where it dangled among the rest of her beads and belts. Then I gathered up Billy and Lucky and hightailed it to our rendezvous point before Lala returned from the river, where she had been washing clothes.

We stopped at Four-Mile Waterhole long enough to water the horses and for Billy Waters to consider, out loud, his good fortune. Not only had he survived the fatal bite of a rattlesnake, he had awakened in a real-life Gypsy camp, and was now standing side by side with the infamous outlaw, Judd Brooks. Billy was growing up fast. By the year's end, he would be a man. He'd have interesting stories to tell and be able to cuss all he wanted without asking anyone's permission.

Four tired men and one spry girl limped into Broken Wagon Wheel in late afternoon. A small herd of longhorns waited near Pappy's livery stable, which meant Josh Reynolds was in town, but the streets were vacant. Most folks had been chased indoors by a low sun that still blazed against the dusty streets. When we were halfway up Elm Street, people began to leave their shadowy doorways and cool abodes. Josh Reynolds and a handful of his rangy cowboys stepped out of the Crow. They had been drinking, and they moved up Main Street looking angry, harsh, with trouble on their minds. Soon all the saloons, the bank, and the stores emptied and a small mob crowded our horses as they tried to get a closer look at a condemned man. Cameron didn't stop.

He rode through the mob calmly as they trailed us down the street.

"I say we lynch him now," hollered Josh Reynolds as he glared angrily at the outlaw.

"Why wait until tomorrow?" one of his rangy cowboys yelled.

Sam Bradford left his tanning shed and marched up Sycamore Street carrying his rifle. "Drag him to the gallows! We'll have this done with once and for all."

Wordlessly, Cameron continued to push his horse through the crowd until we reached the jailhouse. We came to a standstill and the mob surrounded Judd's horse. The rangy cowboy grabbed Judd and tried to pull him from the saddle. Cameron dismounted, looped a rein around the hitching rail, then stood defiantly on the porch to confront the crowd.

"Gentlemen," he said, calmly. "This man is in my custody. He'll hang Friday at noon, not a minute before."

"Friday will be too late. Let's have it done with before Juan Caballe rides into town," said Sam Bradford.

A drunken Clem Bradford stumbled through the crowd, all red-eyed and smelly. "What about Jennifer? Did you find Jennifer?"

"Sorry, Clem," said Cameron, shaking his head.

"Sam's right," said Josh Reynolds. "Why give Caballe a chance to spring him again? If you can't do your job, Marshal, then get out of the way and let us do it for you." Josh took a short rope from the marshal's horse and charged up the steps. Cameron cocked his rifle. Josh froze on the second step.

"Dammit, Josh, I mean it." His voice was low and stern. "No one touches my prisoners. Now you men go on back to the Crow and buy yourselves a bottle. Tell Catherine it's on me."

Mayor Joseph Bagley was suddenly standing next to Cameron, nervously pulling at a fluffy sideburn. "Stop this nonsense," he demanded weakly. "Broken Wagon Wheel will not become a town of vigilantes."

"Vigilantes, my ass," Reynolds growled. "We're just aiming to do what should have been done weeks ago. Just remember, Bagley, there's an election coming up." He backed down the stairs, not because the mayor told him to, but because Cameron's rifle told him to.

Catherine Waters, with Richard Mecum following behind her like a long, thin cord, pushed past Reynolds, and headed straight for Billy's horse. "Billy? Lucky? Where have you kids been? Half the town has been out looking for you."

The hard ride back to town drained most of the sap out of Billy and he looked gray and sickly as he held fast to his saddlehorn. His face was so white his freckles looked like measles. Before Catherine reached his horse, Billy's head lolled backwards, his eyes rolled up in his head, and he fell off his horse. The boy just plumb fainted.

"God Almighty," squeaked Mayor Bagley, stepping off the porch. "What is wrong with him?"

The mob temporarily forgot about Judd Brooks and surrounded Billy instead, fawning over his fallen body. It was the diversion Cameron needed to pull Judd off his horse and hustle him into the jailhouse, kindly leaving me to deal with Catherine Waters and an angry mob.

"A rattler nailed him," I informed them. "He damn near died."

Richard leaned over Billy and fanned his face. "Oh, dear," he murmured. "Oh, dear. Help me take him to his room."

None of the men responded. They lost interest in Billy and were looking around for Judd Brooks.

"Come on, you men," Richard demanded. "Help me lift him."

What the men really wanted to do was hang Judd Brooks, but Brooks was already safely locked in a cell, and since they couldn't deny a sick boy, Josh lifted Billy off the ground, swung him over his shoulder like a sack of grain, and carried him down the boardwalk to the Crow.

Catherine followed behind them, breathing deeply and blinking her red lashes to keep from crying. "Apaches and rattlesnakes," she said, softly. "This country has been forsaken by God."

"Yes, ma'am." I put my arm around her shoulder to settle her. "Don't you worry, young Billy will be just fine."

She smiled faintly. "Marshal Graves calls him young Billy."

Curious about the commotion going on outside, Bennie Colsen stepped out of the Crow just as Josh was lugging Billy through the door. I dropped my arm from Catherine's shoulder and started to turn tail and run back to the jailhouse, thinking I might be a bit safer locked in a cell with Judd. I expected Bennie to be madder than a watchmaker after being left alone for a couple of weeks in a sweaty little room in a God-forsaken country, but curiosity was Bennie's ruling emotion. He took one look at Josh carrying Billy's limp body into the saloon and forgot all about me and my shortcomings.

"What happened to Billy?" he asked.

"He was bitten by a rattlesnake," Richard Mecum volunteered. "Take him to his room, Josh. Hurry."

Horror crossed Bennie's fine features. The boy had an irrational fear of snakes. Back at our ranch in California he usually took an axe to any unfortunate reptile that crossed his path, even if he had to run a couple of yards to do it.

Bennie moved out of the way as Josh carried Billy upstairs and finally settled him onto his fine goosefeather bed. Catherine immediately chased us out of the room.

"He needs rest," she said, herding us out the door. "You men go on now."

"I'll sit with him," said Richard. The banker pulled a chair next to the bed and took Billy's hand.

Billy wasn't the only one who needed rest. Wearily, I dragged myself down the hall and into the hot, airless room above the kitchen. At that moment, the room looked like a cool palace; the mattress looked as soft as water. Groaning slightly, I sat on the edge of the bed and tugged on a boot.

"Poor Billy Waters," said Bennie, taking one last look down the hall before closing the door.

"We were damn lucky the Gypsies were nearby," I said, still tugging on the boot. They were too hot and sweaty to come off. I gave up and decided to sleep with them on.

"What Gypsies?" asked Bennie.

"There was a band of them camped near the Pecos. They saved Billy's life." I didn't say anything about Sitka breathing life back into Billy. It was so peculiar, Cameron and I had quietly decided not to mention it to anyone.

"My family visited Spain when I was a child," said Bennie. He knelt near the bed and pulled off my boots for me. "A huge caravan of Gypsies came through Barcelona while we were there. There must have been a hundred of them. They came on horseback, in wagons, on foot. They were so beautiful and colorful I dreamed about running away with them."

I yawned, but not because his story was boring me. Bennie often talked of faraway places that strained my imagination and made me wonder how one man, so young, could have traveled to places I didn't even know how to pronounce. Sometimes he talked about India and China and Persia, places he'd visited with his father, who'd had a tea-import business before dying a miserable death in the deserts of Arizona. Bennie spoke of strange people with strange cultures and customs, and it made me curious to know how, at the end of it all, he'd ended up in a dusty little room in south Texas.

Nope, I yawned because it felt as if there was a sack of dirt on my eyelids, making them heavy. "You would have made a fine Gypsy, Junior."

"I don't think so. I probably would have run home at the slightest discomfort. God forbid, if I should see a snake." After pulling off my boots, he sat next to me on the bed and rubbed my shoulders.

It was truly gratifying to see that he wasn't mad. In fact, he was being downright nice, and was cheerful and talkative. Bennie had missed me, or he had missed someone to talk to. Hard to say which. I was not cheerful or talkative. I could still see my Colts slipping down the cliff and smashing into pieces. Between being tired and the loss of my guns, I was one sulking companion to try and hold a conversation with. I told him about losing the Colts, just to let him know it wasn't his stories that were bothering me.

"It was the curse," I said.

"The what?"

"The Gypsy curse. Lala put a curse on us."

"Dakota, really," Bennie laughed.

Yeah, hell, everybody laugh. But I was convinced my Colt .44s would be sitting in their holsters right now if the witch hadn't put a curse on us.

After letting me sulk in silence for a few seconds, Bennie said, "Maybe we should have a funeral for your guns." Then he laughed some more.

"That's dern amusing, Junior."

Smiling casually, he leaned over and kissed my shoulder. Actually, he kissed my dirty shirt. In case he decided to do it again, I unbuttoned the shirt and threw it on the floor.

"I stink," said I.

"Would you like me to pour you a bath? I could bring up the washtub."

Geezus, he was being nice. Too bad I was too tired to take advantage of it. "Nah, I think I'll just rest a spell." I settled back on the bed and let out a painful groan. Straw or not, the bed felt finer and cooler than a cloud. "After the hanging, we'll go on to New Jersey."

"Why do we have to wait?"

"Well ... he's going to hang Friday at noon. The stagecoach doesn't leave for San Antonio until then." That may or may not have been the truth – I didn't know what the stagecoach schedule was – but I wasn't going to tell him I wanted to watch Judd Brooks hang. He might think I was morbid. Worse, he might think I was uncivilized. The truth was, I did want to watch Brooks hang. There was a certain satisfaction in knowing your work was finished, and there was no bigger finish than a hanging.

"I'm going to stay in this room until it's all over," said Bennie. "It's beastly the way people behave."

I nodded off. It was just a quick doze because Bennie started rubbing my feet, waking me right up.

"Guess who I saw leaving Catherine's room at a questionable hour of the morning?" said Bennie.

"Cameron Graves?" I asked, hopefully.

"Cameron Graves was with you. How could he be in Catherine's room?" Bennie looked puzzled, but carried on with the game. "Go ahead and guess."

"Junior, I'm too tired to play."

"Richard Mecum. The banker."

"Well, shit."

"This town has more scandals than Boston. Hattie told me that Richard Mecum has been sneaking into Catherine's boudoir at all hours of the night for months now."

I grunted. Life was truly unfair. You could love a person until you ached, only to be cast aside for the puny likes of Richard Mecum. Cameron Graves was a truer man than Mecum. Cameron was young, handsome in a rugged sort of way, and hard-working. He was willing to give Catherine the world. All she had to do was stop being so stubborn and take it. Maybe Cameron was a little slow and he couldn't afford a decent hat. Maybe Richard Mecum was smart and was wealthy enough to grow palm trees in south Texas. But Cameron was still the better man. "That's probably why he's chummy with Billy," I said. "He gave him a gold locket, like the one your friend, Timothy Addams, gave to Clay James. The locket was inscribed and everything."

"Hattie told me that Richard's been practically living at Catherine's since Billy disappeared last week. Offering her consolation, of course."

I grunted again, feeling a sudden fierce loyalty towards the marshal. "While Cameron was getting shot at trying to save Billy's life, Richard Mecum moves in to offer consolation. Love is a kettle of pure disillusionment, Junior. Pure disillusionment."

Bennie stopped rubbing my feet, then worked his hands up my legs. Now I wished I had taken off my jeans. "Hattie doesn't understand why they don't just get married. They're both unattached. They don't need to be sneaking around in the dark."

"Who? Richard and Billy?"

"Don't be dense," Bennie laughed. "You know I mean Richard and Catherine." He suddenly stopped massaging my legs. "Why would Richard give Billy a locket? Why didn't he give it to Catherine?"

I tried to shrug, but my shoulders were weighted down with the same sand that made my eyelids heavy. "Don't know. And I don't care. Maybe he wanted to make an impression on the kid. Lucky says he's sweet on Billy." I yawned and started to drift.

Straddling my waist, Bennie shook me awake. "You're not going to sleep after being gone for two weeks."

I opened one eye. "Why not? Do you have something else in mind? If you do, it had better be good."

He lowered his mouth to mine, kissing deeply, probing with his tongue. "You do stink," he said when he came up for air.

"Sorry." I wrapped my arms around him and rolled him onto the mattress. "You sure smell fine, just like lilac."

"I borrowed it from Hattie Liverpool."

"Hattie Liverpool," I said, doubtfully, as I removed Bennie's shirt. "Did you move in with Hattie Liverpool while I was gone?"

"She's the only person in town who can string a complete sentence together."

"That right?" I unbuttoned Bennie's pants and he lifted off the mattress so I could pull them down around his ankles. Then I kissed him again, not caring a half-hoot how articulate Hattie Liverpool might be. My mouth slid down to Bennie's neck where most of the lilac lingered.

"Hattie and Elizabeth have lived together for over twenty years. Can you imagine that?" said Bennie.

"Nope. I can't imagine living with anyone for twenty years." Hoo-boy, that was the wrong thing to say. I felt Bennie's entire body stiffen. "Except you," I added, quickly, staring into eyes as dark as India ink. "I could spend a hundred years with you and it would seem like an hour."

Like I said, Bennie was in a good mood, and he actually smiled. "If you're going to lie, you shouldn't do it in such a big way."

"That's the only way to lie, Junior. Otherwise, what's the point? Besides, I'm not lying. I'm just exaggerating a little."

"A little." His body softened and he kissed my eyes, letting his lips move lightly over my brows. Then he abruptly stopped. "Do you think it's the same locket?"

"Don't know. Don't care." I reached his chest and was rooting into the tight muscles around his breastbone with my nose and lips.

"What sort of inscription did it have on it?"

"Shut up, Junior." Now I had reached his stomach. Pleasure was only inches away and I would not be sidetracked by small talk.

"What did the inscription say?"

No answer from me. I was too busy.

"Dakota, what did the locket look like?"

I lifted my head and said angrily, "Dammit, Junior, stop trying to carry on a conversation in the middle of important things."

"Don't you find it curious that Billy Waters would be in possession of Clay's locket?"

14

I slept away the following day, drifting in and out of a hazy, lazy consciousness. I didn't know the streets of Broken Wagon Wheel were once again crowded with visitors from out of town. I scarcely remembered Bennie's presence as he came into bed, then out of bed, and as he tried to shake me awake to eat whatever Cookie had sent up from the kitchen. I wasn't hungry, I was tired, and pushed away the food. I slept into the night, until well into the next morning, washed away by the heat, and the perfect comfort and solitude the cramped little room above the kitchen provided.

A sandbag fell through the trapdoor of the gallows, making a heavy thudding noise that echoed down Main Street. The hangman, Eli Butcher, who also served as the town's blacksmith when there were no hangings to be done, repeated the exercise over and over to make sure the rope wouldn't break or the door didn't jam. Because of a loose noose, a slack rope, or a faltering door, a man could take a painfully long time to die. The operation had to be done swiftly to avoid unnecessary suffering. If the condemned man was lucky, his neck would snap instantly and death would come quickly. If not, he would suffocate slowly. Hangings were sanctioned by most western citizens, but no one wanted to watch even the meanest outlaw suffer needlessly. That wasn't

Christianly. To assure a merciful death for Judd Brooks, the hangman dropped the bag again and the trapdoor snapped open, the heavy burlap bag dangling beneath the gallows floor. Everything was working just fine.

I followed all this in a dream – a dream encouraged by the sound of the sandbag falling outside at the end of Main Street. In my dream, instead of the sandbag, instead of Judd Brooks, Eli Butcher was tightening the noose around my neck, and it was my body dangling beneath the bare planks, my spurred boots swaying back and forth beneath the trapdoor. I awoke in a sweat, breathing hard, and blindly patted the mattress, searching for Bennie. He wasn't there. I peered over the edge of the bed to see if he had fallen onto the floor. The bed was small and it had happened before.

Outside, I heard the clamor of wagon wheels, muffled voices, and abrupt laughter. I bolted upright and looked at the clock sitting on the small desk in the corner. It was eleven-thirty, Friday. I'd overslept by a full day. Dammit, anyway. Quickly, I pulled on my pants and hopped to the window. Where the sun had baked the floor planks was blistering hot and burned my bare feet.

Main Street, the secondary streets, and the alleys were crowded with horses, buggies, and wagons. People were still riding in from as far away as Laredo and San Antonio. Cookie had constructed a rock spit and was roasting one of Josh Reynolds's steers. The clearing around the gallows was shoulder to shoulder with spectators and picnic-goers who'd spread their blankets and sat under parasols. In front of the bank, a sharp-dressed salesman was selling balloons and taffy candy. Children ran up and down the boardwalks carrying a balloon in one hand and taffy in the other.

A warm wind blew down Main Street, making the day almost pleasant, and gently cooling off women in their oversized hats and layers of garments. Men lingered outside their shops. Both saloons had their doors wide open and were selling a month's worth of liquor in one morning. To add to the chaos, a herd of cattle mingled unperturbed among the hitched horses and populace. The cowboys were camped ten miles south of town. They didn't want to miss the hanging, but they couldn't leave the cows for rustlers, so they'd brought them along.

It was a glorious day for a hanging.

I searched under the bed for the rest of my clothes, then went to find Bennie. Now, the boy said he was going to stay locked in his room until the hanging was over, but I found him outside in front of the Crow, playing checkers with Elizabeth. Catherine had positioned the tables outside where, from under the Crow's sagging awning, a person had a bird's-eye view of the gallows.

Hattie sat on a bench in front of the Crow sewing silk flowers onto a bonnet. A parasol was mounted to the back of the bench to protect her from the sun. Hattie pricked her finger with a needle and let out a string of curse words. She looked up at me, smiled sweetly, and apologized for her profanities.

"Count my words," she then said to Bennie. "Judd Brooks will not hang on this day."

"And why not?" said Bennie, seriously studying the checkerboard.

"Juan Caballe will rescue the jasper's hide at the last minute. Just wait and see."

"Impossible," said Bennie. "The jailhouse is like a fortress."

"It is?" I said. It annoyed me that I always managed to sleep through the best part of the morning.

"Oh, yes," said Bennie. "Take a look."

I stepped off the porch and squinted down Main Street. Armed guards stood on both ends of the street. Men were perched in the shadows of rooftops, and I could barely see their silhouettes through the windows of attics. Josh Reynolds, Sam Bradford, and Clem Bradford paced the boardwalk in front of the jailhouse carrying rifles. The cowards of Broken Wagon Wheel had developed teeth overnight and there was no doubt their bites would be dangerous this time. Even Juan Caballe wouldn't be foolish enough to cross the border and ride into a compound as fortified as Broken Wagon Wheel.

Elizabeth wiped the board clean of Bennie's checkers. "I win!" she said triumphantly. "Again!"

"I'm going over to the jailhouse," I said to Bennie.

Bennie leaned back in his chair and frowned at the checkerboard. "Fine," he said, then began to set up the board again.

"Don't let that little bandit get away!" Hattie called after me.

"No, ma'am. I mean, yes, ma'am." It didn't matter what I meant. Judd Brooks wasn't going anywhere but to the gallows.

I passed nonchalantly through a throng of well-wishers. Women nodded at me friendly, and said, "Good morning, Deputy," as I touched the brim of my hat. Children giggled and pointed at me. In front of Eli's blacksmith shop, a group of children staged a mock hanging with a real rope. Placing their fingers around their necks, they made choking sounds and rolled in the dirt, pretending to die. One of the mothers ended the game before they succeeded in hanging their pretend prisoner.

As I walked passed the Wagon Wheel Inn, Mayor Bagley slapped me on the back and invited me into the Wagon Wheel Saloon for a drink. "It's perfect weather for a hanging, isn't it?" he said, staring euphorically at the sky. Then he leaned over and whispered discreetly, "I'll be damn glad when this is over and we can get back to normal around here."

"I know what you mean," I agreed. I declined his offer for a drink since it was still early and I was eager to get to the jailhouse, turn in my badge, and say good-bye to Cameron. Once that was done, I'd happily take my drinks, and Bennie and I would leave on the afternoon stage.

"What do you say, Dakota?" said Josh Reynolds. A few minutes earlier the cattleman had been guarding the jailhouse, but now he was standing in front of the inn drinking whiskey and conversing with some of his cowboys. "You think Brooks will hang this time?"

"I'll personally see to it," I said. Hell, I felt bigger than a bull elephant. Bragging wasn't a natural habit of mine, but given the opportunity I could boast with the best of them, and the good people of Broken Wagon Wheel were giving me plenty of opportunity.

Richard Mecum slipped out of the bank, catching the end of my conversation with Reynolds. "Not if Caballe has his way," he said.

I took a long, hard look at Richard Mecum, comparing him to Cameron. Richard Mecum wasn't a handsome man, but he wasn't an ugly man. He was just a man. He seemed nervous, nervous all the time, and he didn't blink as often as most people did, causing his eyes to look watery and red-rimmed. He was maybe twenty years older than Cameron. He was thin, but not soft, and had thick white hair and dirty fingernails from digging in the soil, though he apparently made an unsuccessful attempt to keep them clean and polished. There wasn't anything unpleasant about him, but I still couldn't see why Catherine Waters would choose him over the big marshal. Cameron said Catherine preferred educated men, which would exclude Cameron and just about every other man in Broken Wagon Wheel. Women's taste in men usually dumbfounded me anyway. Richard was tall, thin, and gray. Cameron was strong and rugged and deeply tanned. Richard was persnickety, concerned primarily about his own comforts. Cameron was easy to please and as loyal as a puppy. Hard choice.

"Caballe be damned," Josh argued. "He's powerless against a gunfighter like Dakota guarding the jail doors."

"You're supposed to be guarding the jail," Richard reminded him.

"Ah, Mecum," said Josh. "Take the thorn out of your ass and have a beer. We got nothin' to worry about." Josh threw his arm around my shoulder to prove his point.

All bets were on. It was down to Juan Caballe versus Dakota Taylor. Caught up in the excitement of the moment, I finally accepted a glass of frothy ale from Josh. Then I accepted another. And another. Then, in good spirits, I sauntered down to the jailhouse to get rid of the badge.

When I stepped into the jailhouse, I overheard a raucous argument taking place in the back room. One of the voices belonged to a woman – Catherine Waters. The other voice was unmistakably Cameron's. I hesitated before stepping farther into the office, but I didn't back out completely.

"If you would stop encouraging him, he wouldn't follow after you," Catherine said loudly.

"I don't encourage him, Miz Waters. Time after time, I've sent that boy home. I can't help it if he wants to be my deputy."

"And get himself shot ... or worse!"

"I've warned him of the dangers. Young Billy has to grow up and make his own decisions."

"He's my baby brother and I'll say when it's time for him to grow up. Until then, I'll make his decisions for him. And I'll thank you to mind your own business."

"I reckon it's none of my business that you've been keeping indecent hours with Richard Mecum." Cameron's voice was reaching its bellow stage.

Well, this was getting good. I stepped quietly over to Cameron's desk and sat down in his wooden swivel chair.

"What do you mean by that?" Catherine whispered viciously.

"People are talking..." Geezus ... the cowardly marshal was starting to back down.

"You mean, Hattie Liverpool is talking."

"Welp, people are..." Now Cameron was starting to stutter. I shook my head in disgust.

"If it's any of your business, Marshal, which it isn't, Richard was concerned about Billy disappearing for two weeks. No one knew where he was. If Hattie — and the rest of the people in this town — want to make something of that, so be it."

"Was he worried about Billy on all those other nights he spent in your room? I ain't no fool, Miz Waters. I might look like one, but I ain't."

I chuckled and rummaged around in the drawer until I found a match. Then I put my feet on the desk and relit a cigar Cameron had been smoking before Catherine came by to chew him out.

"Marshal Graves, you *are* a fool, and you're stubborn to boot. Mr. Mecum has graciously shown fatherly interest in Billy. He's the only man Billy has had in his life since Father was killed."

"What about me? You know how fond I am of Billy. I'd happily step into that position if you would let me."

"And teach him what? How to catch outlaws?"

"It's a damn sight better than growing flowers!"

Catherine hit something and I cringed. I don't believe she hit Cameron; it sounded more like she had hit a table or a stack of papers. "I will raise my brother as I see fit. I certainly don't need to explain anything to you."

"No, you don't."

"I'll take my leave, then."

"You just do that."

Catherine slammed out of the back room. When she saw me sitting at the desk, she quickly straightened her bonnet — a Hattie Liverpool bonnet with big yellow daisies on it — and her composure. "How do you do, Deputy Taylor?"

"I'm just fine, ma'am."

She went out the front door and bumped into Clem Bradford, still doing his rigid march up and down the boardwalk.

"'Scuse me, Miz Waters," said Clem.

"Excuse me, Mr. Bradford."

Cameron emerged from the back room, all red-faced and embarrassed. "Brooks wants to see you," he said.

"What does he want?"

"Hell if I know." He was staring out the window, watching Catherine move up Main Street towards the Crow. "He doesn't want to talk to me and he doesn't want a preacher. Guess you'll have to do."

Cameron removed a ring of keys from his pocket and turned the lock on the outer door that led to the cells. There were two small cells at the back of the jailhouse. I followed a short corridor past the first cell. A Comanche was lying facedown on a cot, snoring loudly, and reeking of alcohol. He was wearing pants and a baggy vest and a dirty bowler. I grunted irritably when I passed his cell. He had probably been a proud warrior at one time. Now he was sleeping off a drunk in Cameron's hot cell.

When I reached Judd's cell, I found the outlaw sitting on his cot gobbling down fried chicken and potatoes like he was half-starved. Chicken grease dribbled down the stubble on his chin.

"Graves said you wanted to see me," I said.

"I sure do." He cast aside the napkin he didn't bother to use and approached the bars. His face was so thin his head almost slipped through the bars. "You're still a dern sight riled at me for taking your guns, ain't you?"

"A dern sight."

"I sincerely apologize fer that."

"What do you want, Brooks?" I said, gruffly. The sight of my Colts slipping down the cliff and smashing into pieces was too fresh of a memory for me to be standing next to the man responsible for their destruction. Judd was damn lucky Cameron had the keys to the cell and I couldn't reach him.

"I didn't kill that boy."

"Well, I believe you. I know an honest man when I see one," I smirked.

"Lissen to me, Dakota." Judd grasped the bars with his greasy fingers and stared at me with the frightened intensity of a man who knew he had twenty minutes left to live. "You're the only chance I have left."

It shook me. Not the death stare in his pale eyes, or the desperation in his voice. I was shaken by the fact that he was calling out to me for help. Why me? I didn't know the man, felt no sympathy towards him, couldn't care less if he hanged.

"What makes you think I'm going to stand here and listen to a low-life liar like you?" I asked. Yet, I was compelled to lean against the bars and listen.

"You and me," he said eagerly, his pale eyes casting a sudden glimmer of hope. "You and me. We're cut from the same cloth. Mebbe you look all respectable with that tin star and all, but deep down you ain't much different from me."

"Keep insulting me, Brooks, and I'll twist your neck before Eli Butcher gets a chance to."

Concerned that he might anger me or that I might leave before he had a chance to tell his story, concerned about the seconds ticking away his life, Judd spoke quickly, almost like a telegraph machine. "I saw the man who kilt that boy. I was up in the canyon, bunking down. I saw him ride onto the flats in a wagon and dump the body."

"What were you doing in the canyon?"

Judd paused. "I were doin' some scoutin' for Caballe."

"Scouting what?"

Another pause, then he said impatiently, "What's that got to with anything?"

"You can tell the size of a man's lies by the size of his story."

"Oh, hell, what difference does it make now? We heard soldiers from Fort Davies were transporting guns and ammunition to El Paso."

"I see," I nodded, thoughtfully. "And Caballe was going to ambush them."

"That's right. They was supposed to be carryin' hundreds of rifles through the canyon," said Judd.

"What is Caballe going to do with that many rifles?"

Judd licked his lips and glanced nervously up and down the corridor. The man was running out of time. It was ten minutes before noon. "He was fixin' to sell them to Juh."

"The Apache?" I shook my head violently. "Geezus, Brooks, why does Caballe want to arm him? Juh will take a Mexican scalp as quickly as a white man's."

"Let's jist say we do some tradin' with the Injuns. We do them favors and they don't raid Caballe's camps in Sierra Madre." Judd shrugged. "Call it a peace treaty, if you want. The soldiers took another route; they didn't come through the canyon. But the old man did."

"What old man?"

"The one who kilt the kid," he said irritably, as if I was too stupid to follow his rambling story. "It was nearin' sundown. I never saw him before."

"What did he look like?" My gaze shifted towards the window at the end of the corridor. Someone lit a string of firecrackers and attempted to throw them through the window. But the window was closed, locked, and the firecrackers just popped and cracked and died away in the sand outside.

"He was a tall fella, taller than you. He was thin, old. His hair was whiter than snow. I remember that."

My gaze was steadily fixed on the window. The shadow of the noose was swaying on the adobe wall of the jail cell. "You would say anything to keep your neck out of that there noose."

"Hang me fer robbing banks. I done that. Hang me fer stealing and for rustlin' a gent's cows. I done that. But I ain't kilt nobody 'cept in an honest-to-goodness gunfight. Same as you."

"You're a damn sight meaner than me. You murdered your own *compadre,*" I reminded him.

"Frank would have kilt me!" Judd said indignantly. "He shore would have, if'n I wouldn't have given him the gun. Look, Dakota, after these folks get through hanging me, that old man with the white hair is going to be walkin' 'round pretty as you please. He's gonna get away with murder."

"Uh-huh. I bet it'll just break your heart to not see justice done."

"It ain't my heart I'm worried about, it's my neck."

Slowly, I moved away from the bars. I didn't like the funny feeling pricking at me. My sixth sense was sneaking up on me, whispering to me, against all good judgment that maybe, just maybe, Judd Brooks was telling the truth.

"Dakota, I got me a wife and a brand-new baby. I ain't ready to die yet."

I hated the hesitation in me; hated the lack of clarity of my thoughts. I didn't owe Judd Brooks the smallest of thoughts. In fact, he'd made the fatal mistake of picking at my bones, and I wanted to watch him die as much as the next man. On the other hand, I owed the citizens of Broken Wagon Wheel a good deal.

"You're a bandit and a horse thief and a woman stealer and a watch stealer. You've been a pain to these good people long enough. No, sir, you deserve to hang." Shaking the irritating suspicions from my head, I stomped down the short corridor, my spurs singing wildly.

"Dakota!" Judd shrieked. "Dakota ... ya cain't hang a man fer being a pain!"

The drunken Comanche stirred, grunted, then fell back into his stupor when I closed the door on them both.

I stepped into Cameron's office. He was sitting at the desk with his feet up, chewing on the cigar. Wordlessly, I crossed the room and turned the doorknob.

"Where are you going?" asked Cameron.

With my back to the big marshal, I said, "You're going to hang the wrong man." Then I stepped out onto the boardwalk and was blasted by a hot gust of wind.

15

"We have to do something." Bennie sat stiffly on the edge of the bed and chewed his fingernail. "We can't just sit here and let an innocent man hang."

"Does Judd Brooks look innocent to you?" I asked.

"Sweetheart, you don't look innocent to me. That's irrelevant. The point is, he may be innocent and we have to do something."

"What do you suggest we do?" I wheeled on my heels in the cramped, stifling room. I felt confined, trapped, and needed to get out of there, but there was no place to go. Outside, there was a party going on, a party I no longer wanted to attend, and the only way to avoid it was to stay confined to this room.

"What about an appeal? I could telegraph the governor and request a stay of execution."

I checked the clock on the desk. Five minutes before noon. "I reckon it's too late for that."

Bennie sighed, dropped his hand in his lap, and watched me try to maneuver around the room. "I reckon."

I should not have told him about my conversation with Judd. Still convinced there was some sort of complicated government conspiracy involved in Clay James's death, Bennie was all too eager to accept Judd at his word. I wasn't so sure. My judgment was based primarily on instinct. Admittedly, my instincts were good. Too damn good.

Walking to the window, I leaned against the frame and looked down on the street. The crowds, which had been scattered throughout town, were now gathered around the gallows, their numbers swelling as the execution grew nearer. At this moment, inside the jailhouse, Marshal Cameron Graves would be unlocking Judd's cell, shackling his hands and ankles, and leading him down the short corridor, past the drunken Comanche, and through the outer door.

Right on schedule, the door to the jailhouse pushed open and Cameron stepped out onto the porch with his prisoner in tow. Sam and Clem Bradford flanked the criminal with loaded rifles. Josh Reynolds walked in front of Judd, while Cameron stepped aside and brought up the rear. Judd stood paralyzed for a second, blinded by the sun. He blinked the scene before him into focus, then let his gaze sweep the streets. Perhaps he was looking for the Gypsy wagons; more than likely, he was looking for a sign of Juan Caballe and the mad dogs he rode with. I, too, searched the streets, on the lookout for Caballe. He had been bold enough to attack an armed stagecoach and free his gunman. Would he be bold enough to attack an entire town and do the same?

But there was no one there: no Gypsies, no Mexicans. No one but two hundred or so angry Texans and a herd of longhorns.

"Move ahead." I watched Cameron mouth the words. When Judd didn't move quick enough, Clem roughly shoved him with the rifle. The filthy tanner was obviously enjoying his role as prison guard.

Judd squared his thin shoulders and shrugged his baggy clothes into place. "I'm movin'," he complained. "Ya don't hafta shove."

Upon seeing Judd Brooks, the boisterous crowd fell silent. Quietly, almost reverently, they moved aside as Cameron and his guards pushed Judd through them and up the four steps to the gallows.

Then someone shouted, "Hang the sonofabitch!" and the eerie, respectful silence was broken as the crowd murmured among themselves in agreement.

"This is grotesque," said Bennie. He reclined on the bed, folded his arms under his head, and stared at the watermarked ceiling. "Dakota, close the curtains."

I glanced over at him. Geezus, he was a dramatic one. There weren't any curtains, just a yellow, cracked shade. I ignored him and turned back to the window.

"You're not going to watch," said Bennie when I ignored his request to pull down the shade.

I attempted to open the window, but it was sealed shut by a dozen coats of paint and wouldn't budge. I pulled out my knife and peeled away the numerous coats of paint, then banged at the window again. It slid open six inches before it stopped. Six inches was all I needed.

"You're not going to listen," said Bennie, his voice full of disgust.

Kneeling in front of the window, I pulled the peashooter out of its holster and stuck the barrel out the window. I snorted and reholstered the pistol. "Hand me my Winchester," I said. "I couldn't shoot a bird with this thing."

"Dakota," said Bennie warily. "What are you going to do?"

"Darlin', hand me the Winchester, would you please?" Politeness usually made Bennie respond quicker than demands. If you talked mean to him, you could wait a lifetime for a response.

Still questioning me, Bennie handed me the rifle. "Are you going to shoot Brooks? I suppose it would be more merciful. Good Lord..." Bennie flopped back down on the bed. The straw cracked under his weight, and he let out a small yelp when a piece jabbed him in the neck. "I wish I was in New Jersey."

"We'll be headin' that way come this afternoon. That's a promise." Carefully, I balanced the rifle on the windowsill and scoped in my mark.

"Really, Dakota, you can't just murder the man in cold blood. You can have your Colts remade. There's a gunsmith in San Francisco who is quite good. We can make duplicates."

Bennie talked. I didn't listen. My precious Colts were this morning's troubles, and I had more serious trouble on my mind right at the moment. Trouble like ... Marshal Cameron Graves. When I finished doing what I knew I had to do, Marshal Cameron Graves was guaranteed to be six feet five inches' and three hundred pounds' worth of trouble. Just thinking about it made me grit my teeth, but I kept my scope leveled just the same.

Eli Butcher positioned Judd directly under the noose. Then the blacksmith, sometimes executioner, lowered the rope and looped it around the outlaw's skinny neck. Even from where I squatted, I could see Judd's Adam's apple bob up and down as he tried to swallow. Once again, the crowd fell silent. Some bowed their heads in prayer. I held my breath, my finger gradually squeezing the trigger of the Winchester. Timing was crucial.

Geezus ... Timing was crucial!

The ground began to rumble as a dozen horsemen rode wildly down Main Street, suddenly appearing out of the flatlands like a cloud of locusts. They whipped their horses into the middle of the longhorns and fired over their heads. The cattle circled uncertainly, bellowed in panic, then stampeded. The horsemen took up a shout and guided the cattle straight into the crowd in front of the gallows. Men, women, and children immediately scattered, diving for cover wherever they could find it. The cattle trampled wagons, pushed over water troughs, ran onto the boardwalks, and busted into shops and buildings. One fellow attempted to cross the street to safety and was instantly overtaken by dozens of cows.

"Sonofabitch," I whispered.

Bennie was off the bed and stood by my side. "What is it?" He leaned over my shoulder and peered out the window. "Good Lord, it's Juan Caballe. He's stampeding the cattle."

"Don't touch my shoulder," I said, calmly.

I looked up, just for a second, and squinted at the carnage below me. The bandits fired indiscriminately, not caring whom or what they hit. Cameron's men opened fire from the rooftops. I recognized Kalei, the young Gypsy, as he turned his horse and shot at the guards on the rooftops. One of the guards dropped from the rooftop, rolled across an awning, and fell to the ground. Josh Reynolds shouted something and opened fire on Kalei. The Gypsy boy fell from his horse and was lost in the dust from the cattle.

"Sonofabitch," I whispered again, shaking my head. The beautiful Gypsy boy had sacrificed his life for the likes of Judd Brooks.

Soft, rose-colored dust lifted from the street and the hot wind whipped it into a miniature funnel cloud. It was difficult to see anything five feet above the ground. The cattle were nothing more than a blur of clacking horns. Soon the gallows would be obscured from view. I looked back across the barrel of the Winchester.

Viciously, Juan Caballe spurred his horse towards the gallows. Clem Bradford leaped from the bottom step, eager to finally get a shot at the Mexican who had stolen his wife. Clem fired two rounds and missed both times. With his wicked dragoon dancing in his hand, Caballe wheeled his horse and fired on the tanner. He didn't miss. Clem Bradford dropped to the ground in a heap of dirty furs.

"Drop the gawdamn door!" Cameron bellowed at the executioner, who stood dazed by the attack.

Eli Butcher shook himself and, with the cool precision of a gunfighter, pulled the lever and released the trapdoor. Judd dropped, falling lighter than the sacks of sand. I fired the Winchester. The bullet sliced the rope and it snapped under Judd's weight. Judd landed on his knees in the dirt under the platform. Looking somewhat disoriented and mighty surprised, he scrambled to his feet and frantically looked around him, the noose still looped around his neck.

Juan Caballe galloped up to the gallows. "Get on, *hombre!*" he shouted. He grabbed Judd by the arm and lifted him onto the back of his horse.

Cameron thumbed back the hammer of his pistol and fired furiously at the bandit. Juan spurred his horse again, kicking up more dust, and with Judd bouncing on the back, they galloped south, out of Broken Wagon Wheel. He was soon followed by the rest of his men. Dozens of the townsmen's bullets burned at their backsides, most of them missing by inches.

I leaned away from the window and pushed my hat back off my forehead. "Junior, I do amaze myself."

"Why did you do that?" asked Bennie, confused.

He wasn't the only one who was confused. Frankly, I didn't have the slightest idea why I had saved Judd's life.

Except, well ... the outlaw had asked me to — begged me to, in fact. Maybe I did it for Sitka Rudshika ... maybe for Lala. Maybe

I did it for that squalling little baby in the back of the Gypsy wagon. Or maybe I did it because Bennie Colsen was expecting me to do *something*, and not a day went by where I didn't try to live up to Bennie Colsen's expectations. I knew one thing for sure: I didn't do it solely for Judd Brooks or the possibility that he was innocent.

"I don't know," I said quietly, resting the Winchester against the window ledge. "But I do know you'd better pack your bags, and fast. There's over six feet worth of trouble heading this way."

And he was heading down the boardwalk as we spoke.

16

Bennie had just snapped the buckles of his satchel when there came a pounding on the door of such force I thought the thin door would splinter. I glanced at Bennie. He glanced at me.

"Too late," I said. "We are in trouble."

"*We*?" he smirked.

I hesitated. Denial seemed to be the safest course of action. I surely did not want to fight the big marshal; I was bound to lose. Being beaten senseless in front of Bennie Colsen for doing what I felt was right might have earned me points in his eyes, but I was already hot and sweaty, the room was airless and sultry, and I wasn't in the mood for a bloody battle. Even one guaranteed to get Bennie's sympathy.

Cameron didn't give me time to think of a proper excuse. He angrily pushed through the door. "Gawdamnit!" he snorted as he roared around the room. "Gawdamnit, anyway." His ruddy face was flushed, his teeth clenched, his hands two powerful balls of fists. Once again, I thought of how similar those hands were to the paws of a bear. I'd been mauled by a grizzly once and the fight had been sadly one-sided.

"I've chased that sonofabitch to hell and back again, and my deputy sets him free," Cameron bellowed.

Play dumb, I thought. The only way I'd survived the battle with the bear was when I wised up and played dead. Playing dumb just might work with the marshal. "Did the bullet have my signature on it?" I drawled.

"No one but you could split a rope like that."

"Marshal, you know I couldn't hit a snake with this here toy pistol. I've tried and failed."

Cameron pushed past me and picked up the rifle. He sniffed at it as if it were a daisy. "This has been fired recently. I'd call it evidence."

"Circumstantial, at best," said Bennie, helpfully.

Cameron stared at him, dumbfounded all the way around.

"He thinks he's going to be a lawyer someday," I explained. "So far I've been able to keep him from that shameful profession."

"Instead, he's aided in the release of a dangerous criminal," said Cameron.

"Not necessarily," Bennie protested.

"Be a smart man and don't get him started," I warned Cameron.

Holding the rifle, Cameron sat on the edge of the bed and rubbed his forehead as if he had a serious headache. Sweat trickled down his nose and he took a deep breath, either in an attempt to calm himself or to get some air. "It's hotter than the underworld in here."

"Cookie's making corn bread," said Bennie.

"Why?" Cameron said, now looking more like a little boy than a bear. "Why did you do it?"

"Geezus, Graves, he's innocent."

"Innocent of what? There's no one more guilty than Judd Brooks. He, along with Caballe and the rest of his bunch, have been terrorizing this town for years. They have stolen people's cattle, molested the women, even taken children into Mexico."

"But he didn't kill Clay James," said Bennie. "You can't hang him for something he didn't do, even if it puts everyone at ease."

Cameron walked to the window. Josh Reynolds had gathered up his cowhands and they were mounting their horses in front of the Crow. They weren't going after Brooks. They were going after Reynolds's scattered cattle. The rest of the townsfolk were busy cleaning up the streets after the brief gun battle.

"It's the second time them people have come to see a hanging. It's the second time I've disappointed them," said Cameron.

"They got to see a cattle stampede instead. Not everybody gets to see that. If they're patient they can watch the cowboys round them back up again."

"You're taking this very lightly, Deputy. You broke the law. You're lucky I don't hang you instead."

"If it will make you feel better ... I'll go along to the gallows with you," I said.

"We're leaving on the afternoon stage," said Bennie. "We'll be out of your way then, Marshal."

Cameron's threat had made Bennie nervous and he began to pick at the buckle on his satchel. But Bennie didn't know Cameron Graves the way I did. The big marshal was no more capable of hanging me than he was capable of hanging Catherine Waters. We had ridden together, been shot at together, sweated and shivered together. Nope, we were tied together with a hemp rope stronger than the one the noose was made of.

Cameron shook his head. "The stagecoach isn't going anywhere as long as Caballe is in the area. I won't have him bushwhacking my coaches, and I don't have enough men to ride shotgun."

"How many did you lose?" I asked. In my mind there were swift, fleeting images of men dropping, falling, rolling during the worst of the gun battle, and I had to remind myself the gun battle was not my fault – Juan Caballe was responsible for their deaths. I was responsible only for Judd's escape.

"Clem Bradford is dead."

"Well, he was a miserable sort."

"Three others were wounded, but they'll survive. The rest of them ran."

"Good for them. What about the Gypsy boy?"

"What Gypsy boy?"

"Kalei. I saw him fall."

"If he did, they picked him back up."

That was comforting news. If Kalei was dead, the bandits would not have bothered with him. If he was wounded, he had a good chance of surviving with the help of Sitka and her magic.

"Judd is the luckiest outlaw I've had the misfortune to cast my eyes upon," Cameron continued. "He has Juan Caballe standing in front of him and Dakota Taylor standing behind him."

"He didn't kill Clay James," I said. "That's the only reason I'm standing anywhere near him."

"Why? Because he said so?" Cameron shouted angrily.

"Because my gut says so," I said, rigidly, once again preparing to flank his anger. My reason sounded lame and I knew it, but it was all I had to go on. Cameron needed assurance. It was the best I had to offer.

"I'm supposed to trust your gut over the judgment of twelve jurors? I'm supposed to trust your gut over all the evidence?"

"Yeah, you are."

A part of him did. Despite his better judgment, despite the evidence, I had successfully planted the seed of doubt in Cameron's stubborn mind. He knew me. He knew I wasn't prone to casual impulses. A pitcher of water sat on the table beside the bed. Cameron poured a glass. "You got any whiskey to put in this?"

"Junior, here, doesn't allow me to imbibe."

"He sounds like more trouble than Catherine."

"He is." I leaned against the windowsill and enjoyed the hot wind pressing against my back.

"He had the dead kid's watch on him, for chrissake."

"I know. And he was riding a horse that was missing a shoe. I've ridden a few three-shod horses in my lifetime and I've stolen a few watches. It ain't a hanging offense."

"It is if you're Judd Brooks."

"Look, Marshal, a gunfighter with the skill of Judd Brooks would not have wasted time strangling the kid. If he'd wanted the watch, he would have called him out and shot him. Or he would have won it in a poker game."

"And there's the letters," said Bennie.

"What letters?" asked Cameron.

"Didn't you tell him about the letters?" Bennie couldn't believe my negligence sometimes.

"They slipped my mind," I lied.

Bennie walked to the dresser. "Clay James left some letters behind. You might find them interesting."

Cookie's oven was suffocating us all. "Come on," said Cameron, wiping sweat from his brow, "let's go downstairs. I need a real drink."

"Bring the letters, Junior," I said.

The Crow was more crowded than it had been that morning, but now, instead of talking about the hanging, the men were talking about Caballe's attack on the town and Judd's escape. When we descended the stairs, two men approached Cameron to discuss the incident with him, but when they saw the surly look on the marshal's face, they wisely backed away and returned to the bar where they resumed conversation with other willing men. With the same surly attitude, Cameron ordered a group of men to surrender a table to us, then he ordered a bottle of whiskey. The only time his demeanor softened was when Catherine brought the whiskey and two glasses.

"You can't fight the fires of hell on your own," she said in an attempt to placate him. She threw a look at me and frowned. "Especially when your deputy is helping to stoke that fire."

I coughed and studied my thumbnail. It was turning blue over some mishap I hardly remembered. By this time, I reckon everyone in Broken Wagon Wheel knew I was the one who'd fired the bullet that freed Judd Brooks. I was getting angry glances from the men at the bar, questioning glances from the men at their tables, but when I returned their glances, they quickly looked away. Anyone who could split a rope with a bullet wasn't a man you wanted to look mean at.

"Thank you, ma'am," said Cameron. "You can rest assured – you can all rest assured," he added loudly, "I'll bring Judd Brooks back in to hang. Again."

"You've done it before. I don't doubt your ability to do it again." She smiled sweet at him, then frowned at me again. "And without his help." Then she returned to the bar. Catherine Waters sure wasn't afraid to look mean at me.

"See there?" I grinned, cheerfully. "She has complete confidence in you. I think she likes you."

Cameron growled and snatched the letters out of Bennie's hands. He started with the first letter – Bennie had meticulously kept them in chronological order – and slowly read through them, drinking half the bottle of whiskey before he came to the end of them. His face reddened as he threw the letters, not so meticulously, back to Bennie. He leaned across the table and whispered loudly, "Why, he was a whore!"

"That's right," I said.

"I mean, he was a *man*-whore who favored other men."

"That's right," I repeated.

He leaned back in his chair. "By God, men don't do such things."

"There's nothing a woman does that a man ain't capable of doing," I said. "And I reckon the opposite is true."

"Bear children," Bennie corrected. "Men can't..." He saw the look in my eyes and stopped. It went without saying.

"Small detail, Junior," I said, annoyed at his constant preciseness.

Bennie waved at Catherine to get her attention. "Would you bring another glass, please?" Catherine brought him a smoky-colored glass, looked sweet at him, looked mean at me, and returned to the bar. Bennie waited until she was out of earshot before continuing. "I've read over and over those letters. I believe Clay James had a companion here in town."

"Here? In Broken Wagon Wheel?" Cameron scoffed. "There's none of them kind of folks around here."

"They're all around you," I said. "Like ticks on dogs."

"No, sir." Cameron wouldn't hear of it. "Maybe in New York City. Maybe in San Francisco. But not in the state of Texas."

"Graves, you're so damn dumb...," I said with exasperation.

"And you're facing a hanging, fella. I wouldn't push it if I were you."

Bennie nudged me under the table. Not only did the subject of hanging make him nervous again, he was eager to get on with his theory now that he had someone to hear him out. And he was afraid that by obstinately trying to prove my point I might expose us as "them kind of folks," and we would both be lynched. Cameron *was* dumb, for chrissake. Even Hattie Liverpool had us figured.

"It's quite possible the killer wasn't a Texan. He might have come from back East, like Clay James did," said Bennie, to satisfy Cameron's patriotism.

"That might be," Cameron agreed.

"According to the letters, Clay James was extorting money from dignitaries in Washington, D.C. It's possible he was doing the same here. Clay may have threatened to expose him and, in desperation, the man he was blackmailing killed him."

"Sounds kind of farfetched." Cameron shrugged. "There's no evidence besides the letters here."

"Judd Brooks provided the evidence. He was in the canyon when Clay's body was disposed of. He saw the killer," said Bennie. "He stole the watch after the fact."

"Then why didn't he come forward with the information?" asked Cameron.

Bennie poured himself a whiskey and took a tentative sip. "If you were an outlaw on the run, would you step foot in a jailhouse? Judd was probably more interested in pocketing the watch." Bennie downed the whiskey.

"Brooks described the killer to me when I talked to him in his cell. He said he was tall and thin, an older fellow with a shock of white hair," I said.

"It's a good description," said Bennie, pouring another drink. "Still, there's a lot of tall, thin men with white hair."

"You'd better be careful with that, son," said Cameron. "It has a kick to it."

"Think hard," said Bennie, ignoring Cameron's warning. "Did any strangers come to town fitting that description during the time Clay James was killed? Did anyone leave shortly thereafter?"

"No," said Cameron quickly.

"Are you sure?" Bennie pumped him.

"Son, I'm the marshal. It's my business to keep an eye on anyone who steps off the stagecoach, anyone who rides in alone or with a group. No one came. No one left. I'd stake my badge on it."

Bennie frowned, thoughtfully. "That means he's still here."

"I'm telling you there's none of them kind of folks around here. There's no one in Broken Wagon Wheel who wasn't here before I became marshal."

"They might have met outside of town. Perhaps near Dead Horse Canyon, where the body was found," Bennie insisted. I grinned. I had to admit, I admired his tenacity. He wasn't going to let Cameron buffalo him out of his pet theory. Good. Let him pester Cameron for a while. "There's one way to find out if the killer is still in town."

"How?" asked Cameron.

"Find him another boy."

"Where are we going to find a man who's willing to..."

I was as familiar with the way Bennie's mind worked as I was with the way his body worked, and I knew what was coming next when he got that smug look on his face.

"I'll do it," Bennie said, all pleased with himself.

"Ah, geezus," I said. "He's drunk. No more whiskey for you." I took Bennie's glass from him.

Cameron pretended to like the idea, if for no other reason than to annoy me. He was going to punish me for my part in Judd's escape. "It might work," he said.

I took Cameron's glass. "You're drunk. No more whiskey for you."

"Why not?" They both chorused.

"The last boy who crossed this fellow is dead," I reminded them.

"We'll keep an eye on him. Nothing's going to happen to him. We're lawmen, for chrissake," said Cameron, then winked at me. He had no intention of going along with Bennie or his plan. He didn't believe any of it. As far as Cameron was concerned, Judd had killed Clay James. His mind was set on that. He was just being polite ... or trying to irritate. One or the other.

"Here," said Bennie, filling an empty glass. "Have a drink. You'll feel better."

Before the night was over, Bennie had lost what was left of my money in a poker game. Then he found a tuneless piano in the corner of the Crow and started singing Irish love songs. Just before midnight two of Josh Reynolds's dusty cowboys came into the saloon after spending most of the evening rounding up longhorns. One was a lanky, red-haired wrangler who happened to be Irish. After purchasing a bottle, he joined Bennie at the piano, woefully wailing along with the songs. Soon the second cowboy joined in. They had come in only to wet their dust-parched throats, but midbottle, they were both stricken by the doe-eyed beauty holding court on the piano bench, and started jostling for his attention, nearly starting a brawl. Not in Texas, my ass.

I knew I had to get Bennie Colsen out of there and upstairs into bed before all hell broke loose and I was forced to shoot two good-spirited, fun-loving wranglers. It would have been a damn shame. Though the wranglers protested and threatened, I half carried Bennie upstairs and he spent what was left of the night vomiting over the rail of the upstairs balcony.

"Put a bullet in me," Bennie groaned, his head hanging over the rail. "Please, put me out of my misery."

"My killing days are over. Come on, you'd better lay down." I took him by the arm and tried to lift him up.

Sloppily, he pushed my hand away. "I can't lay down. Everything spins when I lay down. If you love me, you'll kill me."

I took my tobacco out of my pocket and rolled a smoke. "If I loved you I would have sent you to New Jersey where you belong. Wan' a cigarette? Tobacco settles the stomach."

"Why not? I might as well finish myself off." He tried to focus on the cigarette, but was blinded by whiskey. I lit it and handed it down to him. He was still on his knees, hanging onto the railing.

"Junior, I want you to forget about Clay James and finding his killer."

"It's forgotten. I doubt if I'll remember my own name after tonight."

"Good boy.

Bennie groaned and held out his hand. "Help me up, please."

"Are you finished getting sick?"

"I should be. I don't have any insides left."

He wobbled like a sick pony down the hall and into our room and collapsed on the bed. "Good Lord ... what a bed."

I cradled him in my arms, kissed his sweaty forehead, and straightened his mussed-up hair. "The bed would be soft in New Jersey."

"The bed would be empty in New Jersey."

17

I finished my breakfast and pushed the plate aside to make room for the newspaper. President Grant was sending a delegation to the Black Hills of the Dakota Territory to try to persuade the Sioux to turn over the hills – and the gold that the miners had recently discovered there – to the government. I chuckled and took a swallow of hot, thick coffee. Good luck, buddy.

It was early and the Crow was empty. Catherine and Cookie were out back where I could hear them arguing over the installation of Catherine's newfangled hand pump. Cookie didn't want the damn thing in his kitchen, I heard him say loudly. He wanted it out back near the horse trough where it belonged.

Bennie stepped weakly down the stairs. He looked as if he was sick with fever. His bronze cheeks were yellow, his black eyes red-rimmed and bloodshot. I swear, I could hear his chest rattling from where I sat at the table. Bennie had had a hell of a night.

"How ya doing, Junior?" I moved the newspaper out of his way and handed him my coffee, figuring the boy needed it bad.

"I've seen better mornings," he said.

"Want me to call Cookie in and have him fry you up some eggs?"

His face turned from jaundiced yellow to gray ash. "No, thank you. I find it perplexing how you men drink the way you do. Whiskey is lethal. It should be outlawed."

"There's a trick to drinking," I said.

"What is it?"

"It helps to have a hole in your gullet."

"I see."

"You look worse than Billy Waters after he'd been snake-bit," I said.

"It's mighty kind of you to point that out." Tentatively, he took a sip of the thick coffee. "Speaking of Billy, I just passed him in the hall. He was rosy-cheeked and dressed for a picnic."

"Glad to hear it." Billy had quickly recovered from his snake-bite. Like most boys his age he was strong, durable. The morning following our return to Broken Wagon Wheel from the Gypsy camp, Billy was on his feet, riding his horse, playing with Lucky, and generally causing Catherine trouble.

"I'll miss him this morning," said Bennie.

"How so?"

"Well, normally when I come down for breakfast, he runs to my table, pulls out my chair, then proceeds to drop my fork, spoon, and knife on the floor. In that order."

"Clumsy kid."

Bennie managed a tight smile. "I think he's in love."

"With you?"

"It's happened before."

"And to bigger men than Billy Waters." I grinned. "Well, you're a damn sight prettier than Sally Reynolds."

"Thank you, whoever Sally Reynolds might be."

"I sort of had my suspicions about young Billy. I tell you, Junior, I can spot a man who fancies another man across a ten-mile stretch of desert."

"You cannot." Bennie laughed, immediately regretted it, and pressed his fingertips against his temples. "Good Lord, my head."

"You can inform Miz Hattie that Richard Mecum is making those midnight visits to Billy, not Catherine. That's one less scandal in Broken Wagon Wheel."

"Really? Why, ain't you a well of information this morning." Bennie mocked a slow, Texan drawl and I almost suggested we return to our hot, little room upstairs.

"I overheard Catherine telling Cameron the very same. I was eavesdropping. I'm picking up your bad habits," I said.

"Why would an old man like Richard Mecum want to visit with Billy Waters?" If Bennie's black eyes had not been dulled by whiskey poisoning, they would have flashed with a sudden excitement. "Dakota, you don't suppose..."

"Forget it, Junior." I knew exactly what Bennie Colsen was starting to imagine, and I wanted nothing to do with it. I reached for the newspaper and held it in front of my face, pretending to be absorbed in the headlines. "Look at this, Junior. They're sending government boys up to the Dakota Territory to try and talk the entire Sioux nation out of their gold. They'll start a gawdamn war is what they'll do."

Bennie wasn't the least bit interested. He lowered the paper. "Think about it. Richard Mecum apparently has an interest in young boys. Look at the attention he's paying to Billy Waters. And ... his hair is as white as snow. Am I right?"

"No, you're pitifully wrong, and I have a feeling you're just going to get more wrong as the conversation goes along."

"What about the locket?"

"Lots of folks have lockets. I'd have one myself if I could afford one."

"That locket belonged to Clay James," he insisted.

"You don't know that for sure."

"It matches the description of the locket Timothy Addams sent to Clay. Although it has been altered, it's basically the same inscription. You said so yourself."

"Okay. Fine. What if it is the same locket? What if Clay James needed money to get out of Broken Wagon Wheel? What if he sold the locket to Richard and Richard turned around and gave it to Billy because he might — and I'm just saying he *might* — fancy the boy. There's nothing murderous about that."

"But he told Billy that he bought the locket in Washington, D.C."

"No, Billy said the locket *came* from Washington, D.C. You're getting your facts confused."

Bennie paused to rearrange his mental arsenal, and within seconds he was ready to attack again. "Richard Mecum is a wealthy man. He's a banker. That's a prominent position."

"He's an accountant, for chrissake."

"Accountants are important," Bennie said indignantly, mainly because he'd been employed as one during his university days. "Dakota, what if Clay James was blackmailing Richard Mecum?"

"Look, Junior." I grinned. I had to admit, the way his mind worked kept me more entertained than the newspaper did. "Whoever killed Clay James – and I seriously doubt it was your bank accountant – is a dangerous fellow. I know you're bored, but you promised me you wouldn't fool around with this."

"When did I promise you such a thing?"

"Last night when you were puking over the balcony."

"Whiskey talk."

Bennie learned fast. Whenever he held me accountable for something I said that I didn't really mean, I blamed it on whiskey. Now he was doing the same.

"A man who kills once is likely to kill again," I warned.

"Well, you're the one who started it all," he said, exasperated.

"Me? What did I do?"

"You freed Judd Brooks. If you hadn't we could have left on the stage yesterday afternoon."

"You're right. I should have let him hang. He's been a source of pure irritation ever since we crossed into Texas." I glanced around the saloon to make sure no one was there. I leaned across the table and kissed him lightly, tasting the bitter bite of coffee on his lips. "It's a real shame you have a headache, Junior."

"It goes beyond a headache." He smiled faintly.

I kissed him again, my mouth probing deeper this time. The door to the saloon swung open, filtering in a harsh glare from outside, and before I could pull away, I noticed the shadow of a tall, thin man standing in the doorway. Richard Mecum's face turned as white as his hair.

The banker cleared his throat and quickly crossed the room. "Excuse me, gentlemen, please excuse me." He scuttled up the stairs and disappeared down the hall.

"Guess we spooked him," I laughed.

Bennie lifted the coffee cup to his lips. "And so begins our plan."

"You stay away from him, Junior. Now, I mean it."

Bennie's gaze drifted away from me and rested at the top of the staircase at the entrance to the hall. "Of course ... whatever you say."

Shit.

✦

The problem with Bennie Colsen was once he put his mind to it he was perfectly capable of making any man fall in love with him – Josh Reynolds's wranglers, Billy Waters, and old gunfighters. We had been in Broken Wagon Wheel for only three weeks and he already had young Billy Waters dropping silverware and tripping over tables. And Hart McCall, the barber back in Two Rivers, California, didn't give Bennie a shave and haircut at discount because he was a generous man. No, like the rest of the us, the barber was smitten. If Richard Mecum was the sort of man Bennie insisted he was, the poor fellow didn't stand a chance. Hell, I wasn't worried about Bennie. It was Richard Mecum who needed protection.

Just thinking about it made me irritable as I plodded down the boardwalk to the marshal's office with the tin star in my hand. Cameron could have his badge and his peashooter and his hot, dusty town. My duties here were finished. It was time to move on.

I pushed open the door with more force than was necessary. Cameron stood by the gun cabinet buckling his holster. "Mornin', Deputy Taylor. You're up bright and early."

I flipped the badge on his desk as Cameron shoved his six-shooter into his holster. "What do you need that for?" I asked.

"Get ready to ride."

"Where to?"

"Mexico." He fanned a piece of paper in front of my face. "The warrant from the governor just came in. We're bringing back Jennifer Bradford, even if we have to go into Mexico to do it."

"I thought you said Jennifer Bradford didn't want to be rescued."

"Maybe she does. Maybe she doesn't. But it's a damned good excuse to go after Caballe." He grinned a lopsided grin. "Especially while you're still in town."

"I ain't still in town. I'm turning in my badge and leaving on the afternoon stage. And don't tell me the stage isn't running. I already checked with Riker Sims."

"Welp," he said, slowly, thoughtfully rubbing his chin, pretending he was worried, though he wasn't. "You can do that. You can go to New Jersey and sip tea with a poet. Or you can ride with me to the Sierra Madre. Few *gringos* have been there and lived to tell the story."

"Tea with a poet doesn't sound half-bad anymore," I said.

"Yeah, but the Sierra Madre..." His eyes glazed over. Cameron was a man after my own heart. And he knew it.

I had to admit, it was mighty, mighty tempting. The great mountain range of Mexico was one of the few land masses left that hadn't been stomped on by explorers or settled by farmers. Everywhere a man went, out here, even in the most remote regions, he was bound to stumble upon a cabin, some fencing, a township, or a way station. When Bennie and I settled in Two Rivers, California, four years ago there wasn't another soul for miles. Now scarcely a week passed when I wasn't chasing homesteaders off our land. Scarcely a week passed when I wasn't watching more wagons full of men, women, and children moving into the area with their belongings. But the Sierra Madre held only the ruins of ancient civilizations; only the most cunning Mexican bandits; Indians as wild as the animals who prowled the mountains. It was the ultimate test of man's courage, and Cameron was anxious to meet the challenge.

"Think about it," Cameron goaded me on, sensing my indecision. "One last ride before you're too old for the saddle."

"Geezus, Graves, I ain't that old," I said.

"You're beginning to sound like it. 'Tea with a poet ain't half-bad.' For chrissake, Dakota, you're starting to sound like Catherine Waters. I'm offering you a chance to travel one last untraveled trail before the railroads cover every square inch of this country."

It was true. It was happening as we spoke. Soon mile-long trains would be chugging through the Sierra Madre as if it were a busy city street, instead of a wild, lost country.

Slowly, I reached for the badge. "I'll help you bring in Juan Caballe," I said. "I can't stomach the thought of you stumbling through the Sierra Madre for the next ten years. I reckon you'll get lost at the first bend, scalped or shot at the second bend, then I'll feel regret for the rest of my life."

Cameron slapped me on the back. "You're a fine deputy. Loyal and steadfast. You should have been a Ranger." He opened the gun cabinet and started removing rifles. "How's Junior feeling this morning?"

"Pretty useless. I don't appreciate you encouraging him like you did."

"Me?" Cameron looked at me innocently. "I didn't do anything but let him talk."

"That was your first mistake. Then you started feeding him whiskey and teaching him how to play poker."

"I shared my whiskey and got out the cards. Hang me." Cameron shrugged.

"Now he's got some fool idea about Richard Mecum and he ain't going to let it rest. He's going after him."

"Richard? Why?"

"Because he's a banker and he has white hair. Our killer."

Cameron's laugh was like thunder. "He's as harmless as a ... tulip."

"I ain't real eager to chase Caballe up and down the Rio Grande if my boy's going to be strangled by your banker."

Another thunderous belly laugh. He placed the palm of his hand against the gun cabinet to steady himself. "Trust me. Richard Mecum isn't capable of killing anything but flowers."

"So you say. You also said Jennifer Bradford was kidnapped."

"She might have been. She might not have been."

"You also said Judd Brooks was guilty."

"I still say he is, despite the pity you've shown him."

"Well, that's another thing. I'm not bringing Judd Brooks back to town just so you can hang him. You gotta promise me he'll get another trial."

Cameron shrugged again. "Promise. But it isn't just Judd Brooks I want, this time. I want them all. Juan Caballe. Pole. Carlos Coria. All of them. And the two of us are going to do it, son."

I nodded, doubtfully. "And the Sioux are going to sign over the Black Hills to the American government."

"Damn right."

18

I still had Juan Caballe's shaggy bay and the thought brought me almost wicked pleasure. She had been stabled at Pappy's for a few days, was well rested and well fed. Stable life made most horses fat and lazy. It had only made this mean little mustang more durable, more restless. Having the bay gave me an advantage. She had traveled the Sierra Madre more than once. She knew the trails. She would think she was simply heading for home.

Pappy stood at the barn entrance loading two pack mules with two weeks' worth of supplies. The old man had taken the trek into the Sierra Madre once, into the mountain town of Durango, and lived to tell about it. He grumbled and scolded us as he loaded the pack mules, making it no secret that he thought the big marshal and I were crazy for going after Caballe in his own territory.

"Find an Apache trail and stay with it," he grumpily advised us. "You'll find water. And watch for animal trails."

"Thanks, Pappy," said Cameron.

"You have two canteens each. They won't last across the Chihuahua Desert, so you had better damn well find an Apache trail. Once you reach the mountain, water won't be a problem. Bandits will."

"Thanks, Pappy," Cameron said again.

"Don't be thanking me, you damn fool. If you were smart — which you ain't — you'd wait until Caballe crosses the border again."

"There's no time for that. My deputy, here, is itching to get to New Jersey."

"Your deputy is itching to die." He handed Cameron the reins to the mules. "I reckon I won't be seeing either of you again. It's a damn pity. This town needed a good marshal." Pappy moved away from the pack mules and nodded towards the corral. "Take one of them mustangs," he said to Cameron. "It will give you a good run when you come across Injuns." Then the old man entered the barn and disappeared into a dusty, filtered light.

We led the horses and mules to a water trough on the other side of the corral. Lucky was squatting next to the trough. She ran a stick through the water, watching it ripple, looking lonesome.

"What's the matter with you, girl?" asked Cameron.

"Nothin'." Her stubborn jaw clamped shut, then just as quickly reopened. "Billy's havin' a picnic with Richard Mecum and I wasn't invited."

Cameron grunted and wagged his head at me. "I reckon Miz Waters will be pleased." Then he stomped back towards the barn, leaving me to water the mules.

Lucky lifted her head and looked at me. "Can I go to Mexico with you? I can shoot Apaches."

"I don't doubt that for a second. I'd be proud to have you along. But we're going to be gone for two or three weeks, and Pappy's getting feeble. He needs you to run things for him. "

"I reckon you're right." She looked back down at the rippling water. "I sure ain't speaking to Billy Waters no more. Now that he has fancy friends."

"Do me a favor, Lucky. Keep an eye on one of those fancy friends while I'm gone."

"The purty one?" She squinted towards Mecum's pond, didn't see anything but palm trees and a dusty haze.

I nodded. "I'll tell you about Mexico when we get back." I sat on the edge of the trough and shared a smoke with her while the shaggy bay sucked deeply at the water. More than likely, it would be the horse's last pure drink of water for a spell.

"Welp, Deputy," Cameron hollered from the barn with false bravado. "Let's ride."

Once again, it was a pleasure riding the bay. She was a rough rider, gave no thought to the comfort of the man straddling her back, but she walked with her nostrils permanently flared and her ears held high as if she was constantly on the alert. This was a horse that would be able to smell water, wild animals, and Indians from miles away. And she wouldn't panic when things got rough. Course, like most mustangs, she was an ugly critter. She had a block head, short legs, a sharp, painful backbone, and a barrel-round body. But what the hell. We weren't riding in a horse show, and Apaches weren't frivolous enough to snicker at the sight of a man's horse. Besides, it would give me more wicked pleasure to run this horse straight into Caballe's camp. I patted the horse's muscular shoulder in appreciation.

Riding at a leisurely pace down Main Street, we passed Richard Mecum's pond and flower garden. Cool afternoon shadows crept slowly across the pond. The sweetness of the irises and lilies blooming against a dry countryside never failed to fascinate me. Apparently, it fascinated Cameron, too. We stared at the flowers, twisting our necks to take a longer look as we passed by.

Sitting underneath the boughs of a thin willow were young Billy and Richard Mecum. They were having their picnic. Richard sat on a bench while Billy was sprawled out on a blanket at Richard's feet. Lying next to Billy on the blanket was a third man. He looked familiar and I squinted into the shadows. It was Bennie Colsen. Upon seeing me, Bennie sat up and threw me a cheerful wave, looking all pleased with himself.

Fine. Bennie had finagled his way into a picnic. If he wanted to play sleuth with Billy and the banker, let him. At least it would keep him occupied while I was in Mexico.

✦

Ten miles north of the Rio Grande we came upon tracks: wagon wheels cut deeply into the ground.

"What is it?" said Cameron.

"A wagon. It's hauling a heavy load. Two single riders are flanking each side of the wagon, and there's another horse coming up the rear. But it's not carrying a rider."

"Are they Caballe's tracks?"

I shook my head. "They don't appear to be."

"What about the Gypsies? Is it their wagon?"

"No, the wheels are squat and wide." I pointed at the deep gouges in the ground. "It's moving real slow, like it's carrying too much of a load."

We followed the trail the wagon left behind for another four miles, slowly gaining on it. The wagon was a mile or two ahead of us. If the land had been level we might have seen it traveling against the horizon. But there were too many swelling ridges and twisting bends in front of us.

Suddenly, the tracks of several men on horseback appeared on one of the ridges to our left. According to the tracks there were seven men in all. From the looks of it, their horses had swooped out of a hollow, startling the driver of the wagon and the riders following close behind. The earth was scarred and churned over where the riders fought to steady their horses. Then the tracks of the wagon became erratic. It had taken off in a run, darting in and out of mesquite brush.

I loped ahead of Cameron, following the trail where the wagon disappeared into the mesquite. I found signs, the empty shells of spent cartridges, and returned to Cameron's side.

"The wagon took off in a southern direction. If I had a couple of poker chips, I'd bet the horses trailing it belong to Juan Caballe and his men." Actually, it was an easy bet. The men in the wagon would have come face-to-face with only two enemies: Caballe or Indians. The horses were shod. Few Indian ponies were.

"No bet," said Cameron. "I never bet with a man who knows his signs."

"They're making a run for it." I dropped the cartridges in the palm of Cameron's hand. "And putting up a good fight."

Off in the distance we heard the faint, hollow sounds of dying gunfire.

"Can we catch up with them?" asked Cameron.

I shook my head, slowly. "Not before it will do them any good."

Miles later, a sharp, narrow ridge rose to the west of us and the wagon tracks led us up it. The trail into it was littered with sharp rocks. Small landslides obstructed the path in some places. It was no place to take a wagon. It was certainly no place to try and outrun men on horseback. But, apparently, the driver had felt he had no choice.

"They lost a wheel," I said to Cameron. There was a deep gouge in the short bank where the wheel had broken off and the axle had dug into the earth. There was another churning of dirt where the horses had tried desperately to get their footing. The horses had broken free of the harness, but they hadn't been able to hold back the heavy weight of the wagon and it had catapulted over the edge of the steep ravine. Cameron and I galloped to the ravine, halted, and looked down at the wreckage.

The wagon was still intact, but it was lying on its side, its back wheel slowly spinning. A saddled horse was standing ten yards from the wreckage, nonchalantly nosing the ground. Two men were sprawled facedown in the dirt. A third man was sitting up with his back resting against the wagon. All three of the men were wearing blue uniforms.

"Them look like soldiers," said Cameron. Quickly he kicked his horse down the ravine. I followed behind.

When we rode upon the wreckage, the soldier who was leaning against the wagon dropped to the ground and tried to crawl towards a rifle lying a few feet away from him.

Cameron reined back his horse. "It's all right," he called to the soldier. "I'm Marshal Cameron Graves from Broken Wagon Wheel. We're friendly."

The soldier relaxed. Exhausted from the gun battle and from loss of blood, he collapsed on the ground, only inches from the rifle. We swung off our horses. Cameron hurried to the soldier's side while I checked the condition of the two men lying in the dirt. They were dead. Their bodies still held warmth, suggesting their deaths were recent. There wasn't anything I could do for them. Squatting on my haunches, I patted the closest soldier on the back and swiped horseflies away from his face.

"What happened here?" Cameron lifted the wounded soldier back up against the wagon and began to feed him water from his canteen. The water would do little more than offer comfort. The soldier was gutshot. It was only a matter of minutes before he would join his comrades.

"We were ambushed coming over the ridge," he whispered in a gravelly voice too weak for speech.

"Was it Comanches?" asked Cameron. We were still too far east for Apaches.

The soldier winced at the fire burning in his belly. "Juan Caballe." He winced again. Talking was painful, but he was a veteran soldier. His sideburns were the same steel gray as his eyes, and his skin matched the color of the earth. The yellow patches on his sleeves indicated he was a sergeant. He had fought his share of battles. He had fought Indians, Mexicans, and men of his own nationality. If this was to be his final battle, the old veteran would make damn sure he took his enemies to hell with him. "We were carrying ammunition to Fort Davies."

"Ammunition?" Cameron repeated, fearfully.

"And rifles. Over a hundred of them. Caballe's been arming the Apaches. You gotta..." The sergeant grimaced and dug his bloody fingernails into Cameron's forearm.

"Don't talk anymore, Sergeant. We'll get you to a doctor," said Cameron.

The soldier held fast to Cameron's arm. "It's too late for that, man. Go after Caballe. Juh and his warriors were spotted along the Arizona border. They're moving this way. You gotta stop them before they get the rifles."

What the sergeant said made sense. Even if we could repair the wagon, his wounds were such that he would not make it a mile down the road. Broken Wagon Wheel was fifty miles behind us, El Paso fifty miles ahead. If Caballe was hauling ammunition and rifles, it would slow him down considerably, and if we moved quickly, there was a chance we could catch up with him before he became entrenched in the Sierra Madre.

Yet, a man should not be left to die alone. So we waited. The marshal waited quietly next to the sergeant's side, listening to his shallow, raspy breathing. The sound of death made me restless, angry, so I tried to make myself useful by digging three graves. But the ground was too hard. Inches below the loose sand was hard granite. I retrieved blankets from the pack mules and covered the two soldiers; then I laid rocks over the blankets. I placed a large boulder at the base of their heads and set their caps on the boulder, just to let any passerby know that these had been fighting men. Then we waited some more.

Twenty minutes after we'd arrived, the soldier's hand slipped from Cameron's arm and he died without complaint. We never asked him his name.

19

We reached the Rio Grande at dusk. The sun was sparse and pale upon its flat surface. We didn't enter the water, but continued along the banks for the next twenty miles. Eventually we became engulfed in darkness, with only the sound of the water as our guide. Traveling away from the damp banks of the river, we found a dry place to camp. Once we reached the harsh Chihuahua Desert we would travel by night and rest in the day. This would be the last campfire we would dare to build, the final night we would dare to rest.

Sleep came quickly and easily. The ride to the river had been uneventful and we had traveled at a slow, easy pace, but my muscles ached from the rough ride of the shaggy bay and I was grateful for the cool of the night and the comfort of my bedroll. Cameron snored loudly beside me, and I wondered, with a snore like that, how we would ever cross the desert without attracting every Apache within a twenty-mile radius.

By early morning, we were back in the saddle, moving along the river again. Somewhere along the way we passed El Paso, north of us. Since leaving the dead soldiers we had not encountered another living soul, and it was lonely knowing there were people nearby.

Soon after we skirted past El Paso, we left Texas and entered New Mexico. We didn't figure on finding tracks this far west. Caballe and his gang would probably cross the Rio Grande in Texas and travel the entire distance of the Chihuahua. But we needed to be more prudent. There was already enough desert ahead of us and caution warned us to run the river for as long as possible.

Once we reached New Mexico, it was time to cross. Twilight settled on the Rio Grande and the wide, flat shallow waters were prettier than they were at most times of the day, except for maybe at daybreak. What was left of the melting sun splattered long, golden light across the water like a colorful Navaho blanket. It shimmered, rippled, changed colors, looked cool.

The pack animals were old Mexican burros who had waded across the Rio Grande a dozen times in their ancient lives and they did so again without hesitation. The shaggy bay complained about nothing. Heat, harsh traveling, tight reins left her unaffected, and a little bit of water didn't bother her none. We were wet up to our knees when we reached the opposite bank. Twenty feet off the banks of the river, our clothes were dry again. The sun, even in its final descent, was still hot enough to dry a man's clothes within minutes.

A slim, silver moon hung in a starry sky and the heat finally diminished along with the light. We were in desert country, somewhere. We had crossed the borders of Texas, New Mexico, and Mexico in less than twenty minutes' time.

Though I was familiar with the Sonora Desert west of the Sierra Madre, I was not familiar with Chihuahua. I asked Cameron. Neither was he. We rode blind, hoping to put as many miles behind us as we could before the sun reappeared and made travel impossible. Imagining in my mind that this desert was like all others – Death Valley, the Mojave, the Sonora – I avoided the silvery shadows of cacti, skirted through prickly pear and pumice, and let the self-assured animals be our guides.

It wasn't long before the slim moon bade farewell and was once again replaced by a threatening sun. Still we rode on, for the morning sun was pleasant and the animals uncomplaining. Traveling as we were, slow but constant, we put the miles behind us without being aware of how far we had come.

Midday we found tracks belonging to Juan Caballe and his entourage. Dismounting, I carefully studied the tracks and was soon convinced that not only was Caballe burdened with guns and ammunition, he was now traveling with the Gypsies. Earlier that morning, north of the Rio Grande, we'd picked up the tracks of the Gypsy wagons, and now, far south of the river, they merged with Juan Caballe's.

I squatted next to a burned-out campfire. The ashes were barely warm. A pot had been left behind and I found a wooden doll lying among the brush. Little barefoot prints, and the flat-heeled prints of a puppy were scattered around the doll. Children, Gypsies, guns ... the load was so great, Juan Caballe would be lucky if he was able to travel ten miles in an afternoon.

Something else was in our favor. Caballe didn't know about the warrant, didn't know we were coming, and was making no attempt to cover his tracks. The bandit was in his own territory and was in no hurry. He was riding straight into the mountains, leaving a path more noticeable than if a cyclone had passed through.

"You would think," I said, grimly, "after killing them soldiers he would watch his back more carefully."

"Nope," Cameron responded. "Even after murdering our soldiers, Caballe knows the Mexican generals won't allow a regiment of American soldiers to cross the border. The Army won't respond. They can't respond. There's just the two of us. An old Ranger and an old gunfighter."

"Well, that makes a man feel real confident."

"How many of them do you reckon there are?"

"Marshal, I'd say we are sadly outnumbered. Including women and children, I'd guess about twenty. And they have guns. Geezus, do they have guns." I pointed to deep slashes in the sand caused by a ruggedly built travois. "They're still carrying the weapons."

"That means they haven't rendezvoused with Juh, yet. Let's see if we can keep it that way." Cameron lowered himself out of the saddle. "We'd better get a couple of hours of sleep and let these horses rest. The sun will only get hotter."

Cameron picketed the animals in a shaded area while I rekindled the fire, boiled coffee, and fried bacon. Then we found shade near the horses and slept. I slept deeply, toasted comfortably by a warm ground, and sheltered nicely by thin cacti. The land around us was quiet, tranquil, still, and allowed a man a good sleep.

But we didn't sleep long. As the sun sank low behind the plateaus, Cameron tapped me on the shoulder. "Let's go, pardner. I reckon we've rested enough."

I reckon we hadn't. But the Apache, Juh, was a stringy fellow who didn't need much rest either. It was a good bet Juh was following Caballe's trail as closely as we were and it was wise to stay way ahead of him. The most honorable revenge for the death of the sergeant and his infantrymen was to retrieve their guns for them; or, at least, keep them out of the hands of the Apaches. Since we couldn't give them a decent burial, revenge was the next best thing.

We made good distance under a moon that was maybe a fraction of an inch smaller than the previous moon. The following day, when the sun hung low and mean, we stumbled upon what Pappy had called an Apache trail. Actually, it was an animal trail that would eventually lead us to water. Our canteens were low, holding maybe an inch of water between them. We were grateful to find the trail. It meant we could fill our canteens, give the horses a good watering, and soak our scorched, dusty bodies. But the trail spoke of danger; a danger that made your skin prickle and hold your breath a mite longer than normal.

"Welcome to Apache country," Cameron said solemnly.

Only Apaches could live in such a land. Juh's tribe, the Chiricahua Apache, were without argument — though the Comanche and Sioux were sure to argue — the hardiest group of warriors known to mankind. And the sneakiest. In order to make their homes in the Sierra Madre and to travel the deserts as if they were cobblestoned streets instead of wild, dangerous land, they had to be. A single man couldn't fight them, the gawdamn United States Army couldn't fight them. A single man couldn't outrun them, the gawdamn United States Army couldn't outrun them. All you could do, if you were almighty lucky, was to avoid them. And it was hard to avoid them when you were riding straight into one of their watering holes.

Well, damn the Apaches. Damn them to all hell. One reason I had settled in California was that I was pretty much guaranteed to never run across another Apache. Now here I was traveling through the main artery of the Chiricahua. I could almost hear their collective breathing; almost see the sands move as each shadow, each wind drift, became an Apache warrior.

If Cameron was worried, he didn't show it. The sun was up, sparkling pretty, and he was feeling like a free spirit. In fact, he started whistling a tune, a spry little tune an Apache's ears could hear all the way to Arizona. Well, damn the Texans, too. Like the Apache, they possessed no fear. Unlike the Apaches, they possessed no sense. A handful of Texans had conquered the Mexicans and the Comanches, and now, because of their accomplishments, they were complacent, and far too cocky for my taste. It wasn't until I sidled my horse over to his and slapped him in the knee with the ends of my reins that Cameron stopped whistling.

"You worried, son?" Cameron asked, quietly.

"Oh, hell, no. There's probably more Indians crawling through this brush than there are reptiles. I don't believe it's necessary to entertain them."

Cameron grinned. "Welp, if they're out there, a little music ain't going to change our fate none. Might as well die singing."

That was a Texan's logic for you.

As we'd anticipated, we came upon water. There wasn't much of it, only a stagnant pool that mainly served as a breeding ground for mosquitoes and centipedes. But, in this country, you took what you could find wherever you could find it. And you took it without whining. Whether it was a tough old jackrabbit or raw rattlesnake meat, you learned to eat it as if it were steak and potatoes at the Crow. If you were smart enough to find water, you couldn't worry about getting a little mud in your canteens, nor be overly concerned about typhoid. Nope, you counted your blessings, lapped up the water as if it were pure mountain springwater, bathed in it as if it were drawn from a freshwater well, and moved on, a grateful man.

Before we indulged ourselves in the water, I studied the tracks around the pool. There were plenty of bird, deer, and coyote tracks, but there were no signs of Indians or their horses.

The horses and mules waded into the water until it was up to their bellies. Cameron and I did our share of drinking, then filled our canteens. I took off my shirt and, using my bandana, washed the first two layers of dust off my skin. Cameron removed his boots and waded into the water fully clothed, splashing alongside the horses and mules.

We stayed in the water for ten minutes, then reluctantly led the animals out, put on their saddles and packs, and climbed back aboard. We rode westward, moving deeper and deeper into Indian territory and closer to the Sierra Madre.

Purposely, we avoided the desert towns, riding clear of them by miles. Most of the Mexicans who were stalwart enough to make their homes in the more remote regions of Chihuahua were as lawless as Juan Caballe. More than likely, they were friendly with the cheerful, generous bandit and would, somehow, get word to him that two *gringos* with United States badges were on his trail. So we avoided everything, everyone, even the smallest indication that civilization lay nearby.

We passed the hulls of burned-out villas — stone-wall fortresses that had been abandoned years ago by Mexican land barons who'd grown weary of fighting Apaches or been killed. The stone walls, built twenty feet high, had not been able to hold the Apaches back, nor had well-armed *vaqueros*. They'd simply climbed the walls and slaughtered entire families while they slept. Then, one by one, they'd picked off the *vaqueros* as they sat in their saddles staring at the hind ends of cattle.

On the third night of our journey into Mexico, we spent the night inside the ruins of a *rancheria*. It, too, had been protected by twenty-foot walls. It, too, had fallen under the violence of an Apache assault. Few remnants were left over from the people who had made their homes there. A torn blanket was partially buried in the sand. Broken pottery lay smashed on the ground, old cooking utensils still hung from the adobe walls, but everything else had been carted away by the Indians.

Building a low, smokeless fire behind an eastern wall, we ate our first real cooked meal since leaving New Mexico, but we cooked it fast, ate it partially raw, put out the fire mighty fast, and spent a restless night behind the useless walls listening to the sorrowful spirits of the people who had tried to live and sleep there before us.

Back on our horses while the moon was high, we left the walls behind. It was the last time we watched the sun lift its massive, fiery head; the last time we saw the moon cast its bluish glow across the plateaus. Miles ahead of us was the stark elevation of the Sierra Madre.

We reached the mountain mass at early dusk. Out on the desert, the sky was still bright, the sands bleached white. Darkness settles quicker in the mountains. Scarcely a thousand feet above the flatlands we became shadowed by immense lava rocks and ancient pines. The sun's rays, which had lain flat and brutal against the desert floor, were now impotently eclipsed behind black volcanic ridges. We spurred the horses onward, quickening our pace, hoping to reach the top of the mountain before the light disappeared completely and we were forced to ride the steep, slippery trail in the dark. It was hard to say which was worse – the mountains or the desert. For a California man like myself, the mountains, as gnarled and dank as they were, offered an almost intangible relief. Despite better judgment, I felt my body relax, my spirits soar. Conversely, for the first time on our journey, Cameron sat upright, stiff and rigid in the saddle.

"Sonofabitch," he growled when his horse faltered on the slick lava rock. "At least in the desert you can see them coming."

"See who coming?" I asked, listening to the sweet chirping of birds and, somewhere off in the distance, a waterfall.

"The Apaches, that's who. They can come slipping out of the trees before we could even get these horses turned around." He looked straight down into the bluff below us. "And there ain't no place to turn around."

He was right, of course. But whether they came out of the trees, or lifted from the sands of the deserts, it made no difference. They were flat-out dangerous regardless of the terrain you had to fight them on. The big marshal was getting skittish because his view was restricted; restricted by moving shadows, darkened hollows, and sheltering trees. Personally, I was thankful for the shade. I'd reached a point 140 degrees ago where I didn't care if five hundred Indians were lurking in the mountains. I just wanted its shade.

Not to say a man didn't have to stay alert. He had to stay mighty alert and not be numbed by the beauty or the coolness of the Sierra Madre. For, if the truth be told, the mountain itself was more dangerous than five hundred Apaches.

The shaggy bay began to pick up speed, climbing like a bighorn, and I suddenly found myself fighting to rein her back. "She's rearin' to go," I said.

"Go where?" asked Cameron.

I looked at the big marshal and grinned. "Home."

Not only was she a damned good desert animal and a fearless Indian-fighter, this ugly little horse was going to lead us straight into Caballe's camp. I let the shaggy bay have the rein, and she trotted — as solidly as she could against the conditions of the land — ahead of Cameron.

Take us on home, little horse.

20

I heard the faint sound of a dulcimer. The shaggy bay suddenly sidestepped and blew nervously, her ears twitching. I reined her to an uneasy halt. "Do you hear that?"

Cameron nodded. "It's coming from the valley."

We dropped off the horses and picketed them behind round, swollen boulders that stood taller than a man. The horses were far enough away from Caballe's camp that no one could hear if they whinnied or stamped around, but they were close enough to get to in a hurry, if it should become necessary, and I was sure it was going to be necessary.

Walking a quarter mile to the valley's rim, we heard the music get louder, along with the boisterous voices of men calling back and forth, of women laughing, of children squealing, all speaking in the Spanish tongue. We squatted on our haunches behind thick bulberry and piñon, and gazed into the valley.

Caballe's hideout – like the old bandit himself – was clever. It was sparse, practical, and self-sufficient. There were permanent corrals made from pine poles; there were lean-tos and tents and badly constructed tepees. Everything had been built for mobility. Mexican women, like Indian women, were capable of breaking camp, packing up their belongings, and disappearing within minutes, leaving nothing behind but empty corrals.

The Gypsy wagons rested under a thick stand of trees off to the side. Catherine's steers were still alive and grazing, fat and healthy, in northern Mexico.

I tapped Cameron's forearm. "Over there," I said.

West of the camp, nestled against the flat side of the valley wall, were a half-dozen pine crates with the telltale words U.S. ARMY stamped on their sides.

"How are we going to get them guns out of this valley?" asked Cameron.

"We ain't," I answered. The valley walls were too steep, the trail we had traveled too narrow, and our retreat would no doubt have to be made too swiftly to be worrying about guns. "They'll have to be destroyed."

I let my gaze shift around the rim of the valley. Apparently, Caballe's hideout had served him well through the years. There was no way to approach the valley floor without being seen. An attack from above would only send the bandits scrambling into the underbrush. I didn't like the idea of firing into a camp where there were women and children, and I expressed my concerns to Cameron.

"We could wait for the men to ride out and ambush them then," said Cameron.

I shook my head. "They know these mountains better than we do. We'll lose 'em in the forests. We'll wait until dark, then we'll surround them."

"'*Surround* them'?" Cameron chuckled quietly.

"Sure." I grinned and nodded across the valley. "You on this side, me on that side. I'm going around. Keep your head down until dark."

"You're a lunatic," Cameron grumbled with affection. "We can't surround..."

But I had already ducked low and was moving silently down the hillside. The brush was thick, the rocks slippery, and there were secret caverns where the ground had split open by some great quake centuries ago. I damn near broke my leg in a six-inch crevice and had to stop and wrestle my ankle free. It would be dangerous to run this valley wall in the dark.

Within twenty minutes, I was on the northern side of the valley. I found a comfortable location where I could follow the men in the camp and see Cameron's position on the other side. He moved down the hillside, closer to the camp.

The final hours before night completely enveloped the valley moved slowly, but after days of hard traveling, to sit among the pines and do nothing was a pleasure most men couldn't comprehend. I cradled my Winchester in my arm and benignly watched the shenanigans going on down below. A couple of women danced to the music of the dulcimer. Their men, cradling whiskey bottles like I was cradling the rifle, joined them, and they gaily danced, arm in arm, in a circle. Geezus, they looked happy. I tapped my foot to the music, and felt like a big, black spider ready to sweep down and ruin their party; ruin their lives, for chrissake.

So what the hell was I doing here? I hated it when the law swept in and ruined my parties; now here I was about to do the same. I didn't particularly have anything against Mexican bandits, just like I didn't have anything against Apaches, as long as I was in California and they were in Arizona or New Mexico. Juan Caballe hadn't done me too much dirty. It was Judd Brooks who'd stolen my Colts, and I'd had the opportunity to watch him hang and I'd spoiled that, too. And now, as I sat among the cool pines, relaxing, the death of the soldiers didn't fester in me as much as it had. Soldiers were fighting men. They knew the risks they were taking the second they signed their names on the line and enlisted. War was war – every soldier knew that. And, even if it wasn't official, we were still at war with renegade Mexicans and Apaches.

I didn't have the slightest idea why I was hiding among the brush like a black widow, but as I looked across the valley and saw the bulberry rustling slightly as Cameron, pushing his luck, moved in closer, I was pretty well convinced that he had something to do with it.

Night closed its tender arms around the valley. Below me, the Mexicans built a huge fire and continued with their party. Food was put on the fire and more bottles of whiskey and wine were opened. Late into the night they played. Then, finally sweating out the last of their merriment, they gathered around the campfire and spent more hours smoking and talking.

The children curled up under the wagons to sleep. They were far from the center of camp, from the tents, and for that I was grateful. After dark settled, the air began to chill and the mothers covered the children with blankets, then disappeared into the tents. One by one, the men began to straggle off to bed.

Four Mexicans, carrying rifles, broke from camp and walked halfway up the hillside. One of the them I recognized as Pole. I could almost see his white eye shining in the moonlight. The men took positions at all four corners of the mountain, one on each side, one on each corner. One of the bandits settled dangerously close to Cameron. Each corner of the valley walls now had a guard posted.

This wasn't good; it was unexpected. To successfully control Caballe and his men, we needed them all bunched up in one place. The guards would have to be removed before we could attack the camp. And they had to be removed quietly.

Apparently, Cameron had the same thing in mind. Sucking in my breath, I watched as the big marshal stepped gingerly down the slippery incline with all its concealed gorges and gouges. Despite his size, Cameron could be graceful when he wanted to be and I watched as he maneuvered up behind the first guard. The guard silently slumped over. The marshal reappeared and moved agilely to the second guard off to his right. Within minutes, that guard rolled onto the ground. Cameron notified me that all was well by waving his floppy hat. It reflected the moonlight.

Now it was my turn. The third guard had settled somewhere below me. Carefully I climbed over craggy boulders until I came up behind him. He was a hefty man, stocky and muscular, but he was rendered lazy by too much food and drink, and he snored like a bull as he slept deeply against the trunk of an oak. Easily I sneaked up behind him and cracked him in the skull with the stock of my rifle. He dropped without knowing what had hit him.

The final guard was on the western face of the valley wall, in a more hazardous location. The moon temporarily disappeared behind a black cloud. I climbed over another sharp rim of rocks and slid in the slick grass. The noise was slight, but it was enough to alert the fourth guard. He turned suddenly, his profile visible as the moon slipped out from under the cloud. It was Pole. Lucky me.

Like the timber wolf he resembled, Pole instantly sensed my presence and walked towards the brush where I was crouching from his view. He unsheathed his hunting knife and carefully inspected the brush, coming in close. I leaped from behind the brush, catching him around the waist and throwing him off balance. We hit the ground and tumbled together down the face of the hillside, catching on a plane above the valley floor. Pole was a scrapper, a confident fighter, and instead of calling out a warning to his buddies only twenty feet below us, he chose to fight me on his own.

When we stopped tumbling, he was on top of me, and he brought the knife plunging down. I twisted my neck and he buried the blade in the dirt. Just as quickly, he pulled it out. I grabbed his wrist, holding the wicked knife inches above my chest as he forced it towards me. His strength matched mine and our hands began to shake as I pushed his wrist away from me. With his left hand, he punched me in the jaw, and I lost my grip on his wrist. The knife thrust forward, snaring my vest, and cutting into my shirt.

I rolled him over, and with me now on top, I slugged him in the face, hearing the crack of his cheekbone as his head pushed into the dirt. Once again, I reached for the knife, grasping it below the handle. The sharp edge of the blade cut into my hand, into my fingers, and I bit down hard on my lip to stifle a shout. Roughly, still holding on, I bent the blade until it snapped, then with one sudden thrust, I pushed what was left of the blade into his heart. Pole grunted, his good eye fluttered, and his body went limp underneath me. I stood, my knees shaking, and nudged him gently with my boot. The one-eyed bandit was dead.

Knotting my bandana around the palm of my hand, I pulled at the ends with my teeth to make a tourniquet. Then I looked around for something to signal Cameron that I had succeeded. Barely. I was wearing my fancy, go-to-meetin' black hat, hard to see in the dark. Cameron would just have to trust that I had gotten the job done.

He did. Cameron climbed even closer to the camp. Concealed behind low-lying manzanita, he sprawled out on the ground and leveled his rifle. On my side of the valley, I did the same. I balanced my rifle on a deadfall and unholstered the peashooter.

The peashooter wasn't going to do me any good at this distance, but it would make noise, and I wanted to make so much noise the Mexicans would think the United States Army was converging on them. With all of our weapons firing at once, there was a slight chance the bandits would think they were outnumbered and surrender without too much bloodshed. Real slight.

I was about to open fire into the valley when a loud voice broke the silence.

"This is Marshal Cameron Graves of Broken Wagon Wheel..."

Shit.

"You men are surrounded. Put down your weapons and..."

Before Cameron could finish declaring official orders, all hell broke loose. Caballe and his men now had all the blessed time they needed to reach their weapons. They rolled out of their blankets and fell out of their tents as if a prairie fire was racing through camp. These men were not stupid. They were hunted men, outlaws on the lam, and a hunted man never sleeps without his gun inches from his grasp, ready to go into battle.

The element of surprise was no longer on our side. The Mexicans hit the ground running. They stumbled in the darkness, firing at the hills, blue fire streaking from their guns.

Cameron and I were well covered and Caballe's men were shooting in the dark, shooting at shadows. I fired over their heads, more interested in making noise than in bringing any one man down. Fearful that if I shot at a shadow running along the valley floor that shadow might belong to a child or a woman, I kept my bullets aimed high.

I scrambled behind one tree, opened fire, then scrambled behind another, in a pitiful attempt to make it sound as if there were dozens of guns on the hillside. I noticed the shadowy figures of three men running up the hillside towards Cameron, and I no longer aimed high. I scoped the first man in, dropped him, then took down the last two before they reached Cameron.

With Cameron once again safely covered, I turned my attention back to the camp. The crates of guns and ammunition were less than a hundred feet to my left. Close enough to make a try for it. Crawling on my hands and knees through the wet brush, I reached the valley floor and came out into the camp. I crouched low, jumping along the ground with my knees bent, my Winchester ready, until I reached the smoldering campfire. I pulled a long stick from the fire. When it got oxygen, it burst into flames and I swiftly ran towards the crates of ammunition. I shoved the torch between two crates, then dove for cover.

The ammunition exploded. Hundreds of bullets popped and cracked, sending shrapnel into the night sky, sounding like Mardi Gras in New Orleans. Caballe's men hit the ground, scrambling for cover as the bullets whizzed and cracked past them. No one had seen me torch the ammunition, and the bandits were fooled into believing they were being fired on by dozens of lawmen.

A thin Gypsy child, frightened, panicked by the gunfire, bolted from the protection of the wagons. Then she stood paralyzed in the circular light of the campfire, crying out for her mother. Making a desperate run towards her, I swooped her up in my arms, then dropped on top of her, the bullets from the crates whistling around us.

When the popping died down and the smoke cleared, Juan Caballe and his men got to their feet and lifted their hands in the air, surrendering.

I released the child, aiming her in the direction of her mother. Cameron stepped out from his hiding place, our rifles trained on the outlaws. Juan stood passively, only his eyes moving as he surveyed the hillside, waiting for the rest of the American posse to march out of the brush.

"Where are the others?" he asked.

I grinned. "No others."

"It is only the two of you?" He looked at me in disbelief.

"Yep," I said. "Pretty embarrassing, ain't it?"

"Holy Mother of Jesus." He laughed and let his hands drop to his sides. He was dressed only in threadbare long johns. His stomach was so big the buttons stretched across his belly.

"I wouldn't do that," I said, motioning for him to put his hands back up.

"Ah, what do you think? That I have a dragoon down my pants?" He looked down at his crotch.

I grinned again. "It looks like it."

"We're taking you back to Texas to stand trial," said Cameron, all professional and growing impatient with our good-natured sparring.

"For what crime?" Juan shrugged. "As you can see, the little criminal is not here."

He was right about the little criminal. Judd Brooks was not among the bandits, though the Rudshikas were huddled around their wagons, looking frightened. To my relief, Kalei, the Gypsy boy, stood with them. The wound he had received in Broken Wagon Wheel while helping Brooks escape was wrapped in a dirt-gray bandage. I nodded friendly at him. He nodded friendly back.

"For the abduction of Jennifer Bradford." Cameron reached into his pocket. "This here is a warrant. Signed by the governor of Texas."

The bandit stared at the paper and scoffed, "I do not abduct women. They come freely or they do not come at all."

Cameron looked around him, studying the faces of the women. "She's a *gringo*. An American. With yellow hair." He was speaking to the dark-haired, dark-eyed women. Except for the Gypsies, they were all Mexican nationals.

"Look around you. Do you see anyone with yellow hair?" asked Juan.

Caballe was right. No Judd Brooks. No Jennifer Bradford. Cameron was going to have to do some quick thinking if he wanted to cross the border with the Mexican bandits in tow.

"What did you do with her?" Cameron asked angrily.

"I did nothing." Juan smiled widely. The campfire spontaneously ignited. The flames illuminated his wide, grinning face and turned his salty beard yellow, then orange, then red. "If there was an American woman in camp, she would not be my prisoner. She would come and go as she pleased. Is this a crime, Marshal?"

"Then I'm taking you back for questioning for the murder of three American soldiers. Where I come from, killing soldiers is a hanging offense." Cameron's chest was rumbling. I could almost feel it about to explode with anger.

"Soldiers?" Juan looked at his men, feigning ignorance. "What soldiers? We did not see any soldiers. Perhaps it was the Apaches, no? I hear rumors that Juh has crossed the border."

Cameron took a step forward, ready to punch him in his grinning face. "And you stole them rifles over there for Juh."

Juan shrugged again. "Rifles? What rifles? I do not see any rifles. I see only smoke and flames. The rifles we carry we bought from the Apaches."

"Apaches don't sell guns, Mister. They buy them. And you've been supplying them with weapons," said Cameron.

"I don't know what you are talking about," said Juan. "Perhaps you should take it up with General Diaz."

General Porfirio Diaz. A powerful military man with ambitions of being the next president of Mexico. He would not get there by the common man's vote. He needed revolutionaries like Caballe and his outlaws to help him achieve that goal, and it was no surprise that Juan considered the general his friend. And it would be no surprise if the American government avoided hostile involvement with the Mexican military, despite the brutal deaths of its soldiers.

Again, Cameron was ready to pounce, his thick hand doubling into a fist. I held his arm to stop him. Two great bears were about to tangle, which would leave me with the impossible task of guarding two dozen little bears with one rifle.

"It ain't worth it," I said to Cameron. "Let's just take him in."

Cameron relaxed, turned professional again. "You're right, son. We'll let a judge and jury decide."

"Gentlemen..." It was a woman's voice, soft and quiet, almost a whisper. Then came the sharp snap of a rifle being cocked. "Put down your guns."

Without turning, we slowly let our rifles slip from our hands. Almost in unison, Caballe's men snatched up their weapons from where they had thrown them and pointed them at us. Carlos Coria, a stocky, handsome man, picked up our rifles, then relieved us of our six-shooters. The woman stepped around us, becoming visible in the partial moonlight and firelight. Her long, blonde hair was untied and hung loosely around her shoulders. In the moonlight, her skin was the lucid color of milk.

"Miz Bradford," said Cameron, his voice a mixture of relief and surprise. "We've come to take you home."

"I am home, Marshal Graves," she said with the same light whisper.

"Clem's dead. He was killed when Judd Brooks made his escape," Cameron explained.

"I see." She smiled wanly. "You rode all this way to bring me good news."

Juan settled his bulk against a wagon wheel and lit a cheroot. "As you can see, Marshal Graves, I do not capture women. It is just a story. Carlos, take them to the..."

"Two riders coming from the north!" a Mexican on lookout shouted from the bottom of the hill.

And every single man holding a weapon slapped back the levers.

21

With little regard for their horses or for themselves, the two riders bolted down the slippery, rocky slope, then galloped across the valley straight into Caballe's camp. Carlos was standing protectively next to Caballe. He lifted his rifle to his shoulder and aimed.

"Muchos gringos," he muttered.

Recognition of the two riders softened Jennifer Bradford's features, and she placed a hand on Carlos's rifle and lowered the barrel.

"They're kids," she warned. "I know them."

And, indeed, they were just kids.

"Sonofabitch!" Cameron hollered and pitched his floppy hat to the ground. "It's young Billy and ... Lucky."

Billy wildly reined to a halt in front of the campfire while Lucky gradually pulled the reins. Their horses nearly collapsed under them, no doubt permanently injured from the pace of their run. Billy fell out of the saddle, then scrambled to his feet. He seemed blind, oblivious, to the armed Mexican bandits surrounding him.

"You gotta come," Billy mumbled, breathlessly.

Cameron grabbed the boy by the collar and shook him. He lifted the palm of his hand to give him a smack. "Dammit, Billy, I told you to stop following us."

Billy ignored him and continued to babble incoherently. "You gotta come."

"What are you trying to say, boy?" Cameron did slap him, lightly, on the cheek, just to settle him.

"It's Bennie. He's in trouble," said Billy.

Lucky peered down from her broken horse. "Richard Mecum has your friend. He's gonna kill him."

Roughly, I pulled Billy from Cameron's grasp and shook him myself. "What the hell happened?"

"Bennie found out about Richard." Billy was nearly crying, making his words even more unintelligible. "Richard took him into Dead Horse Canyon. I swear, Richard's going to kill him. He had a gun."

Grabbing the reins to Billy's horse, I swung into the saddle and pulled its head around.

"Hombre," said Juan Caballe. "You're not going anywhere."

"Is that right?" I looked at the bandit with cold disregard. "The only way you're going to stop me is by putting a bullet in my back." I spurred the horse towards the mountain.

Caballe motioned for Carlos to shoot, but once again, Jennifer Bradford intervened. "Let them go," she said. "They won't be back."

Juan nodded at Carlos and Carlos lowered the gun. The old bandit let me ride away. I reckon it wasn't wise to anger a woman with yellow hair.

Billy's horse couldn't travel. It was slowly dying beneath me. When I reached the top of the hillside, I returned to where we'd picketed our horses and mules behind the lava rocks. From the mules I took a canteen and a box of cartridges, leaving the food and supplies for Cameron. My only real need was the shaggy bay.

Once I'd positioned myself in the saddle, I ran the tough little mustang down the Sierra Madre. Texas now seemed farther away than New Jersey. I rode hard and dangerously, not stopping, the miles passing beneath the horse's heavy hooves a darkened blur. I didn't know what sort of terrain I was asking the horse to cross at high speed, and I didn't care. All she had to do was cover it.

By morning, I was out of the mountain range and racing down the sweeping, rolling dunes at the bottom of the Sierra Madre, then across the flatlands. After hours of running, the shaggy bay began to falter. It wasn't the miles slowing her; it was the heat. Her neck was bathed in lather and deep, guttural noises came from her lungs. If I didn't stop, the horse would die, then I would die, then Bennie would die. Reluctantly I slowed to a walk, then stopped altogether and dropped from the saddle.

Restless and angry, I stood alone in the vast plains of the desert, waiting for the horse to breathe normally. The distance I still needed to travel stretched out in front of me, seemingly without end. The sun blurred the horizon, smeared the sky with blue fogs and strange, purple rings of fire. Beyond the smear of the horizon was New Mexico, El Paso, Broken Wagon Wheel, Dead Horse Canyon. Miles.

Cameron was somewhere behind me, I had no doubt of that. I knew the man well. And I knew, if it weren't for the two youngsters now in his care, he would be running just as hard beside me. I couldn't allow myself to be concerned for his safety or for that of the kids. They would make it across the desert without me; they had enough supplies, enough water. If they ran into trouble, Cameron would have Lucky's buffalo gun to back him up. Bennie Colsen had no one but me. I was who he counted on, depended upon. And I was standing helplessly in the Chihuahua Desert, hundreds of miles away.

Realizing I'd been standing on my feet for hours, I squatted on my haunches and built a small fire. Not to eat. I had no appetite for food, and my mouth was too dry for the bitter taste of coffee. I built the fire hoping the smoke would guide Cameron's way. Removing the canteen from my saddle, I watered the horse, generously wetting her muzzle, then took a swig of water in an attempt to remove the dryness from my mouth. I spit the water on the ground.

As I sat impatiently by the fire, waiting for the sun to cool, I glimpsed a spare figure on the horizon. Quickly I looked up, studied the horizon. Nothing. There was no one there. I took another swallow of water and stared into the fire. Then I glanced up again, sure, this time, I had seen something.

There he was. A lone Apache rider shadowed against the graying light. Almost like a ghost, he nonchalantly walked his horse along the rim of the sweeping sand dune.

Geezus ... this wasn't any old Apache – though any old Apache was one too many Apaches for my taste. He sat on his horse as straight as a lance, as silent as a whimper in a thunderstorm, as cool as an icy stream. The Apache, Juh.

Slowly, very slowly, I capped the canteen and inched closer to the shaggy bay, never taking my eyes off the Indian. He continued on his journey across the dune as if he didn't see me, but that was the Apache way. Of course he saw me. He had smelled the smoke from my campfire, had heard the breathing of my horse, had probably heard the violence of my thoughts from miles away. I reckoned the rest of his warriors had seen and heard the same and were hidden behind the breast of the sand dune.

In a situation such as this, a man has very few options. He can run, which innate fear and instinct compel him to do. But that only delays the inevitable. When an Apache is as close as the horizon, you cannot outrun him, not even on a horse as fast as the shaggy bay. The horse would be shot out from under you, clean and simple.

A man can stand and fight them. To an Apache that means you have grit, and the Apaches admire a white man with grit, since so few white men maintain it in the face of an Apache attack. During a fight, the Apache does his damnedest to capture you alive. Not only do they admire a man with grit, they admire a man who dies hard, and they can spend two or three leisurely days putting you to death.

The smartest thing to do, the most merciful thing to do, I thought, was to end my life right then, while Juh waited on the horizon. It would irritate the hell out of him, spoil his fun.

Run. Fight. Put a bullet in my head. Those were my options. If it weren't for Bennie Colsen, I would have opted for the bullet. Many times in the past, I had ridden up on the gruesome results of a white man who'd lost a fight or lost a run against the Apaches. As I inched towards the shaggy bay, I made the decision to run, knowing damn well it would end in the horse's death. Once the horse was down, I would turn and fight. But at the end of it all, when I was down to my last bullet, I would use that bullet on myself.

When I reached the horse, I glanced to my left, my gaze drawn there by a sudden movement. The sky was dotted with brilliant red and orange hues, the bluish haze becoming dim and shadowy. On the horizon stood dozens of warriors.

With a sickening thud, an arrow slipped past me and struck hard into the cantle of my saddle. There were more Indians surrounding us. The startled horse jumped, and I grabbed its reins to keep it from bolting. A high-pitched cry pierced the quiet desert air, and the Indians galloped down the sand dune. Another cry and they tumbled from the surrounding brush.

"Ah ... geezus." I swung into the saddle and ran. The shaggy bay had been running hard for the last twelve hours, and I pushed her as desperately now as I had when Billy and Lucky first brought news that Bennie was in trouble.

Arrows slid past me like sleet, cutting the air, thumping the ground, and the Indians were gaining on us fast. Another arrow struck and the shaggy bay grunted, stumbled, then righted herself and kept running as if her life depended on it. It did. As expected, they were aiming for the horse. She was a bigger target than I was.

I felt moisture on my leg, seeping through my pants, trickling down my shin. I was afraid to look; afraid I might see my blood, or blood from the horse. Dropping my right hand to my knee, I wetted my fingers in the moisture, then took a quick look. It wasn't blood. It was worse. It was water. I glanced past my leg. The arrow had struck my canteen, and water poured down the horse's side, down my leg, onto the ground, until the canteen was empty.

I was a dead man. Deader than if the arrow had struck my heart.

The Apaches were now within rifle range, but, so far, they had not fired their guns. They were armed — I saw their rifles swinging in their hands as they galloped behind me. But they were using only arrows and lances.

"Shaggy bay," I shouted. "They don't have any gawdamn bullets."

It stood to reason. Juh was on his way to Caballe's camp to retrieve the rifles and ammunition. They probably had a few bullets left on them, enough to kill me with, but I was only one lone White Eyes. Why do with their rare, precious bullets what they could very easily do with an arrow?

Spotting an arroyo off to my right, I violently jerked the horse's head in that direction. The bay labored when we reached the edge of the slope, her hooves burying deep in the sand. We descended the arroyo and I jumped from the saddle, grabbing only my rifle, and slapping the horse on. She continued to run across the desert with frantic speed as if the Apaches were still chasing her. They weren't. They saw the horse gallop away without a rider and were no longer interested in her.

Quickly, I shoveled out a shallow hollow with my bare hands, then burrowed into the sand. I centered the Winchester in its own little burrow. The Apaches were still coming straight on. As soon as they came into range, I shot the closest one off his horse. They came on. I fired again, killing another.

As suddenly as they'd appeared, the Indians disappeared: the whole lot of them, along with their horses. Ghosts. I smiled with twisted admiration. The bastards were like ghosts. They had risen from the desert sand and they had returned to the desert sand. Even a man with good eyesight could not see them.

I fumbled through my pockets for the spectacles Bennie had bought from the optometrist. I needed all the help I could get. I found the spectacles in my bottom pocket, but the glass in the left eye was shattered and the frames were bent. When I'd dropped off the horse and rolled in the sand, I had accidently crushed them.

Fine. I didn't need the eyeglasses. If the sand moved, I would shoot it. That was my strategy. The sand moved. I fired. A cry instantly followed my gunfire. Three Apaches down, I'd say about twenty more to go. No problem.

A mesquite bush off to my left rustled. I shot at it. They were moving in closer, sneaking up on me as invisible as the wind. Soon, in unison, the ghosts would leap from the earth and drag me off to their fires.

And that's the way it would end: Dakota Taylor found dead in Mexico, tortured by twenty Apaches; Bennie Colsen found dead in south Texas, strangled by a spooked banker. Somehow my death would read more interesting in the local papers.

The light call of a bird broke the silence, followed by the call of another bird off to my right. The Apaches were calling back and forth, signaling their next moves. Again, the twisted smile. "Come on, boys," I grunted. "I ain't that stupid."

A small tidal wave of sand rolled into the underbrush a few feet away, rolling towards me. Rapidly I fired into it. My bullets were answered by another slew of arrows sailing into the arroyo. A shadow leaped from the sand and, with a teeth-grinding shriek, somersaulted into my hollow. Scrambling to my knees, I whipped him fiercely with the rifle. He pulled his knife and slashed at my chest, ripping open my shirt. I flung myself at him, knocking him off balance, and together we went rolling down the sand dune.

I lost my rifle, though I desperately tried to hang onto it with one hand, and keep the Apache from burying his knife into me with the other. Two knife fights in less than twenty-four hours. My luck was running low.

The warrior fought savagely, gouging my eyes with his fingers, biting into my neck, my shoulders, as we continued to roll. I heard the shouts of the other Apaches coming towards the hollow, and, jerking my knee, I kicked the warrior in the groin. He released his grip, slightly, then swung the blade at me. I butted my head into his chest and the knife struck sand.

Gathering a handful of burning-hot sand, I threw it in his eyes. He screamed, freed one hand to wipe at the sand, and held me down with the other. I struggled to reach the peashooter in my holster, brought it up to bear in his midsection, and fired. The strength left his body instantly and he slumped forward, rolling in the sand for the last time.

The Winchester rested fifteen feet up the banks of the arroyo. I scrambled for it, grabbing it up just as the other Apaches reached the top of the arroyo. Crouching in the open, I fired wildly, the spent cartridges kicking from the gun and dropping into the sand. Two more Indians fell into the arroyo, but the mass of them kept coming, running straight into my bullets.

From across the flatlands, another rifle sounded, followed immediately by another, then another. The Indians turned to fight the assault from the rear, giving me a chance to hunker back into the burrow I had hastily dug. I squinted towards a ridge on the south side where the rifle shots were coming from. Cameron Graves and his young Indian-fighters were behind that ridge.

Without ammunition, the Apaches were not prepared for long-range fighting. They sprinted towards their horses and galloped south, riding towards the Sierra Madre.

Four Apaches were sprawled in the sand; I checked for signs of life as Cameron and the youngsters trotted across the flatlands with the two mules in tow. Three Apaches were dead, one was seriously wounded. When I touched him, he swung his arm at me angrily, his deep eyes burning with pure hatred.

"It's all right," I said. "Let me take a look at that wound." Again, I reached out, and again, he kicked away from me, spitting in the sand as he did so. I didn't need to get any closer to see the extent of his injuries. They were fatal.

With his eyes still burning into me, he grunted something in Apache. I knew the language well enough to recognize his request. I stepped away from him, pumped the lever on the Winchester, and shot him. He had asked for an honorable death. I gave it to him. The only other choices were to leave him there to die a slow, painful death under a scorching sun or to drag him across the flatlands, a prisoner of the white man until death overcame him.

Cameron appeared at the top of the arroyo astride his horse. When he saw the dead Indians, he held out his arm, stopping the kids from coming any closer to the massacre.

"You're hurt," he said, solemnly staring at my blood-stained shirt.

"Them's the finest soldiers there ever was," I said, dabbing at my chest with a dirty neckerchief. "They'd be roasting me by the fire about now if you hadn't showed when you did."

"Welp," said Cameron, gazing at the bodies with blank, tired eyes. "Even the finest soldier is close to useless without a bullet."

Wearily, I climbed to the top of the arroyo. Billy and Lucky had kept their distance, Billy fidgeting nervously in the saddle. Without warning, I grabbed Billy Waters off his horse and threw him to the ground. Cameron's horse spooked and danced a jig as I lifted Billy by the collar.

"You'd better start talking and you'd better talk fast," I growled.

"It wasn't my fault!" Billy cried. "I didn't know nothing, Deputy Taylor. I swear!"

Cameron regained control of his horse and trotted towards me. He rammed me with the horse, knocking my feet out from under me. I hit the ground, but was back up before the slow

Texan had dismounted. Lowering my head, I plowed into him. The big man didn't even sway. I circled his waist with my arms and attempted to push him off his feet. Strength normally accompanies largeness, and Cameron's strength matched his size. He grabbed my wrists and pried me loose, holding me at arm's length. I swung at him, my fist barely missing his broad nose.

"You calm down," he demanded. "Dammit, Dakota..."

"You said Mecum was harmless. Said I had nothing to worry about. You let me ride out of there thinking Bennie was safe." Out of pure frustration, I swung again and missed again. Cameron held me at bay, as if he were holding a wild opossum by the scruff of the neck.

"I'm plumb sorry your boy turned out to be right about Richard Mecum and we left him on his own. That ain't no reason to be whupping on Billy. He didn't know any more than you or me."

"I swear, Deputy Taylor," Billy said. He was still sitting in the sand where I had dropped him.

I threw one last pointless punch at Cameron. He swung me around, shaking the fight right out of me. "Now, Dakota, you calm down," he kept hollering.

Finally, I did. Winded and tired, I unstrapped a canteen from Cameron's saddle and flopped on the ground next to Billy. I took a long drink, then handed it to Billy.

"Talk," I commanded.

"We were visiting around Richard's pool having a picnic, talking about flowers and such. Bennie knows a lot about flowers..."

"I know that part," I said, impatiently.

"It was getting hot and Richard said to come in for drinks. We sat there till near evening. Bennie told us that he found some letters written by Clay James in a bureau at the Crow. I swear..." Billy's voice faced away and I glared at him angrily before he continued his story. "Bennie said one of the letters mentioned who Clay James was planning to visit the night he was killed."

"They didn't say anything about that," said Cameron.

No, they didn't. Damn that Bennie Colsen, anyway.

"Richard started getting real nervous and started asking a lot of questions about Clay James and the letters."

"Then what did he do?" I goaded him. Billy was taking too long to tell the story. He was like Bennie, taking time to decorate it instead of just telling the facts.

"Nothing. We went back to the Crow."

"'We'?"

"Yes, sir. Me and Bennie. It was late. Bennie said he had some things to do, and I reckoned Catty would be looking for me, so we went back to the Crow."

"How did..."

"I'm getting to that," Billy interrupted me. "I went to bed, but I couldn't sleep. I kept thinking about what Bennie said, about the letters and all. I ain't real quick, but eventually I put the pieces together. Richard killed Clay James." Billy took a drink from the canteen. "I swear."

"What did you do then, Billy?" Cameron asked quietly.

"I went to Bennie's room. I wanted to see the letters for myself, but Bennie wasn't there and his bed hadn't been slept in. It gave me a fright, so I went and got Lucky."

Cameron and I both looked up at Lucky, who was still slouched in the saddle. "We sneaked over to Richard's," said Lucky, taking over the story. "They were gettin' on horses when we got there. Richard had a gun. We followed them to Dead Horse Canyon, but lost their trail."

"I reckoned the smart thing to do," said Billy, "was to come for you."

Cameron patted the boy's shoulder. "You done right."

"I dunno," he said, miserably. "Maybe we should have kept following them like Lucky said. Maybe it's too late."

"How long ago did they go into the canyon?" I asked. I was on my feet now, looking down into the arroyo for a glimpse of the shaggy bay.

"Four days," said Lucky.

"Geezus...," I muttered. There was no sign of the horse.

"We rode as hard as we could," said Lucky.

"I know you did," said Cameron. "I know you done your best. Son," Cameron was now addressing me. "I know you're itching to ride, but these horses are plumb tuckered out and so are these youngsters. None of us are going anywhere if we kill these animals."

"You're right." I turned away from the arroyo. The shaggy bay, even if I did find her, was ridden through. Along the flat, four Indian ponies forged the desolate ground. They were wilder than fire, but there was one truth to an Apache pony: they were more durable than the Apache themselves.

"Young Billy?" I said.

"Yes, sir?" He jumped to his feet, eager to please.

"You ever ride an Apache horse?"

"No, sir."

I grinned at him. "Well, unsaddle them horses: you're about to learn."

22

I could feel the pull, hear the long-distance whispering from across the Chihuahua. The Apache ponies took a long time to catch, the sun took a long time to cool, Cameron took a long time to fry the youngsters some bacon. I wanted to go. Go now. I could feel the pull.

But I couldn't leave them. Not now. Juh was now aware of us. He knew we were out here. I had killed four of his bravest warriors and he would not forget. He would come back to avenge their deaths, to finish the job he'd started. Odds were better if we stuck together. If I left Cameron, I'd leave him burdened with two kids. He could not successfully fight off an attack by himself.

"The two of you single-handedly captured Juan Caballe?" asked Billy Waters enthusiastically.

Cameron squatted on his haunches in front of the campfire, shifting the bacon around in a fry pan. "Young Billy," he said, calmly. "Did it look like we had Juan Caballe captured?"

"Looked like he had you captured," snickered Lucky.

"He did. Let that be a lesson to you all." Cameron studied the bacon, being careful not to burn it. "What I don't understand is how you two kids made it across the desert on your own."

Lucky shrugged. "Just followed the 'Pache trails like Pappy said."

"Welp, you're damn fortunate the Apaches aren't eating you for supper."

Billy's eyes grew round with wonder. "Do they really eat folks for supper?"

"Just the young and tender ones," said Cameron.

"Boy-howdy," said Billy, shivering slightly in the warmth of the afternoon.

"For chrissake, Billy Waters," said Lucky impatiently. "Can't you see he's just joshin'?"

I could feel Billy's eyes on my back as I continued to stare across the desert. "How many of the 'Paches did you kill?" he asked me.

I stared across the desert, ignoring his question. The sun was beginning to drop, turning the desert sky into ever-changing colors. This was not the Apache's homeland. Once, their lands had stretched across Arizona, New Mexico, Texas. They'd been chased into this mean, harsh land by soldiers, by white settlers, by bankers and railroad tycoons, by men like me. They returned to the States to carry out their raids, to make a concentrated but pitiful effort to reclaim their homeland. It would never happen. The Apaches now had only the mean Chihuahua, the brutal Sonora, to call home. And vengeful Mexicans who didn't want them around any more than the bankers and railroad men did. In this desert the Apaches would take their last stand. In this desert the Apaches would die trying.

How many 'Paches did I kill? I had killed too many.

Lucky nudged Billy. "Can't you see he ain't in the bragging mood?"

Glancing over my shoulder at Lucky, I found nothing more than a pile of rags sitting in the hot sand. She had little sticks for arms, little sticks for legs, and a sunken, pale face with eyes already deadened by the hard facts of life. I felt a sudden smidgen of affection for the desert orphan. Briefly, very briefly, I considered taking her back to California with me. Junior wouldn't mind much.

The small, one-room cabin we'd built four years earlier was now a proper house with a proper kitchen, bedrooms, and a parlor, where Bennie had lined the walls with his books. The three hundred acres we'd staked a claim on were now twenty thousand acres. I was running cattle, making a good, honest living. There was plenty of room for a sixty-pound kid. She would make a sturdy cowhand and Bennie would have someone besides me to irritate, for I was mighty convinced Lucky would find Bennie Colsen irritating.

Suddenly I turned and kicked sand on the campfire. "Let's ride."

✦

The horses splashed casually through the shallow waters of the Rio Grande. The Apache ponies rode rougher than any horse I had ever ridden, including the shaggy bay. It felt like I had a Brahma bull between my legs instead of a thin-boned pony. It took most of the following day to reach the river, and Dead Horse Canyon was still a day's ride away. By that time, Bennie would be long dead.

We were halfway across the river when gunfire erupted nearby. Cameron and I pulled our pistols, swung the horses in the water, and tried to find something to shoot at in return. The bullet churned the water a good ten feet in front of us. The gunman was either a poor shot or he'd purposely missed.

"Hold your fire!" a voice sounded from the Texas side of the river.

"Hold *our* fire?" Cameron muttered.

"Who's out there?" I shouted.

From behind a gently sloping bank the barrel of a rifle lifted straight into the air. A filthy white cloth was tied to the end of the barrel. A sign of surrender.

"I'm coming out. Hold your dern fire."

A scrawny man showed from behind the bank, fitfully waving the white flag.

"It's Judd Brooks," said Billy. "I swear."

"Why is he surrendering to us?" asked Cameron, warily.

"Maybe he ain't surrendering," I said. Despite the white flag, we kept our pistols forward and ready to fire.

On foot, Judd tentatively tiptoed down the bank of the river, slipping slightly in the mud. He kept his rifle straight in the air, but he still had a long-barreled six-shooter dangling from his side, the leather thong looped securely around the handle. A man, even one as fast as Judd, could not draw with his gun secured like that.

Cautiously, we led our horses across the river to meet him. Now, everyone knows you are not supposed to fire on someone when you're carrying a white flag. And you sure as hell ain't supposed to fire on someone carrying a white flag. Those are the rules, and even the rankest outlaw respects the rules of surrender. But just in case Judd had never heard of the rules, I kept a sharp eye on his free hand.

"What do you want?" I asked as we climbed out of the river. Water cascaded off the horses and they shook like wet dogs. "If you were smart you would get your skinny ass to the other side of the river."

"I saw him!" Judd said anxiously.

"Saw who?" asked Cameron, unimpressed.

"The white-haired feller who kilt that kid. I swear, by Joseph, it was him."

"Where? When?"

"In Dead Horse Canyon. The night 'fore last."

"Was there anyone with him?" I tried to disguise the desperation in my voice, not wanting Judd to know how badly I dreaded his answer.

Judd ran dirty fingers through dirty hair. "Yep. A fancy feller. A purty one."

I turned the Indian pony's head, pointing it towards Dead Horse Canyon. "Was he alive?" There was more fear in my voice, more fear of the answer.

"Well, yeah, they was both alive. I'd have kilt the white-haired feller myself, but I reckon I'll keep him alive jist long 'nough for him to do some talkin'."

Cameron was suspicious. "Why are you telling us this? Why aren't you in the Sierra Madre with Caballe and the Gypsies?"

"The sonofabitch was willin' to let me hang fer his crime." Judd looked up at me. "And you saved my neck. I owe you one."

"Thanks." More chitchat was time-wasting. As of the night before last, Bennie Colsen was alive. I spurred the pony into a run.

"Just a dern second," said Judd as he tiptoed back up the bank. "Let me get my dern horse."

"Are you riding with us?" asked Billy, stunned that once again he was riding alongside the infamous outlaw. Only they were riding as partners this time.

"I owe that white-haired feller one, too," Judd hollered over his shoulder.

"Is he riding with us?" Billy asked Cameron.

"Appears to be," said the big marshal, as puzzled as Billy. "Boy-howdy."

We stopped in Broken Wagon Wheel just long enough to get supplies and fresh horses. Judd waited for us outside of town. The gallows hadn't been dismantled yet and it still waited ghoulishly for his return. I left it up to Cameron to inform Catherine that Billy was riding with us, warning the marshal to make his argument short and to not turn into a jellyfish. I needed the kids with me.

While Cameron was arguing with Catherine, I inquired at the bank if Richard Mecum had been to work recently. A clerk said no, he hadn't seen him in a week. No one had seen him. Not even Hattie Liverpool, and she was holding a package of tulips for him. The clerk was worried. So was I.

At Pappy's stables, Hattie skirted through loose straw and horse manure to fretfully inform me that she hadn't seen Bennie Colsen in a week. She was worried. So was I.

Ten minutes later, we were on our way.

Time was kicking at me harder than a wild bronc. Time was moving faster than a locomotive and I was keeping pace with it slower than a snail. Judd had seen Bennie alive as recently as the night before last. And that was kicking at me, too. Why was Richard Mecum keeping him alive?

Once we were inside Dead Horse Canyon, Cameron suggested that we stop at Gray Ritter's well, fill our canteens, and rest the horses. Now that Caballe was no longer in the area, the old depot man was friendlier than he'd been at our last meeting, and we ate at his table that night. I ate in silence, slowly chewing my food and my thoughts. Once again, I was pondering the question of why Richard was keeping Bennie alive. It had been a week. One week to do away with the only person who could link him to Clay James's murder. Bennie was a smooth talker, that's for sure, and no doubt he was talking himself into a few more hours of life. But eventually, the talking would come to an end, and a man as smart as Richard Mecum, a man who had as much to lose as Richard Mecum did, would ultimately do what he had to do.

"Sometimes," said Cameron quietly, as if he were following my thoughts, "a man wants to be caught and punished for his crimes. He can't live with himself any other way."

Judd guffawed at that statement. "Not me. No sir, not me."

"You make a career out of breaking the law. You are, by profession, a criminal. It isn't profitable for you to get caught," said Cameron. "Richard is different. He ain't a criminal. What he did was against his nature. Why he did it, nobody will ever know. He probably doesn't even know, excepting he felt he needed to protect himself. There's a part of Richard that would rather be killed than be forced to kill again."

"I'll happily oblige him," I muttered, pushing my plate away. I had no appetite for food. Gray frowned at me, started to ask if there was something wrong with the steak, saw my face, and stayed quiet.

Judd guffawed at that statement, too. "I'll oblige him after you."

"It ain't funny," said Billy. He threw down his soiled napkin, rose from the table, and stared painfully out the window.

"What's eatin' him?" said Judd.

"Richard's a friend of his," Lucky explained.

"Just how close are you and Mecum, anyway?" I asked the boy. Billy instinctively knew what I meant.

"I never bedded down with him, if that's what you want to know," said Billy, still staring out the window.

"Whaddaya mean you never bedded down with him?" Cameron suddenly bellowed.

Sensing trouble, Gray Ritter quickly started clearing empty plates away from the table. Should a fight break out, he didn't want his chipped and cracked crockery to get smashed in anger. He carried the dishes over to the washbucket and started scrubbing them.

Billy ignored the big marshal and continued to stare at the red-rimmed ridges of the canyon. "Richard wanted to. In fact, he pestered me a lot, but I didn't fancy him."

"Of course you didn't fancy him!" Cameron bellowed again. The big marshal was sorely confused, and once again, I felt sorry for him. It's damaging to carry around such a slow wit. "Look, son," said Cameron, rising from the table and talking kind and meaningfully. He reached over and laid his hand on Billy's shoulder. "You have it all backwards again. Men don't fancy men. They fancy ladies. You got it all wrong, son."

"Well, I know that, Marshal Graves," Billy said miserably, shrugging Cameron's hand off his shoulder. "But I just can't help myself. I get a funny feeling when I look at men. I mean, men like Bennie Colsen. I ain't never felt for Sally Reynolds what I feel for Bennie Colsen." Billy finally turned from the window, looking at me imploringly, his face a mask of pain and confusion. "Pardon me, Deputy Taylor. I know he's a friend of yours and all, but I just fancy him something awful."

"Don't we all," I muttered.

"Young Billy" – Cameron's voice was stern once again – "you stop talking like that. It ain't natural."

"Leave the boy alone," I said. "There's nothing unnatural about the way you feel, young Billy."

"Look here, Dakota," said Cameron angrily. "You have some mighty queer ideas about the law, about what's right and what's wrong. Don't be making this boy any more confused than he already is."

"You're the one who's confusing him. You and too many people like you." I looked at the big marshal coldly, feeling that old, familiar chill. A gunfighter's chill.

"But the marshal's right," said Billy, and my cold eyes shifted from Cameron to him. "There's gotta be something wrong with a man who wants another man."

"I'm not riding into Dead Horse Canyon because Bennie's a friend," I said. "Though that would be reason enough. I fancy him something awful myself. And there's not a damn thing wrong with me." The cold eyes shifted back to Cameron again, ready to challenge his next words.

It silenced him. Stunned him. He didn't know what else to say, didn't like the feel of coldness upon him. He respected me. We had ridden long, hard miles together. Had been shot at together. Had protected the other's backside and had been willing to die to save the other. He couldn't go on with the argument and he found his place at the dinner table and fell into his chair. An awkwardness hugged the room. There was only the sound of dishes clinking against the washbucket.

Judd looked up from the steak he was tearing apart with teeth and hands. Grease dripped all the way down his arms to his elbows. "Heck, I ain't ashamed to admit I've bedded down with a few *hombres* myself, 'fore I got hitched."

Gray turned away from the dishpan and said wistfully, "In the old days, when the soldiers came through the canyon, some of them boys were mighty lonesome. And I was a good-looking fellow back then."

Lucky stuffed a wad of chaw into her bottom lip. "Sometimes, when I'm sleeping in the hayloft and the nights are cool, I imagine what it would be like to be married to a proper lady like Catherine Waters."

And Cameron Graves gave up. His big shoulders sagged in surrender and he let out a long, low sigh. "So have I, Lucky Lady. So have I."

23

The darkened spires of Dead Horse Canyon stood before us like great monuments, remote, unapproachable. Riding through the canyon during the glaring light of day was treacherous enough. At night, the sharp-edged buttes, the deeply gutted hollows, the craggy-faced ridges seem to come to life as their moonlit shadows crawled across the canyon floor. The spirits of the men who'd failed to survive the blazing heat or who'd been blinded by the blackness of the canyon howled through the rocks, making the hair stand up on my arms. At least, it sounded like moaning spirits, but it was just the wind. We were all grateful when the sun lifted its mighty head and once again took heavy-handed control of the canyon, making the trail more passable.

We were deep in the canyon, staying on the trail Lucky had etched in her mind. She was a smart tracker, had good instincts, and I trusted her to lead the way. If it had been left up to Billy, we would have gotten lost miles back.

Lucky stopped her horse and studied the landmarks around her. "We lost the trail here," she said. "They just disappeared."

"No, girl, they're here," said Judd. "Up there. That's where I saw 'em." Judd pointed to the top of a wide mesa surrounded by the face of a bulging, bloated mountain. It was a long way up and the trail was steep. We could not approach it on horseback. We would have to scale the mesa on foot, which would slow us down even more.

"You kids stay here," said Cameron, as he studied the difficult climb ahead of us.

The youngsters wouldn't hear of it. They had crossed the Chihuahua on their own. As far as they were concerned, they were old veterans, and would not be left behind. They didn't verbally argue with the big marshal, but they dismounted and followed anyway. Cameron was too preoccupied with the job at hand to bother sending them back.

It took one long, hard hour to reach the top of the mesa. We were bathed in sweat, panting heavily, our hands scratched and torn from the sharp rocks we were forced to hold onto in order to secure ourselves to the mesa wall. I wondered how Bennie Colsen had survived such a difficult climb.

Once again, I questioned Judd, and once again, Judd assured me he had seen two men at the top of the mesa. Both alive.

"They're down there, camped in that hollow," said Judd.

The hollow Judd spoke of was surrounded by a high outcropping of rocks. We took cover fifty feet away from the rocks and drew our weapons.

"Richard Mecum!" Cameron shouted. "This is Marshal Cameron Graves. You are surrounded. Throw down your weapon and come out peacefully."

That was the first time Cameron was able to complete his speech. Usually we were greeted by gunfire halfway through it. This time, we were met by silence. Cameron looked at me expectantly. I looked at Judd.

"Are you sure this is where you saw them?" I asked.

"Dern sure. I'm telling you they was camped in that hollow beyond that ridge," Judd insisted. "It looked as if they were there for a long time."

"Well, they aren't there now." Disappointment and frustration shrouded my face like a death mask.

"They probably moved on," said Cameron. "Let's see if we can pick up their tracks."

Billy grabbed my arm. "Look!"

A vulture lifted its heavy body, flew gracefully a few feet above the wall of rocks, circled, then disappeared into the hollow. It was followed by another vulture, then another. Both circled, cackled, and returned to the hollow. Something – or someone – was dead down in that hollow. I didn't have time to panic. Cameron did it for me.

"They're circling the hollow," he shouted, and ran up the mountain like a buffalo.

"Geezus...," I groaned.

I was no longer concerned about Richard firing on us, for I was now convinced he was no longer at the campsite. If he was, he could have easily taken the big marshal down. Cameron was running straight towards the ridge with no cover, no shelter.

When we reached the ridge, Judd said, "They were camped behind them rocks."

A vulture landed on the wall of rocks. The bird was eyeing its dinner lying on the hollow floor. I shot at it, just because I felt like shooting at something. The bird ruffled its feathers, jumped a few feet, then came back down to light on the rocks.

"Brooks and I will go down," said Cameron, trying to be helpful. "There's no need for you to..."

Valiantly, I moved ahead. "If Mecum's anywhere around I want first crack at him," I responded stubbornly.

"Son, it ain't going to be a pretty sight," Cameron warned.

More vultures swooped down and landed behind the rocks.

"I think I'll stay here," said young Billy, looking sick to his stomach. Lucky trudged ahead, staying close to my side.

After climbing the outcrop of rocks, I looked down into the hollow. Even from that distance, I could smell the nauseating stench of rotting flesh. The camp was still intact; nothing had been moved. A body lay next to a small watering hole just outside the perimeter of the camp. A half-dozen vultures covered the body. I took out my peashooter and emptied the cylinder shooting at the vultures. I missed most of them and they fluttered clumsily in the sky, screeching and squawking, but they were persistent, and not easily deterred from their meal.

"I'll go down," Cameron repeated.

Ignoring him, I jumped off the rock and walked as if in a trance towards the body. I heard a noise behind me, the desperate sound of a man groaning, then of a tin pot being kicked over. Judd and I swung around, our guns zipping out of our holsters.

Bennie Colsen was tied to a cypress stump jutting out of the smooth limestone. The splayed, gnarled branches offered him some protection from the sun. His hands and feet were bound with rope. He had a man's bandana shoved in his mouth and he mumbled loudly, trying to get our attention. He'd managed to kick over a coffeepot resting by the burned-out campfire.

Slipping the peashooter back into its holster, I sprinted over to the cypress and quickly untied his hands. His wrists were raw, swollen from the pressure from the ropes. Briefly I rubbed his hands, trying to get the blood flowing. Men had lost their arms to gangrene because of tied ropes cutting off their blood supply. Then I removed the gag from his mouth.

"What took you so long?" he whispered hoarsely.

"Well, I had to cross a couple of deserts to get here, Junior." I put my arms around him, pulling him close to my chest, and gently kissed the fiery-hot hollow of his neck. He held on tight, as if his life depended on it, and refused to let me go.

Cameron and Judd paid no attention to us. They were more interested in the body lying next to the water. Tentatively, Cameron rolled the body over and grimaced.

"It's Richard," he said. "He's been dead for quite a spell."

"Yep," said Judd, closely inspecting the body, his nose only inches from the dead man's face. "That's him, all right. That's the fella who dumped the kid's body in the gully."

Cameron examined Richard's body for a sign of what might have killed him. It could have been outlaws, maybe Comanches, but there were no gunshot wounds, no knife wounds, no sign of a struggle. Just below the elbow, embedded deep in his flesh, were two tiny puncture marks.

"Looks like a dern rattler got 'im," said Judd.

✦

"Now, admit it, Junior, this was a hell of lot more adventurous than having tea with a poet."

Bennie pulled the last of his clothes from the drawer in our sweaty little room at the Crow. He dropped them in a pile on the straw mattress. "I must say, you and I have extremely differing opinions on what constitutes adventure."

"I don't understand why he didn't kill you when he had the chance. Not that I ain't glad he didn't."

"You are a funny man." Bennie smiled gently. "I've come to realize that the more you joke, the more serious you are. If you ever become serious, I'd probably have cause to worry."

"And you should."

Bennie sighed and stared at the bundle of clothes that waited to be folded and meticulously placed into his satchel. "He didn't have the nerve. He was afraid. When it came right down to it, he did not have the nerve to kill me. Poor Richard Mecum."

I grunted. Poor Richard Mecum, my ass. Because I didn't want Bennie to think I was barbaric, I didn't bother to tell him that I'd been prepared – in fact, anxious – to do the work the rattler had done. Richard Mecum had forced my heart to beat faster than I liked it to beat; forced me to think about what life would be like without Bennie Colsen around to keep me walking straight; forced me to imagine what Bennie's perfect body would look like after being mangled by vultures. I didn't exactly feel sympathy for the man.

"If I hadn't been gagged I would have warned him. I saw the rattlesnake coiled by the water, but all I could do was mumble. It all happened so fast..." Bennie's voice faded off as he remembered the details leading up to Richard's death.

"Don't shed too many tears for Richard Mecum. He had the nerve to kill Clay James."

"That was more of an accident than an outright killing. Richard tried to explain it to me, tried to make me understand how it happened, why he did it. He said he felt cornered, trapped. He didn't know what else to do. Desperate men take desperate action. He panicked," Bennie explained.

"He was going to let an innocent man hang for his crime," I reminded him.

"Of course you're right," said Bennie quickly, and started fidgeting with his clothes.

"Course I am," I said. I wasn't prepared for Bennie to drop an argument that quickly.

"It's all terribly sad. A terrible tragedy."

"Life is a tragedy, Junior. Any which way you look at it, life is a downright tragedy."

Bennie smiled sadly. "Shakespeare said that. In so many words. "

"Well, Shakespeare knew what he was talking about."

Wandering over to the window, Bennie looked down on Main Street. A group of men were dismantling the gallows. I could hear the blows of the hammers, the crashing of lumber. "Why do they bother to take it down? They will probably have to erect it again in a couple of weeks."

"It ain't real welcoming. Would you want to visit a town where the first thing you see when you ride in is the gallows?"

"I don't suppose." Bennie turned away from the window. "The real tragedy in all of this is that Richard chose to kill rather than be exposed for what he was."

"And what's that?"

"A homosexual." It was Bennie's favorite word. It was rare, academic, and he and other intellectually inclined men and women like him sat around our rock fireplace in Two Rivers and batted the word back and forth, savoring its definition, proud of its stature, smug because they'd finally discovered a word that described who and what they were, and no one recognized its meaning but them.

"Nope, the real tragedy is that men like Richard Mecum are lily-livered cowards. They live in fear. And a young boy died because of that fear."

"You are absolutely without mercy," Bennie admonished.

"You bet I am. It annoys me to think we have to ask permission. Go ask Hattie Liverpool for her permission to love me."

Bennie laughed. For the first time since his ordeal there was genuine cheerfulness in his laughter. "I don't know about Hattie, but Elizabeth would give her blessings."

"They should. They've been living in sin for twenty years."

"But people treat them as if they are sisters. Just a couple of old harmless spinsters who never had the opportunity to marry. If people only knew."

"Junior, they do know. They probably knew about Richard Mecum, too. And they probably would have let him go on being their banker and handling their money. If the truth had come out, I doubt if Richard Mecum's life would have changed much."

"It's easy for you to judge, Dakota. You've never been afraid of losing anything."

"Sure I have." I unbuckled the holster holding Cameron's peashooter and dropped it on top of the bureau. "Towards the end there, with all them buzzards flying and circling, I was afraid of losing everything."

Moving away from the window, Bennie didn't bother to fold his clothes. He shoved them into the satchel in one lumpy mess. "Can we go home now?"

"You bet."

I am honored to say the entire population of Broken Wagon Wheel was waiting at the stage depot to say good-bye. I'd be lying if I said there was a brass band and all that. There wasn't. But Hattie Liverpool's Welcoming Committee baked us another pie and a group of schoolkids presented us with a bouquet of flowers that looked suspiciously like they were from Richard Mecum's garden. Sam Bradford was there with his arm in a sling. Josh Reynolds was there with his daughter, Sally, who kept side-glancing sweet looks at Billy Waters. And, of course, young Billy ignored her and gave Bennie a long, drawn-out hug. Lucky sat off by herself in the hayloft, her skinny legs dangling from the window of the loft, pretending not to notice our departure, pretending not to care. Catherine Waters hugged Bennie and pretty much demanded that he take care of himself on the trip home. Bennie hugged Catherine, promising that he would. Then Hattie Liverpool hugged Bennie and started to cry, wiping her pug nose on her lilac-scented handkerchief. Bennie hugged Elizabeth and started to cry. Things were getting all soppy and teary-eyed.

After Bennie stopped hugging everybody, Cameron pushed through the crowd and handed me a package. Then he stepped back, looking as awkward as all hell.

"What's this?" I asked.

"Welp," he said, stiffly, like he was about to give a speech or something. "The citizens of Broken Wagon Wheel all pitched in and bought you a going-away present. It's the least we could do."

"No kidding?"

"To express our gratitude," said Catherine. She looped her arm through Cameron's, letting her hand rest on his solid, muscular forearm, and leaned against him. The marshal looked even more awkward, more sheepish, but downright pleased.

"And for stopping us from hanging an innocent man," squeaked Mayor Joseph Bagley.

"That's right kind of you," I said, feeling a bit awkward myself. "Thanks." Heck, I'd never gotten a present before. A slap on the back would have suited me fine.

The stagecoach rumbled up to the depot. Riker Sims was sitting at his usual place in the driver's box. "Load up!" he called. "Everyone going to El Paso, get on board."

"Welp," said Cameron, holding out a big paw. "Thanks for your help. If you ever a need a job..."

"As a deputy? No, thanks. It's too dangerous." I squeezed his hand firmly. "It's been a hoot."

"I reckon I'll be chasing Juan Caballe until the day one of us dies," said Cameron.

"Hopefully, it will be of old age," I said.

"Load up!" Riker repeated.

Bennie and I climbed into the coach and closed the door. Riker shouted, "Forward Ho!" and the coach jolted forward. Bennie continued to wave out the window until we were halfway down Main Street.

"Sort of makes you feel like a dignitary or something," I said.

"Open it." Bennie tapped the package lying in my lap. He loved wrapped packages as much as I loved whiskey and tobacco.

I untied the string and pulled away the brown paper to expose a leather gun box. I lifted the lid. Two Colt .44s were nestled in the box, lying side by side. They had ivory handles. My initials were inlaid in gold at the corner of each handle. They were a matching pair.

"I'll be damned," I said.

"Catherine hired a gunsmith in San Antonio," said Bennie. "I know they're not the originals, but they are exact replicas."

"You knew?"

"Of course I knew. Hattie couldn't keep a secret if her life depended on it."

I picked up a Colt and rolled it in the palm of my hand. It felt strong, powerful, familiar. "I'll be damned..." was all I could say.

The stagecoach rumbled past the miniature oasis at the edge of town. The pond was murky, but the water looked cool against the brown backdrop of the flatlands. The bluebells had lightly budded. The palm trees swayed gently in the wind, making a lonesome sound.

Alyson Publications publishes a wide variety of books with gay and lesbian themes. For a free catalog or to be placed on our mailing list, please write to:

Alyson Publications
40 Plympton Street
Boston, MA 02118

Indicate whether you are interested in books for gay men, lesbians, or both.